ALL THAT JAZZ

headline

First published in 2008 by
HEADLINE PUBLISHING GROUP

First published in paperback in 2008 by
HEADLINE PUBLISHING GROUP

4

Cataloguing in Publication Data is available
from the British Library

ISBN 978 0 7553 3956 3

Typeset in Palatino by Avon DataSet Ltd,
Bidford-on-Avon, Warwickshire

Printed and bound by CPI Group (UK) Ltd, Croydon, CR0 4YY

Headline's policy is to use papers that are natural, renewable and
recyclable products and made from wood grown in sustainable
forests. The logging and manufacturing processes are expected to
conform to the environmental regulations of the country of origin.

HEADLINE PUBLISHING GROUP
An Hachette Livre UK Company
338 Euston Road
London NW1 3BH

www.headline.co.uk
www.hachettelivre.co.uk

This book is for my granddaughter Emma.
I was so proud watching you get your degree
from university for creative writing. I have
always said you have the perfect name for a
book cover. Love you lots.

I would like to thank Jeanette for her help with
dance steps. I had great fun trying them out
and I still can't master the Charleston properly.

And thank you to Stephen Humphrey at
Southwark Local History Library for the
information regarding the cinemas in and
around Rotherhithe in the 1920s. I enjoyed my
day at the library reading the microfiche papers
to find out what was showing at that time.

Chapter 1

1921

DAISY MAY COOPER sighed softly. She wanted to cry. Why was life so cruel? She had lost her dear dad at the Somme and now her mother was desperately ill with the influenza that was sweeping the country. She held her mother's gnarled hand and looked at the fingers that once did such fine stitches on clothes that were brought to her in need of repair. Daisy May remembered the nights she and her younger sister Mary Jane were in the bedroom and should have been sleeping, but knew their mother was sitting straining her sad brown eyes as she worked by the light of a candle to save the penny for the gas light and help pay for some food to put on the table. Now her breathing was laboured and her eyes closed, eyes that had seen so much pain in her life. Daisy gently stroked the back of her mother's hand. She had been hoping the New Year would have been kind to them, but February was already proving to be bitterly cold.

'Daisy May.'

'I'm here, Mum.' She bent closer to her mother to hear what she was saying, as her voice was very soft and the rattling in her chest frightening.

'You will take care of Mary Jane, won't you?'

Daisy held back her tears. Their mother always called them by their full names.

'Course I will. But Mum, don't worry. You'll be up and around in . . .' Her voice trailed off as she felt her mother's hand go limp.

In the flickering candlelight Daisy sat looking at her mother. She wanted to scoop her up in her arms and run away. She didn't know where she would go; they didn't have any family as far as she knew. She was always told that her mother and father had come from over the Thames. They had been very young when they met and had run away to get married and finished up in Rotherhithe. Daisy always thought that sounded very romantic, but they had never kept in touch with their brothers or sisters. As most people of her parents' age couldn't read or write at the time, Daisy could understand that.

She felt tears run down her face. Who would come to her mother's funeral? And how could she even pay for it? She brushed her tears away with the flat of her hand. She also had to think of her young sister, Mary Jane. How was she going to look after her? She was only six, eleven years younger than her. Daisy's head was reeling as all the problems began to close in on her. She kissed her mother's cheek and noted that for the first time in years all the worry seemed to have disappeared from her face and she looked very peaceful. Daisy blew out the candle and went into the other room they rented. By the light that came from the gas lamp in the street, she looked down on the dark hair of her sister. She managed to stifle a sob. Her mother had always said Mary Jane was very precious, as she hadn't thought she could have any more children because after Daisy she had lost two babies as soon as they were born. She always said she was being punished for running away from home to get married. But then Mary Jane arrived. Daisy had

3

loved her from the first time she saw her. The little girl was now asleep on the battered brown leather sofa that had seen better days. She was covered with a threadbare blanket and her coat. Not that there was much warmth in either of them. This room was freezing, as since their mother had been taken ill, it was only the bedroom they could afford to have a fire in. Daisy would have to shovel up the hot coals and bring them in here to warm this room, and put a kettle on the fire so that in the morning they would be able to have a cup of tea. Her mind had gone into thinking about the practicalities of what was to be their life now.

'Daisy? Is that you?' Mary's voice came through the darkness.

'Yes, love. I'm here.'

'Is Mum all right?'

'No.' Daisy went and sat next to her sister. She put her arms round her and held her frail, thin body close.

'You're freezing,' said Mary, pulling away from her.

'Mary, I'm afraid Mum has gone.'

'Gone? Gone where? I thought she was . . .' She stopped when she heard her sister sob.

'D'you mean she's ...' She couldn't finish the sentence.

'She's with Dad now.'

Mary burst into tears. 'You know I always said my prayers like Mum taught me. She mustn't die.'

Daisy sat holding her small sister and could feel her thin body shaking, but she couldn't find any words of comfort.

'What we gonner do without Mum?'

'I don't know.'

'Will she have to go in the ground like old Mrs Turner from upstairs?'

'Yes.' It was only last week that Mrs Turner had died. She had been interred in a pauper's grave and Mary, along with all the other kids in the buildings, had followed the handcart. She had been full of it when Daisy got home from the greengrocer's where she worked.

'I don't want Mum to go in the ground.' She shuddered. 'Rene Watts said that all the worms will come and eat her up.'

There wasn't any answer Daisy could give her sister. Her mind was full of things she had to do. Tomorrow she would have to go and ask Mrs Wilson to lay her mother out. Everybody in the buildings knew that the widow Wilson did the laying out and bringing the babies into the world and that she always had more than enough work. Daisy's mother had told her that she only charged a few pennies. Daisy knew she had to get to work as soon as it was light. If she was late, she knew that her employer would shout and carry on. She didn't like Daisy and made it very clear by the way she was always going on at her and making her lift heavy boxes when her husband wasn't around. Daisy was a slight, thin girl and Mrs Martin was a big, robust woman who worked on the market before she married Mr Martin. She took great delight in watching Daisy struggle to lift the heavy boxes. But Daisy did not have any option other than to stay there. Jobs were very hard to get, as she was always being reminded, and besides, sometimes Mr Martin, who was very nice, let her bring home any fruit or veg that had gone off and couldn't be sold. Gradually her heavy eyes began to close.

'Daisy, I'm cold.'

Daisy woke with a start. The arm that had been round her sister was numb and her body ached. It was light outside and she began to panic; she would be late for work. 'I've got to go and see Mrs Wilson.'

Mary clung to her. 'Don't go. Don't leave me alone with Mum.'

'I must. I've got to find out what we have to do.'

Mary started to cry. 'I don't want to be left on me own.'

'Well hurry and get dressed and come with me. But please don't get in the way and don't say anything or we'll get into trouble.'

'I won't.' Mary jumped off the sofa and quickly put on the coat that had been covering her. She had gone to sleep dressed. Before putting on her boots she rearranged the cardboard inside them to cover the holes and stop the water wetting her socks, not that it was any good when it rained heavily. 'I'm ready.'

'You'd better run the comb through your hair.'

Mary gave her a warm smile and Daisy's heart went out to her. She was a pretty girl and her big blue eyes were full of expression in the pale face that looked as if she had lived far more than her six years. 'Do you want to see Mum?'

Mary shook her head.

'You will after Mrs Wilson has made her look nice.'

'But she won't bring her back, will she?'

'No. Now come on.'

The stiff breeze cut through their thin clothes as they made their way to the next block of drab redbrick buildings that looked the same as the one they lived in. So many families were crowded into a few rooms. The people who lived here had nothing. Some of the tiny windows had a piece of curtain stretched across, while others had been left bare. Rubbish was permanently blown about and old furniture that was too useless to be taken inside or used for firewood littered the path and was home to the rats that scurried about. Daisy hated this place. They had lived in a nice house when their dad was alive. He had had a good job working the huge presses for the newspapers, but like many others he had chosen to fight for his country and had been killed, and now their dear, wonderful mother who had tried so hard to make ends meet had gone too.

'I think Mrs Wilson lives here,' said Daisy. 'I'd better ask that woman over there.' She went over to a woman who was standing at the door.

'Bleedin' kids,' she yelled up at the windows. 'So help me I'll string the lot of you up one of these days.' She caught sight of Daisy and Mary walking towards her. 'And what d'you two want?'

'Please,' said Daisy in her best voice, 'd'you know what number Mrs Wilson lives in?'

'Number forty-six. 'Ere, you don't wonner for a birth, do you?'

Daisy shook her head.

'Oh, a laying-out. Sorry. 'Ere, ain't you the kid that works in the greengrocer's?'

Daisy nodded.

'Thought I recognised yer. Is it yer mum, love?'

Again Daisy only nodded. She knew if she spoke the tears would fall.

'That missus you work for's a right cow; don't know how a nice bloke like him managed to get tangled up with her. Sorry, love, I'm speaking outta turn.' She stood to one side. 'You go on up. She is in.'

'Thank you.'

Clutching Mary's hand, Daisy began to mount the concrete stairs. Forty-six would be on the top floor. They passed the communal lavatory, and like most of them in these blocks the smell almost took their breath away; there was one on every floor that those families had to share and should take turns in keeping clean, but not many did. Daisy hated it when she had to sit in there while people banged on the door and shouted at her to hurry up.

'This is it,' she said as she knocked on the door of number forty-six.

'Who is it?' came the voice from inside.

'Please, Mrs Wilson, it's Daisy Cooper from Chapel Court.'

The door was opened and a tall, thin-faced lady stood in the doorway. Her white hair had been scraped back into a bun and her slippers were cut away to relieve her bunions. She looked at the two sad-looking girls. 'Is it yer mum, love?'

Daisy nodded.

'Come in.' Florrie Wilson knew Mrs Cooper. She was a good woman who had fallen on hard times. All those men that went off to fight would be turning in their graves if they knew how their womenfolk had finished up. She would always be grateful that her mother had passed on her skills of laying out the dead and delivering babies. She was lucky; she could still make a meagre living, not like some round here.

They walked into a warm, cosy-looking room. Daisy couldn't believe how nice Mrs Wilson had made her home look. Like their block, every one of these flats had only two rooms: a living room that had running water from a tap in the corner over a big white porcelain sink, and one bedroom. In this room Mrs Wilson had put a pretty floral curtain round the bottom of her sink. The dresser that took up a wall had a row of hooks with odd cups hanging from them, and plates were standing neatly along the back. The mantelpiece was covered with a green cloth that had a deep fringe; on top there were little china animals and a clock with the glass missing.

'Right, tell me what's happened,' said Mrs Wilson.

Daisy told her about her mother, and many times she had to stop and wipe her eyes. Mary was holding her sister's hand very tight.

'I see. I can come over now if you like. When I've finished, you'll have to get a doctor to issue a death cersificate, then you can take it to the church and see about getting her buried.'

'We can't afford a funeral.'

'I guessed that. Old Harry Thorn will take yer mum to the cemetery on his cart, and unless you can afford a plot you know that she'll have to go in a pauper's grave?'

Daisy nodded.

'I don't suppose she left any instructions?'

'No.' Daisy thought about last night. When Mary was asleep, she'd gone through the shoebox at the bottom of the cupboard. She knew her mother kept some papers in there and Daisy was hoping there was an address that would tell her where their relations lived. There were some letters from her dad to her mum when he was in the army, but she didn't like to read them as they were very personal. It felt wrong somehow. There were a few photos of happier days, but no address. Mrs Wilson was talking to her.

'Right. I'll just get me coat and 'at and I'll come along with you.'

'Do you need me there?' asked Daisy tentatively.

'Why's that?'

'I should be at work and Mrs Martin will be very cross.'

'That woman can be nasty at times, make no

mistake. But don't worry, I can manage, yer sister can take me across.'

'No. No. I'm not going without Daisy.'

Daisy bent down and held her sister close. 'Please, Mary, go with Mrs Wilson. I can't get the sack, not now, we need the money.'

'Come on, love. You'll be all right with me. Then when I've finished you can go and find your sister.' Mrs Wilson felt very sorry for these girls, who were now left all alone. How would they survive?

Chapter 2

'AND WHAT TIME do you call this?' Mrs Martin shouted as Daisy walked into the greengrocer's shop.

The woman who was being served at the time looked round and Daisy could see the shocked expression on her face at the manner in which she had been spoken to.

'I'm sorry,' said Daisy, hurrying along to the storeroom and quickly removing her hat and coat and donning her sacking apron.

Mrs Martin turned to her customer. 'Would there be anything else?' she asked in a soft, unnatural voice that she could put on when the situation called for it.

All That Jazz

Daisy hadn't seen this woman in here before. She looked very well dressed, not like their usual customers.

'No thank you.'

'That'll be one and six, thank you.'

The woman gave her the money and left the shop.

As soon as the door closed, Mrs Martin turned on Daisy. 'Well, what sort of pathetic excuse have you got today?' She was a large, round woman who because of her fat legs had difficulty walking. Her pale face was always powdered and her grey, hennaed hair sat in a bun on top of her head that wobbled when she spoke. She smelt of strong perfume and sweat.

'Me mum died in the night,' said Daisy softly. 'And I had to find the lady who lays 'em out.'

'So I suppose you'll be wanting time off to bury her?'

'Yes please, but I don't know when that'll be.'

'It 'ad better not be Sat'day, our busiest day.' There wasn't any sympathy in her voice. 'Now you can bring in the box of oranges that's outside in the yard, and don't go pinching any.'

Daisy went outside and cried as she tried to

lift the heavy box. She hated this woman and this job, but what else could she do?

'Hallo there, Daisy. Everything all right?'

She was struggling to pick up the heavy wooden box, and looking up quickly she put it back down again and wiped her eyes on the bottom of her rough apron. 'Yes thank you,' she said softly. She hadn't heard Mr Martin come in from making his deliveries. Every day he went out with his horse and cart doing the rounds selling vegetables and fruit.

'Now what's upset you? Has Ethel been shouting at you again? You know you don't want to take too much notice of her, her bark's much worse that her bite. She likes you, you know.'

Daisy wanted to say that she didn't think so, but instead said, 'It's me mum, she died in the night and I was a bit late coming in as I had to see the lady who lays 'em out.' It was said in a rush before the tears fell again.

'Oh my poor dear, that's very sad. I seem to remember she's been poorly for some time now.'

'Yes she has, but you always hope she's gonner get better.'

'Of course you do. Have you got everything sorted out now?'

'Mrs Wilson's going in this morning. And I hope to do the rest tonight.'

'As I well know, there's a lot to do when someone dies.'

'I know. I'll have to have some time off when we bury Mum.'

'Of course you will. Now let me take that box in for you.'

Mr Martin was a small, slight man next to his wife, and although in Daisy's eyes he was old, he was very strong. He was also very kind and gentle and he had given Daisy an extra shilling a week after her mother had been taken ill; at least that helped pay the rent. He effortlessly lifted the heavy box of oranges. As Daisy followed him back into the shop, she wondered what he had ever seen in this woman. She knew she was his second wife, Daisy never knew the first Mrs Martin; she had died many years ago before they moved to this area.

'William, you're back early,' said his wife as Daisy opened the door for him.

He put the box on the floor. 'Yes, my dear, I've run out of potatoes. Must be this cold spell. Everyone wants more than usual. I'll just have a cuppa before I take a couple of sacks out again.'

'Daisy, make Mr Martin a cup of tea, and you can bring me one in as well while you're about it.'

Daisy didn't bother to answer her.

When she walked in with the tray of tea, Mr Martin was sitting on the bentwood chair they kept next to the counter.

'Daisy, you don't have to worry about taking time off for your mother's funeral. Just let us know what day it will be, and I know you've got a lot to do, so you can go at six tonight as I'll be back be then.'

'Thank you.' Daisy looked at Mrs Martin, whose face was like thunder.

For the rest of the day Daisy's thoughts were on her mother, and she wondered what she would have to do next. Would Mrs Wilson set things in motion? If only she could get away, but the only thing she could do was to try and keep out of Ethel Martin's way.

At six o'clock Daisy hurried home. 'Mary,' she called as soon as she opened their front door. 'Where are you?'

There was no reply. The only light was from the gas lamp in the street. They were lucky; this room was at the front of the building, not like the bedroom, that overlooked the dark eerie courtyard.

Gently Daisy pushed open the bedroom door. As her eyes got accustomed to the gloomy room, she could see her mother lying peacefully with her arms folded across her chest. She went over and took away the two pennies that were on her closed lids. Her mother was very cold. She bent and kissed her forehead and stood for a while just gazing down at her. Suddenly she remembered Mary. Where was she? Daisy knew she wouldn't be that far away and she also knew that she had to go and see Mrs Wilson, so decided she would do that first before looking for Mary. She left their cold, heartless rooms and went to see the widow lady.

She knocked on Mrs Wilson's front door, and when the door was opened, Mary was right behind Mrs Wilson. She rushed to her sister and threw her arms round her.

' 'Allo, love, you're early. Mary said you didn't finish till seven on Mondays. Come on in.'

'Thank you. I don't usually but Mr Martin said I could go.' Daisy stepped into the warm and cosy room.

'I hope you don't mind, but I brought Mary home here with me. Didn't like the idea of her being on her own over there.'

'No. That's very kind of you.' Daisy envied the blazing fire, and the warmth of the room was making her cheeks burn.

'Now sit yourself down and have a cuppa. Kettle's on. What did old misery guts say when you told her about yer mum?'

Mary settled herself down on the colourful rag rug in front of the fire. Daisy sat on the green uncut moquette sofa that had the luxury of two stiff hard cushions behind her. 'She wasn't very happy about me being late for work, but Mr Martin said it was all right for me to have time off for her funeral.'

'I should bloody well think so an' all.'

'Mrs Wilson, what do I have to do now?'

The widow sat down on the sofa next to Daisy and took hold of her hand. 'Don't worry about it, love. I hope you don't mind, but me and Mary here have taken care of everything, ain't we, little 'en?'

Mary nodded and smiled, making her dimples deepen. Her face was flushed from the heat of the fire.

'The doctor came and gave me the cersificate and then we went and saw the vicar and then old Harry Thorn. If it's all right with you, she can be buried on Wednesday morning.'

Daisy could feel the tears trickling down her cheeks. 'The day after tomorrow. Thank you,' she sniffed.

'Well I knew you didn't want to hang about. Is that all right? Is there anybody you want to come?'

Daisy shook her head as she wiped her eyes. 'When we moved here Mum tried to keep herself to herself.'

'You ain't got any relations that might wonner come?'

'No. Mum and Dad didn't come from round here.'

'That's all right then. We won't be upsetting anybody.'

'I wish everybody was as kind as you.'

Mrs Wilson patted the back of Daisy's hand. 'Think nothing of it. I know it's been hard for yer. Now you've got to think of yourselves.'

'I know, and I wish I could get a better job.'

'Well beggars can't be choosers, and let's face

it, you're lucky to have a job at all. There's plenty round here who'd like to be working.'

'I know that. But I wish Mrs Martin was more like her husband.'

'Different breed altogether, that one is. We all know she used to work on the market before she set her cap at him. His first wife was lovely, can't for the life of me understand why he married that one. It ain't as though she's anything to shout about, lookswise that is. Now come on, love, drink up yer tea and I've got you a bit of mutton stew. Is that all right?' Mrs Wilson struggled to her feet.

Daisy broke down. 'I'm sorry.'

Mary came and sat beside her and held her sister close.

'There there, love,' said Mrs Wilson as she hovered over the girls. 'I can understand how upset you are. It's been a very trying time for you. Now come on, dry yer eyes and sit up at the table.'

The smell of the mutton stew had filled the room and Daisy realised she hadn't eaten for a few days, just an old apple that had been thrown out and was rotten.

*

When the girls had finished their excellent meal, they were both very reluctant to leave Mrs Wilson and her warm comfortable room, but Daisy knew they had to.

'Do we have to go home?' asked Mary.

'Yes, we must. We can't stay here with Mrs Wilson.'

'Why not?'

Daisy gave her sister a look that soon put her in her place. 'Now thank Mrs Wilson for looking after you all day.'

'Thank you,' Mary said sweetly. 'Can I come back tomorrow?'

'Mary,' said Daisy, raising her voice. 'I'm so sorry, Mrs Wilson.' She turned to her sister. 'You really should be getting back to school.'

Mary looked up at them both. 'But I want to stay with you.' Large tears plopped on to her hands.

Daisy bent down and held her tight. 'I'm sorry. I have to go to work and I can't take you with me.'

'Look, I have to go out tomorrow but Mary can stay with me, that's if it's all right with you? Just for one day.'

'Oh no. We can't. That's very nice of you, but we can't.'

23

'Why not, Dais?'

'Because I say so.'

'Please. Please.'

'No. Now come on, put your coat on.'

'It's so cold in our house.'

Daisy was beginning to get cross with her sister. Didn't she understand Daisy had to look after her now? 'Mary, come on.'

Mrs Wilson looked at the girls. 'Look, Daisy, why don't you stop here for the night? You can both sleep on the floor and at least you'll be warm.'

'We couldn't. Thank you all the same, but you've been more than kind and we can't take advantage of that.' Deep down there would have been nothing nicer than for Daisy to stay here for the night.

Mary was tugging at Daisy's coat. 'Please, just for tonight. I promise I won't ask again.'

She looked down at her sister's tear-stained face and melted. How could she take Mary back to their cold rooms with their dead mother in the bedroom? 'Well all right. That's if you're sure we won't be in the way?'

Mrs Wilson smiled. 'It'll be nice to have a bit of company for a change.'

Mary threw off her coat and cuddled her sister. 'Thank you.'

'Don't thank me. You must thank Mrs Wilson.'

Mary hugged Mrs Wilson. 'Thank you.'

Mrs Wilson hugged her back and swallowed hard. She would have liked children but it was never to be; that was one of the reasons she loved delivering babies. She looked at the two girls; they had been well brought up and she knew they wouldn't be any trouble.

Chapter 3

T HE FOLLOWING MORNING Daisy was very reluctant to leave Mrs Wilson's warm and cosy room.

'Now are you sure Mary won't be in the way?' she asked Mrs Wilson.

'No. I told you I have to go out to see young Mrs Berry, her baby's due next week and I want to make sure she knows what to do, it's her first. Always frightened when it's their first.'

'Thank you. Now, Mary, don't get in the way.'

'I won't. I promise.'

Daisy kissed her sister and held her tight. She loved her dearly and they only had each other now.

She was deep in thought as she took the short walk to the greengrocer's. How would they manage? It had been very hard after their mother had been taken ill and she'd been unable to do her sewing and help out with money. She shivered as the cold wind went through her thin coat. She was dreading what Mrs Martin would say when she told her what day the funeral was.

'Me mum's being buried on Wednesday morning,' Daisy blurted out as soon as she got into the shop.

'What time?'

'Half past eleven.'

'Well at least you'll be able to come in for a couple of hours.'

'I thought perhaps I could have the morning off.'

'Thought wrong then, didn't you? Couldn't you arrange it for Thursday afternoon when we're shut? Or was you hoping I'd let you have all day off?'

Daisy looked down. 'It was the only time the vicar had.'

'I bet.'

'I was hoping I could go to the second-hand stall at the market and try and get something for me sister to wear for the funeral. She needs shoes.'

'Hard luck. I need you here.'

Daisy walked away. She knew there wasn't any point in her saying any more.

That evening Daisy slowly made her way to Mrs Wilson's to collect Mary. She was tired and hungry after a heavy day when Mrs Martin seemed to want everything moved round the shop. She had dragged heavy sacks of potatoes from one side of the room to the other, only to be told to put them back as Mrs Martin wasn't happy with them after they'd been moved.

The warmth of the room when Mrs Wilson opened the door overcame her and she just wanted to sit down and cry.

'Come on in, love, you look fair whacked out.'

Mary came up to her and hugged her.

'Have you been a good girl?' Daisy asked her.

Mary nodded. Her bright eyes were shining.

'That Mrs Berry's ever so fat,' she said. 'She must be getting ever such a lot to eat.'

Mrs Wilson smiled over the top of Mary's head. 'How did you get on today?' she asked Daisy.

'Not too bad. Tried not to say too much to the missus. Although she did ask why Mum wasn't being buried on Thursday afternoon, then I wouldn't have had to take two hours off.'

Mrs Wilson made no comment; she only tutted. 'Now get your hat and coat off. There's some stew for you. Not got much meat in it, but the veg's good for you.'

Daisy didn't hesitate as the smell from the pot simmering over the fire was making her mouth water. 'This is very kind of you.'

Mrs Wilson smiled. 'As I've said before, it's nice to have a bit of company now and again.'

Mary was sitting up at the small table under the window, ready to eat. 'Will you be cooking like this, Dais?'

Daisy looked at her sister. 'Things will be different when we go home. I won't have Mum to look after and you will have to do a bit more to help me.'

*

After the delicious warming stew, Daisy helped Mrs Wilson wash up and the older woman told her about how lonely she got sometimes. Daisy couldn't understand that, as this woman was so kind that Daisy thought she would have many friends.

At last the time came when Daisy knew they had to go home. She was very apprehensive; she didn't want to go back to those cold rooms.

As soon as they were outside, Mary began whining. 'Why couldn't we stay with Mrs Wilson tonight? I don't wonner go back with Mum.'

'I know. But I have things to do, and besides, it'll be the last time we can say goodbye to Mum.'

'I don't wonner see her.'

'You can't see her. Mr Thorn has put her in her coffin.'

'So she ain't Mum now, is she?'

'Of course she is.' Daisy was almost dragging her sister along. Although she too was very reluctant to go home, she had to get the place tidy before Harry Thorn came and took their mother away, and besides, she wanted to be alone with her and say her last goodbye in private.

Daisy lit the fire, and by the glow of the coals the two girls sat huddled together talking about the good times they'd had when their mum was alive. Although they never had a lot of money they would go to the park in the summer and play in the snow in the winter. When Mary's eyes began to close, Daisy laid her down and, after putting the coats over her, went in to her mother.

She sat on the bed and stared at the cheap coffin. It was going to take her months to pay off the loan she'd had to get to pay for it. Tears dropped from her eyes. She was unable to grasp the fact that her mother was inside it. How she'd loved her mother. Daisy looked round the bare room and thought about how things used to be. Their mother had always been so particular about keeping the place as clean as possible. They always had a clean white cloth on the table, not like some, who only had newspaper. She could almost hear her mother saying: 'Just because our circumstances have changed, our standards mustn't drop.' Their window sills didn't have lines of dead bluebottles, and although the curtains were thin, the windows were clean, apart from where the glass had fallen out or been broken by a stray stone thrown up from the courtyard below. Daisy sighed. How would she be able to keep up her mother's standards? In many ways she was feeling like Mary. She didn't really want to be here, but this was all they had. She knew she would have to look for another job as she didn't earn enough to keep them both, but jobs were hard to get, as she knew when she saw the men back from the war standing on street corners with trays round their necks trying to sell matches, bootlaces and the like. She thought about the past and how things were before the war. Daisy had loved going to school and learning to read and write. That was how she got the job in the greengrocer's: she was one of the few round here that could add up. She would always remember the nights she and her father sat learning together. He would help her with her sums, as he was very good with figures, and she would help him read and write.

Slowly she stood up. She was stiff with cold and her body ached. She bent down and touched the coffin. 'Goodbye, Mum. I will always love you and I promise to look after Mary.' Wiping her tear-stained face, she left the bleak, chilly bedroom and went and sat beside her sister, who was stretched out on the sofa. Mary's tousled hair was over her face and very gently Daisy brushed it aside. 'Oh Mary, how we gonner manage?' she whispered.

The vicar, Mrs Wilson, Mr Thorn and the girls were the only people at the graveside mourning Daisy's mother. There were a few from the buildings who always went to gravesides to see the sort of coffin and where they were being buried. Daisy had been touched when Mr Martin gave her a bunch of flowers to put on her mother's grave. She tossed a handful of earth on the coffin, the vicar shook her hand, and after blessing her he walked away.

'Now you've gotter come back to my place,' said Mrs Wilson to Mr Thorn, and taking hold of Mary's hand, she put her other arm through Daisy's.

'That's very nice of you,' said Mr Thorn, replacing his cloth cap.

'It's only a cup of tea and a sandwich.'

'Will be most welcome, I'm sure. At least the rain kept off,' said Mr Thorn as they began the short walk back. 'Always makes the ground very sticky when it rains.'

'They were lovely flowers that Mr Martin gave you for your mum,' said Mrs Wilson.

Daisy only nodded. She didn't want to speak; her head was full of problems looming up in front of her.

'You're very quiet, little 'en,' said Mrs Wilson to Mary.

'Will the worms eat me mum up?' Mary asked, looking up, her beautiful eyes red from crying.

'No. Course they won't.'

'Rene Watts said they did.'

Mrs Wilson squeezed her hand. 'You don't wonner take no notice of her. How does she know, has she ever been buried?'

Mary shook her head.

'Well then.'

As soon as they entered Mrs Wilson's tidy and warm rooms, the sound of a soft whistle came from the kettle sitting on the skillet in front of the fire. Mrs Wilson rushed over and poked the fire with a long brass poker, causing the coals to burst into flames. 'Kettle's been on all the while we've been out so I'll make the tea right away. Take yer overcoat orf, Harry, otherwise you won't feel the benefit of it when you go out again. Daisy, you can help me bring over the sandwiches. Plates are in the dresser.'

Daisy went over the dresser and took the plates and sandwiches to the table as Mrs Wilson made the tea.

'You always make a lovely sandwich, Mrs W,' said Harry Thorn. 'People round here don't appreciate what you do for them.'

'I only try to do what I can.'

'Yes, I know.' He poured his tea into the saucer and drank it making a loud slurping noise.

For the first time in days, Daisy and Mary smiled.

After a while Daisy knew they had to go. She stood up. 'Come on, Mary, put your coat on.'

Mary pouted.

'And it's no good you pulling that face. I've got to go to work. If you like we can quickly go round by the market and have a look at the stalls.'

'Bit late for that, love,' said Mrs Wilson. 'Most of 'em pack up be lunchtime.'

'You never know, there might be someone still desperate to make a sale,' said Harry Thorn.

Daisy gave them a weak smile. 'I'll pay you as soon as I can,' she said to them both. 'I'm going to ask Mrs Martin for a raise.'

'I shouldn't hold out too much hope in that direction if I was you, love.'

'I know, but there's no harm in asking.'

'No, s'pose not.'

'Say goodbye to Mr Thorn and Mrs Wilson, Mary.'

Mrs Wilson clasped Mary to her. 'Goodbye, love. Pop in and see me now and again, won't you?'

Mary nodded.

'And you as well, young Daisy.'

'We will, and thank you both for everything.'

As Daisy closed the front door, Mrs Wilson turned to Harry Thorn. 'That girl deserves a lot more. She's got a heart of gold and no mistake.'

*

Mrs Wilson was right, most of the stalls had gone, not that Daisy had any money to spend on her sister. She felt so miserable as they wandered around. She didn't want to go back to work. Tonight she would look through her mother's things again. There must be some way she could find out about their family over the river. Then they wouldn't be all alone. As they walked past the town hall, a notice was being put up. In big bold letters it said that a new experience was coming to Rotherhithe: the showing of moving pictures. It was going to be next Saturday at eight o'clock and was going to cost one penny.

Daisy stood staring at the poster. Could she afford that?

She looked at Mary. 'See that? It says that moving pictures are going to be shown here on Saturday. I reckon you and me should come and see them.'

'What are moving pictures?'

'I don't rightly know, but we could do with a night out.'

Mary's eyes lit up. 'D'you mean we could come and see 'em? Could we?'

'Don't see why not.' Daisy's mind was

working. 'We'll be saving our gas and it should be warm inside.'

So despite their shared sadness, hand in hand they made their way home. Suddenly Daisy felt that life might not be so bad. After all, they still had each other.

Chapter 4

AS SHE WALKED to work, Daisy's head was full of what was going to happen at the town hall on Saturday. And what was she thinking about promising Mary they could go when she didn't finish work till nine? The picture show would already have started. Would they be able to get in? She knew she shouldn't have said anything to Mary. Besides, she shouldn't really spend two precious pennies on that sort of thing, but in her mind she felt that she and Mary deserved a special evening out. After all, this was the first time anything like this had happened round here. Perhaps if the Martins went too, then they would shut the shop early.

Later that morning Daisy was intrigued when a well-dressed young man came into the shop and asked Mrs Martin if she would put a poster up in her window.

'What's it about?' she asked abruptly.

Daisy's ears pricked up when he said, 'It's the new moving picture show that's coming here on Saturday. If it proves popular, they could end up building one of them posh cinemas that's all the rage in America and has now come to the West End.'

'So what do I get out of advertising your show?'

'I'd give you two free tickets for Sat'day night.'

Mrs Martin smiled. 'Well I s'pose that's not bad. All right then.'

He handed over two tickets, and although Daisy smiled sweetly at him, he just nodded, touched his trilby and left. There were so many questions she wanted to ask him. How she would have loved two free tickets.

For the rest of the week Daisy was apprehensive. All the customers were talking about what was going to happen on Saturday evening, and it seemed that most of the people round here were going.

'What about you, love, you going?' asked Mrs Bell.

'No,' said Daisy with her fingers crossed behind her back.

'I told me old man but he ain't interested, he'd rather go up the pub. Looks like it'll just be me and me daughter. She's seen 'em before, reckons they're really good. I'll have two of those cooking apples as well.'

Daisy weighed out the apples. All week she had been very careful about what she said, making sure she didn't seem excited, as Mrs Martin would pick up on it and make her work late, since she hadn't mentioned that they were going to use their free tickets. What could be worse was that Mrs Martin would hold her five shillings' wages over till Monday, and then Daisy and Mary wouldn't be able to go out at all.

She needn't have feared for come Saturday morning Mrs Martin was as eager as Daisy was to go to the show. Instead of staying open till nine, she bustled about and shut the door dead on six, almost pushing the last customer through the door. She turned the notice round in the window to Closed and with a big grin said, 'I'll see you on Monday. Don't be late.'

Daisy too had a grin on her face as she hurried home. Tonight they were going out to see a moving picture show.

Mary was at the door waiting for her sister. 'Will we be late?' she asked as soon as Daisy opened the front door.

'No. But we must go soon, as I think a lot of people will be there. So many have been interested in the poster in the window.'

'I'm ever so excited,' said Mary, jumping up and down.

'So am I. I'll just put a bit of coal on the fire and the kettle on, then when we get back we can have a cup of tea, and if you're very good I might buy us a penny bun.'

Mary could hardly contain herself. 'I'm so excited, I hope I don't wet me drawers.'

'Well you'd better go to the lav now. I don't want you sitting around in wet drawers.'

Daisy couldn't believe the number of people

who were waiting to get in to the make-shift cinema. She held on to Mary's hand tightly; she didn't want to lose her in the crush. When the doorman got them into an orderly queue, Mary and Daisy were almost sick with excitement.

They quickly sat down in their seats and waited.

When the lights went down, Mary held on to her sister, squeezing her hand.

A woman seated at the piano began thumping out music. The gasp from the audience was loud as the pictures that were being shown on the big silver screen flickered into life, then for a moment or two everybody was quiet. That was till the music got louder, and then people were shouting and stamping their feet as the baddies with their evil-looking eyes came on the screen. Everybody laughed when one man shouted at the woman in front of him to take off her 'bleeding 'at', and after a lot of turning round and tutting she did, but her piled-up hair was almost as large. They laughed at the policemen on the screen doing silly things. They dabbed at their eyes when the leading lady, who was cuddling her baby, was forced out of the house into the deep snow by her wicked stepfather. Then, all too soon, the magic was over.

It took a while before the audience got to their feet. The lights had gone up, and it was only when the pianist began playing 'God Save the King' that everybody scrambled to stand and sing loud and clear.

'Daisy, can we come again?'

'I don't know when they'll be back.'

'It really was magic, wasn't it?' Mary's blue eyes were large as she looked up at her sister.

'Yes, it was.'

All the way home they talked nonstop about what they'd seen. They stopped at the baker's, and as it was late he let them have two buns for a ha'penny. After a cup of tea and their sticky buns they finally settled down, and when they were in bed Mary went over the wonderful magical evening.

'I'd like to do that.'

'What?'

'Dance like that lady in the long floaty frock.'

Daisy held her sister close and laughed. 'So would I. Now come on, let's try and get some sleep. Remember it's Sunday tomorrow and we can go and see Mum's grave.'

'Do we have to?'

'Yes. We can tell her all about what we saw tonight.'

'But Dais, she won't be able to hear us.'

'I know, but we mustn't ever forget her.'

'I won't. But it ain't a proper grave, is it? Not like those that's got big statues of angels and Jesus looking down.'

'I know, but we can put some flowers on it.'

'I'd like that.'

'That's good. Now come on, cuddle up and go to sleep.' Daisy knew that she too would have trouble sleeping, for what they'd seen tonight would always be with her. How she would love to wear beautiful clothes and dance like that.

On Monday morning Daisy was pleased that Mrs Martin didn't say that she'd seen her and her sister on Saturday. Daisy had made sure she and Mary had kept well back when they arrived and sat low in their seats when Mr and Mrs Martin finally walked in. They'd managed to leave at the end before her employer had finished talking to people. This morning many of the customers were chattering excitedly about what they'd seen on Saturday night.

When Daisy came into the shop carrying a sack of carrots, Mrs Vincent, who was waiting to be served, asked, 'D'you think they'll come again?'

'I hope so,' said Mrs Martin as she started to serve her.

'I'll just have four taters for now.'

Mrs Martin counted out four potatoes. 'Will four be enough for your lot? They ain't very big.'

'They'll 'ave to do. I spent fourpence on going out to that there picture show, not that the old man noticed me and the kids 'ad been out; he went up the pub as soon as he finished his tea and was in his usual state when he got 'ome.' She laughed, showing her toothless gums. ' 'E'd 'ave 'ad forty fits if he knew I took the kids out for a treat. Those carrots don't look bad. I'll 'ave a couple of them as well, and you can knock some of the dirt orf first. I ain't paying fer dirt.'

Mrs Martin didn't argue. 'That'll be tuppence then.'

Mrs Vincent left the shop.

'That woman wants to be careful.'

'Why?' asked Daisy.

'I could stir up a lot of trouble for some of 'em round here if I told their old men what they got up to when they're up the pub. Some of 'em rob 'em blind when the men get back drunk out of their skulls.'

Daisy didn't comment. She knew all about the husbands who came home drunk and beat their wives. She had seen the black eyes, but what sort of injuries were hidden out of sight? Some of the wives took advantage of the fact that the men were only half conscious and proudly boasted that they went through their pockets. Daisy would love to get away from the rows and fights that went on on a Saturday night hereabouts. Worst of all she hated it when robbers ran across the roof of their building with the police after them shouting and blowing their whistles.

'Wake up, girl, you was half asleep then.'

'Sorry.'

'There's some apples outside that need to be brought in.'

Daisy shuddered as she opened the back door. It was freezing outside and she looked at the boxes of apples that were dripping wet. How she would love to get away from here. But where could they go? She often wondered about the aunts and uncles she might have, and what about any cousins? Perhaps when the weather got better she could go over the water and make some enquiries: maybe she would get lucky.

That evening Daisy decided she would look through her mother's box.

'That's Mum's,' said Mary when Daisy brought it from the bedroom.

'I know. I was hoping I would be able to find the address of Mum or Dad's relatives.' She carefully went through everything, but the only clue she had was a letter her mother had received from Daisy's grandfather. It was in a strange spidery writing telling her mother how wicked she had been and that she was never to get in touch with her family again. There wasn't any date or address.

'Well?' asked Mary. 'What does it say?

'Just that Mum couldn't see her sisters or her mother any more.'

Mary threw her arms round Daisy. 'I miss Mum so much, but I'm glad I've got you.'

'I'm glad too.'

*

All That Jazz

It was a long, cold winter and everybody was wrapped up against the rain and wind that seemed to persist all through April. Daisy was finding it more and more difficult to keep their heads above water, and now they'd had a notice to say the rent for their two rooms was going up to four shillings and sixpence. She was worried sick. How would she be able to manage? When she'd mentioned getting a raise, Mrs Martin had refused and she daren't ask Mr Martin as the missus would really go mad about that. She wasn't very pleased after the last time he gave her the extra shilling a week.

She had her head down against the biting wind and her thoughts were as usual on her money worries when she noticed a poster in a shop window telling everybody that the picture show was coming to the town hall again. A tear slid down her cheek. She knew they couldn't go, as she really didn't have the money. She wouldn't tell Mary. She knew that would break her heart, as she was still talking about the last time it was here. As she got closer to the poster she saw that the show was going to be here for a week. A whole week.

*

Everybody who came into the shop was talking about the picture show that was coming again next week.

'Didn't ask me to put a poster up again, did he, the stuck-up little sod,' said Mrs Martin when she heard about it.

'Perhaps he likes to share the free tickets out to all the shopkeepers,' said Daisy.

Mrs M just tossed her head in the air, making the bun that sat on top of her head wobble.

When Mrs Burton came in, the conversation got round once again to the picture show. 'I see they want women to see people to their seats.'

Daisy stood and listened.

'Daisy, those cabbages want bringing in, now.'

Reluctantly she made her way outside to the yard. She wanted to stop and listen to what Mrs Burton was saying. Did they really want someone to show people to their seats? She was beginning to get excited about it. She could do that. Did they pay? She grabbed the cabbages and made her way back inside, but Mrs Burton had left the shop. On her way home tonight she would go to the town hall and ask.

All That Jazz

The rest of the day couldn't end soon enough, and at nine o'clock Daisy quickly put on her hat and coat and left. She had to see the manager before she lost her confidence.

Chapter 5

WHEN DAISY TURNED the corner from the high street, she was surprised at the number of people buzzing around the town hall and for a moment or two she stood watching all that was going on. It was mostly men who went inside. They were wearing black suits and their white shirts and black bow ties looked so out of place round this area. The women escorting some of them were wearing lovely long frocks with expensive-looking furs draped round their shoulders. Daisy stood open mouthed at such a wonderful spectacle. What were they doing round here? She knew that sometimes they had do's at the town hall, but she had never seen anything like this before.

She tried to catch snatches of conversation.

'Fancy old Norman bringing us here for his farewell do,' said one well-dressed man to his beautiful companion.

'Ronnie told me that he wants us to see a bit of the seedy life he'll miss before he goes off into the jungle.'

The man gave a loud, unnatural laugh. 'They do say that he really comes here for . . .' He bent his head nearer to his companion and Daisy couldn't hear what he was saying. But the lady threw her head back and screamed out with laughter.

'Boris, you are very, very naughty.'

'So is Norman, but I daresay he'll get plenty of that where he's going.'

They disappeared through the glass doors.

Gradually the street became empty. Daisy was in a quandary. Should she go inside and try to see the manager, or should she leave it for another night? She was desperate to earn some extra money to keep a roof over their heads. What if there were other people after the job?

The decision was taken out of her hands when the door opened and a man walked over to her. Coming very close, he asked as he took his cigarette from his mouth and threw it on to the pavement, 'What d'you want? This is a private do and they don't want the likes of you 'anging about. And if they fancy a bit of how's-yer-father, they've got their own women. So buzz off.'

Daisy was taken back. 'I ain't here for that.' She was very angry. How dare this man suggest she was a common tart? 'If you must know, I came here to see the manager.'

'Well that's me, so what d'you want?'

Daisy didn't want to talk to him standing here in the street. He was rude and arrogant, but she needed work. 'I was told that you might be wanting people to show the customers to their seats at the next moving picture show.'

'I might be, why?'

'I would like to apply for the job.'

'Have you had any experience?'

'No, but I was here the last time.'

'You would have to work and not just sit and watch the pictures, you know.'

'Yes, of course.'

'Come and see me tomorrow.' He lit another cigarette.

'I can't come till after nine. Is that all right?'

'Why's that?'

'I have to work.'

'And where's that?'

'Martin's Greengrocer's.'

'I know, round in the high street?'

Daisy nodded.

'So why you looking for another job? She give you the elbow?'

Daisy knew it was no good hiding her reason, so she said, 'No. I have a young sister to look after and I need the money.'

In the gaslight she saw him grin. 'There's lots of ways a pretty girl like you could earn a few extra bob, but as I said, come round tomorrow and I'll see what I can do for you.'

Daisy would have liked to run away from this slimy-looking bloke, but knew she had to find extra work. It would only be for a week. Tomorrow she would get Mary to come with her. With her young sister in tow that would make her feel a whole lot safer when she saw this man again. 'Thank you,' she said and walked away.

'Till tomorrow,' he called after her.

*

The following night as soon as she finished work, Daisy hurried round to the town hall. She was pleased to see that Mary was waiting for her.

'I'm ever so cold,' said Mary when Daisy got to her.

'I'm sorry, but you know what Mrs M's like; she makes me stay till the very last minute.'

'Why d'you want me to come with you?'

'I don't like the man I've got to see. Come on.' Daisy pushed open the door and practically had to drag her sister into the foyer. Where did she have to go?

'I'm up here, girl.'

Daisy looked up the stairs.

'Come on up.'

Tentatively Daisy climbed the rough wooden stairs with Mary close behind and they entered a smoke-filled office.

'Who's this then?' asked the manager as he sat behind an untidy desk. He looked very different tonight. Last night he was wearing an evening suit with a bow tie. Tonight he had on a shirt and pullover. He still looked slimy, but Daisy thought that was because of his thin black moustache and slicked-down black hair.

'Me little sister.'

'Does she wonner job as well?'

Daisy shook her head.

'Take a seat.' He motioned to a bentwood chair and Daisy sat down. Mary stood very close to her.

'Now, as I expect you've seen from the posters, the picture show's coming here for one week. And if I play me cards right, we might have them come every week, but a lot of that depends on how I treat the punters. I don't want fights or shouting and the punters chucking things.' He ran his hand over his hair. 'Do you think you can handle that?'

'It wasn't like that before.'

'I know, but when the blokes get used to seeing the same picture they'll get bored. So, what d'you think?'

'How much would I get?'

'Forward little miss, ain't yer? Now let's see. You'd be here for six nights, I reckon, but you've got to show up every night, mind. Sixpence a night.'

'That's three shillings.'

'Quick, ain't yer?'

'I have to be, working in a shop.'

'I suppose you do. So what d'you say?'

'What time would I have to start?'

'Half eight. We open just before nine and finish at eleven, then you'll have to stop and help clear up the mess they leave behind.'

Daisy's heart sank. 'I can't take it, I'm afraid.'

'Why's that?'

'I don't finish till nine.'

'Won't the missus let you go half an hour early? You can't be very busy at that time a night.'

Daisy shook her head and stood up. 'Come on, Mary, we don't wonner waste this man's time.'

'Hold on a minute. Sit down.'

Daisy did as she was told.

'I like you; you're polite, not like some of 'em round here who's been after a job. I could perhaps stretch it a bit to nine, and if you hurry yourself you'll just about make it.'

For the first time Daisy smiled. 'Thank you. I'll take it, Mr . . .'

'Holden to you, and you are?'

'Daisy Cooper.'

He stood up. 'See you Monday night then. And don't be late.'

Daisy could hardly contain herself as they clattered down the stairs. An extra three shillings. That was almost a fortune.

'Can I come with you when you come here?' asked Mary.

'No, I'll be working.'

'But I don't wonner be left on me own.'

'I'm sorry, Mary, but we need the money.'

'I get frightened when I'm on me own.'

'You'll just have to be brave.'

When they were outside Daisy took her sister's hand. She knew by the way she was walking that Mary was sulking, but what could she do? She owed it to her mother to put a roof over Mary's head and food on the table.

On Monday night Daisy ran the short distance to the town hall. The queue stretched right round the corner. She began to panic. How was she going to get in? She walked up to the door and people began shouting at her to join the queue. Suddenly the door opened and Mr Holden called to her.

'Daisy. In here.'

She pushed her way in and he closed the door behind her.

'Right, go in and wait for the rush.'

Daisy walked inside the main hall. All the chairs had been set out in neat lines just like before. She stood at the door and suddenly there was a rush of people and she was almost swept along with them. They fought over who sat where, a couple of chairs were knocked over, and then Mr Holden got on the stage and started shouting for everyone to sit down and be quiet or else there wouldn't be a show. Gradually people began to settle down, and when the lights were turned off a hush settled over the audience and the silver screen burst into life. Daisy stood there. After a while a woman with a young girl came up to her.

'Are you in charge?'

'Well yes, in a way.'

'Iris here wants the lav, can you take her?'

Daisy took the little girl's hand and took her outside. Mr Holden was standing in the foyer.

'What's the trouble?' he asked as soon as he saw her.

'No trouble. She wants the lav.'

'There's one outside. Through that door there.'

Daisy went through, and by the light of the gas lamp she found the lav door.

'I'll wait out here.'

'Don't shut the door,' said a sad little voice.

'I won't.'

'And don't go away.'

'No, don't worry. I'll wait for you.'

The girl was in and out in no time. Daisy guessed she wasn't wearing any drawers to pull down.

'I won't be able to find me ma.'

'Yes you will, I'll take you.' Once again they entered the dark room.

As she stood at the back, Daisy knew this was what she wanted to do. She loved the thrill of being helpful and doing something she enjoyed. Even better, she was getting paid for it.

After everybody had gone, she was given a broom and told to sweep up. An old man who Daisy had seen before began stacking all the chairs away.

'Will you be here termorrer?' he asked.

'Yes,' she said with a smile.

'Me name's Charlie, by the way. You was a bit late getting here.'

'I come straight from work.'

'Straight from work?'

Daisy nodded. 'I work at the greengrocer's.'

'I know the place. You 'ad anythink to eat?'

'No. Ain't got time.'

'Termorrer I'll bring yer a sandwich and a drop of tea.'

'Thank you, that's very nice of you, but you don't have to.' Daisy suddenly realised how hungry she was, and what about Mary? In her haste to get to work this morning she'd forgotten to leave her anything. Guilt filled her. She had left her sister alone in those cold rooms without a fire. She would have to get up very early tomorrow to light the fire and leave her some soup to warm up.

'It's no trouble, girl.'

Mr Holden came up to her as she was putting the rubbish in the dustbin.

'You did well tonight.'

'Thank you.'

'I was impressed with the way you took that kid to the lav and then back to her mum. You didn't make any fuss.'

'I thought it was part of me job.'

'Yes, it was.' He walked away.

All That Jazz

'You must a made an impression; he don't usually hand out compliments,' said Charlie.

As Daisy put on her coat and hat, she called out good night. For just a moment she looked round the large room. She had had a wonderful evening. This was the sort of job she would like, and if they did build one of those big picture houses she would try and get a job there, as she knew this was what she wanted to do more than anything.

Chapter 6

T HE FOLLOWING DAY when Daisy walked into the shop she knew from the expression on Mrs Martin's face that she was in trouble.

'What's this I hear, you bin working round the town hall?'

'Yes.'

'So don't I pay you enough?'

'I do have to find the rent and look after Mary.'

'That's as may be, but it makes me look as if I treat you like some underpaid skivvy.'

'It will only be for a week.' Daisy looked at her hands. 'I'm sorry, I didn't think you'd mind.'

'Well I do mind.'

'It don't interfere with me work here.' Daisy knew she had to stand up to her employer in spite of any consequences.

'That's as may be. And don't go answering me back, otherwise you'll be out on yer ear.' She stormed off.

Daisy feared that the rest of this week was going to be hard. She knew that Mrs Martin was going to be watching her every move and guessed that every evening she would keep her here for as long as she possibly could.

That night Daisy didn't get away till a quarter past nine and was breathless when she almost fell into the foyer. Mr Holden was standing looking at his watch.

'I'm so sorry I'm late. Mrs Martin wouldn't let me go.'

'I gathered that. Get in there and keep an eye on things.'

'Thank you.' Daisy quickly went into the darkened room. There didn't seem to be as many people in here tonight, so as her eyes became accustomed to the dark she was able to relax a little.

After everybody had left she began sweeping,

and Charlie came up to her. 'His nibs ain't very happy tonight,' said Charlie.

'I know, and it's all my fault.'

'No it ain't. It's cause there ain't ser many people. Not many can part with tuppence the beginning of the week.'

'Why did he charge tuppence this time?'

'To do with the big boss. It was a penny before just to get people in and see what it was all about. I told him it'll be different when he changes the films on Thursday.'

'He's changing the films?'

'Yer, so try and get here on time.'

Daisy smiled. 'That won't be a problem, that's me half-day. D'you think he would let me bring me little sister with me?'

'Dunno. I shouldn't ask him tonight; leave it till termorrer. Got a nice bit a cheese in me sandwiches. D'yer fancy one?'

Daisy grinned. 'As if I need asking. Thank you,' she said as she took a large doorstep of bread from his clean white handkerchief.

He laughed. 'You could do with a bit of flesh on them there bones of yours.'

*

All That Jazz

On Thursday, Daisy took Mary along with her to the town hall. Mr Holden looked very harassed and angry.

'Thank God you've arrived.'

'Is there a problem?' Daisy was anxious. 'You did say I could bring Mary with me tonight.'

'Yes. Yes. That's all right, just keep her out of the way.'

Mary, who looked frightened, stood behind Daisy.

'Mary, go and sit in there.' Daisy pushed her sister into the room with the large screen. 'And please don't make any noise.'

Daisy stood around and looked at the people who were beginning to gather outside. 'Looks like we'll have a few more in here tonight.'

Just then the lady who played the piano came in. 'All right then, Georgie boy?' she said to Mr Holden.

'No I ain't all right.'

'What is it? There's a fair few waiting to come in. 'Ere, ain't them there films turned up then?'

'Yes, they're here, but that silly cow Polly who takes the money ain't.'

'Pr'aps she's ill or somethink.'

'She should have let me know.'

'Oh dear. Looks like you'll have to step in, then.'

'I can't. I've got to help the bloke when he loads the films and changes the reels, and I can't be in two places at once.'

Daisy was standing quietly listening to this. 'Mr Holden. Would you like me to take the money?'

He turned on her. 'You?'

'Yes, don't forget I am used to figures.'

He looked at her. 'I suppose I ain't got no option. Right, get behind that desk. Now remember, they'll all be pushing and shoving to get in, but make sure you take their money and give 'em a ticket. I'll take the tickets when they comes through the doors.'

Daisy got behind the desk. She just prayed that everybody would pay; she knew how he shouted at Polly when someone sneaked past her without a ticket.

'Right, I'm gonner open the doors. Are you ready?'

Daisy nodded. She was as ready as she would ever be.

When the doors were opened, people began

pushing and shoving, all shouting at once for a ticket. Fortunately most had the right money and the tuppences were dropping into Daisy's hands very fast. Then gradually the crowd thinned out and only one or two breathless stragglers came racing in, worried that they might have missed the first film.

Daisy sat back and carefully counted the money. She couldn't believe that they had taken ten and six. That meant there were sixty-three people in that room, not counting the piano lady, Mary, Charlie and any that had managed to sneak in. She hoped that would please Mr Holden.

Daisy was a little sad on Saturday night when she said goodbye to Charlie. They had become quite good friends, and while she was sweeping up he would tell her about his life, about his wife, who was an invalid, and how they lived with one of their daughters.

Daisy began putting on her hat and coat. She felt her purse again. She couldn't believe she was going to be three shillings better off this week. There was so much she wanted to do with this extra money. She would get a bag of coal and even some broken biscuits. What a luxury. 'D'you think we might have the films here again?' she asked Charlie.

'I reckon so.'

'Thank you for the sandwiches. I really enjoyed them.'

Charlie smiled. 'You're a good 'en, girl. I hope things work out for you.'

'For you too.'

'I'm gonner miss our little chats.'

'I am as well. I hope your wife gets well soon.'

'Not much hope of that, love.'

'Daisy,' called Mr Holden from the top of the stairs. 'Up here a minute.'

Daisy blanched. 'I wonder what I've done wrong?'

Charlie patted her arm. 'Don't look so worried. I don't think you've done anythink wrong.'

Slowly Daisy mounted the bare wooden stairs.

'I won't keep you a minute. I know you want to get home to Mary.' He stood to one side to let her into his smoke-filled office. 'You've done a good job working here, especially when Polly was off sick. As I didn't have to pay her, I'm gonner give you an extra tanner.'

Daisy could feel herself blushing. She wasn't used to people thanking her and being pleased with what she did. 'Thank you.'

'If they let me have the films again, I'd like you to come and work here in the evenings.'

'I'd love to. Thank you very much.'

'And who knows,' he grinned and puffed out his small chest, 'if they do build a picture house and they make me manager, well, I'd ask you to come and work full time.'

Daisy was beside herself. 'Do you think they will?'

'Dunno. We've done all right and we can only live in hope. Good night now, and thank you.'

'Thank you, Mr Holden.' Daisy hurried down the stairs clutching her sixpence. She would be able to buy Mary a pair of shoes from the second-hand stall now.

'Everyfink all right, girl?' said Charlie.

'If we do have the films here again, Mr Holden wants me to work for him.'

'Good for you, girl.'

'Goodnight,' she called as she hurried through the doors. She was elated. Although it was a cold, damp night she felt a warm glow. She had found a friend in Charlie and Mr Holden had given her hope about a possible full-time job. For the first time in months she felt happy.

Over the next few months Daisy worked at the town hall every time they had the films, and sometimes Mr Holden asked her to help out if they had a do and wanted someone in the cloakroom to take the hats and coats.

As time went on, everybody was intrigued when they started to knock down an old warehouse, and rumours went round that they were going to build a proper picture house in Rotherhithe.

On her afternoon off, Daisy would walk past the site and watch as the building began to take shape. It had such an elegant look about it and everybody was talking about the marble-effect columns and the name 'Roxy' high above. Daisy wanted to jump with joy. Was this going to be her future? But what if Mr Holden wasn't made manager? She would cross that bridge if and when she came to it. For the time being she had a dream to keep her going.

Chapter 7

June 1922

WHEN THE DAY finally came that the Roxy cinema opened in Rotherhithe, Daisy was waiting in the foyer with Mr Holden. She couldn't believe that she was actually here working for him. As she had watched the progress of this cinema being built, she never really thought he would offer her a full-time job. She had been so excited when he got in touch with her telling her the opening date and that she could start work a week beforehand so that she could get used to everything.

Daisy smoothed down the navy skirt that was part of her smart uniform. She pulled at her jacket that had gold braid round the button holes and adjusted the elastic under her chin that was holding her little pillbox hat in place. She held her large torch and waited for the mayor to arrive to cut the ribbon. Her thoughts went to Mrs Martin, who had been furious when she told her she was leaving. Daisy had smiled to herself as she was ordered out of the shop at once, for luckily she had told her employer after she'd been paid.

This past year had been very hard for her and Mary as she found herself desperately trying to keep their heads above water. She would always be grateful to Mr Holden for letting her work at the town hall when the pictures came or when there was any sort of do on and he needed staff. Many times she thought about her relations over the water and knew that if she had the fare she would have gone looking for them. Now she was going to get more money even if it did mean long hours. Although Mary was at school, Daisy did worry about leaving her on her own all evening.

As the band that was accompanying the mayor got nearer, Daisy was feeling more and more nervous. What if she dropped her torch, coughed or sneezed? She felt her stomach tighten. She had never been in such high-up company before. Mr Holden smiled at her and she knew now that he was a fair man who expected a good day's work from everybody. This evening he looked very smart in his evening suit. Mary also looked lovely. Daisy had managed to get her a pretty blue frock; it must have been for someone who had been a bridesmaid. She was holding a bunch of flowers to give to the mayor's wife, and she looked across at Daisy, who could see her young sister was nervous as the flowers were shaking. She smiled reassuringly at her. Mary, now seven, was growing into a beautiful girl with her blue eyes and dark hair. Daisy smiled to herself, remembering last night when she had put Mary's hair in rags.

Mary had looked in the mirror at all the strips of rag in her hair. She turned this way and that. 'Will it work? Will I have curly hair in the morning?'

'I hope so,' said Daisy as she damped the last strand of Mary's hair and wound it round and round the rag.

Now the soft curls rested on her shoulders. Their mother would have been so proud of them.

All That Jazz

Charlie, who had been promoted to being the doorman, gave Daisy a wide grin. He looked smart in his navy blue uniform with gold braid on his hat, collar and cuffs, and when he opened the door the mayor and his wife swept in. First the mayor shook Mr Holden's hand, then the manager handed him the scissors. Mary gave his wife a little curtsy and the flowers. When the ribbon was cut, the mayor posed for the photographers. 'This is a wonderful thing to come to the district,' he said, beaming at them.

Then the doors opened and the invited customers filed in. Daisy thought she was going to explode with happiness. She expertly tore the tickets in half and put her half on the wire she was holding, then she showed people to their plush seats and stood at the back and waited for the curtains to open. As this was the first show, they were going to have a team of local girls dancing on the stage before the films started. There had been plenty of rehearsals and arguments, and as Daisy had watched them she couldn't see how they would ever get it right. Now she stood in wonder at the way they kicked their legs high in the air and danced in a line. She couldn't believe it, it was just magical.

After that memorable day, every afternoon and evening the cinema was full. The films were changed on Thursday. Daisy almost felt guilty at enjoying herself as she laughed along with Harold Lloyd and Buster Keaton. Her eyes filled with tears when Mary Pickford or Lillian Gish, always clutching a baby, were thrown out of their home by their father. The patrons, as Mr Holden called them, could become quite noisy at times, especially when the cowboys chased the Indians or the cops chased the robbers. It was worse when the film broke. The stamping and yelling was frightening, but Daisy coped, threatening to throw them out. Mrs Prosser who played the piano would thump on the keys and everybody would join in with the sing-song till the film was repaired, then a huge cheer would go up and they would settle down again. Daisy didn't have to do any cleaning now, as Mr Holden employed a cleaner. On Saturday nights between the films they had dancing girls, and Daisy was intrigued and spent her time watching them and trying out the routines when she was on her own.

All That Jazz

*

A year had passed since the Roxy opened, and their lives had changed for the better. The hours were long and Daisy was on her feet all day, but she enjoyed her work. She loved seeing the news and all that was going on in the world. She also looked forward to Sundays, her day off. There was a rumour they could be having films on Sundays, but at the moment the Church was very much against it. On Sundays she and Mary would go to the park or wander round the closed shops just looking in the windows and laughing at the latest fashions. Daisy loved being with her sister.

Every morning she sent Mary to school and did the shopping and cleaning of their two rooms. With her wages she had bought some second-hand blankets and washed them as soon as she got home just in case there were any bugs or fleas lingering in them. There was always food on the table now, but Daisy thought there was something missing in her life. She was almost nineteen and felt that life should hold something more than just work. Today was a wet and miserable day and she had come into work early as Mary had gone to the museum with some school friends. She was standing in the foyer looking at the posters for next week's films, which included Mary Pickford in *Through the Back Door*. Mary Pickford, who always seemed to be in trouble, and Rudolph Valentino, with his dark smouldering eyes, were her favourites, and Charlie Chaplin always made her laugh.

'You look a bit down in the dumps, girl, what's up?'

Daisy turned to see Rhoda, the head dancer, standing next to her. On Saturdays Daisy tried to have a chat with her, as she loved to hear about some of the places she'd been to as a dancer.

'Nothing really.'

Rhoda nudged her arm. 'Come on, I know a lovesick look when I see one. So, who's the lucky feller?'

Daisy gave her a weak smile. 'That's it. I only wish there was one, but being here every day I don't get a chance to meet any.'

'What about his nibs?' She inclined her head towards Mr Holden's office door.

Daisy laughed. 'He's me boss. Besides, he's ever so old.'

'He ain't that old and he ain't that bad looking, and I reckon he's worth a bob or two.'

'He might have a lady friend for all I know.' Daisy laughed. 'No. He's not definitely not for me. I want a handsome young man.'

'You don't wonner be too fussy, me girl. Men like him are thin on the ground. I would a thought that with all the blokes that come through that door, someone would snap up a good-looking girl like you.'

'They just see me as someone with a torch who shows 'em to their seats; besides, most of 'em have got girls.'

'Rhoda, get yer arse in here, we're waiting to start rehearsal for that new routine.'

'Coming, Joe,' she called out. 'See yer later, Dais.'

Daisy wandered into the cinema and stood at the back to watch the rehearsal as she often did if she didn't have anywhere to go and Mary was out somewhere. Joe was putting the girls through their paces and would shout at them to keep in line. Several times he'd stop and make them do it again. She smiled. Joe, for all his shouting, was slim and very dramatic; he was also very good looking, with his hair falling over his dark brown eyes. And he was a wonderful dancer.

Suddenly Joe fell to his knees and put his head in his hands. 'What am I gonner do with you lot? You're more like elephants than dancers. Anybody could do this routine, with their eyes shut, but you lot . . . I give up.' He laid down on the stage and the girls began giggling.

'Get up and stop being such a silly bugger,' said Rhoda.

'I'll only get up if you promise to do it properly.'

Daisy began to laugh.

Joe caught sight of her. 'What are you laughing at?'

'I'm sorry.'

'Get out. Get out.'

Daisy turned. 'I'm sorry,' she said over her shoulder.

'Daisy, stop right there.' Rhoda came to the edge of the stage. 'Don't take any notice of him. You come and watch. Come on. Come and sit in the front row.'

Daisy was very apprehensive, but slowly she did as Rhoda told her. Although she was enjoying the banter between Rhoda and Joe, she couldn't help but wish she was up there with them.

At the end of the rehearsal Daisy went over to Rhoda. 'Thank you for letting me watch you. I hope I didn't get you into any trouble.'

'Na, I don't take no notice of him, his bark's worse than his bite. You looked like you was enjoying watching us, saw your foot tapping.'

'It was. I'd love to be able to do something like that.'

'Would you? I could have a word with Joe if you like.'

'No. No. I couldn't.'

'You could always come along to a rehearsal and see if you like it.'

'No, thanks all the same but I don't want Mr Holden thinking I'm doing something behind his back.'

Rhoda gave her a gentle nudge. 'Come on, it'll do you good to do something different.'

'Yes, I know.'

'Well then. That's settled. Next Sat'day come in a bit earlier and we'll give you a go. Who knows? You might be a natural.'

'What about Joe? What will he say?'

'Don't worry about him, I'll sort him out.'

'I don't know . . .'

'Come on, what you got to lose?'

'Only me job.'

'He wouldn't sack you for that, so what d'yer say?'

Daisy shrugged.

'Right then, see you here at ten.'

Daisy watched Rhoda walk away. Why had she agreed? She must be mad. What if Mr Holden caught her? Would he sack her? All these things were racing round her head. She couldn't risk it and knew then that she wouldn't be here early next Saturday.

But all week Daisy thought about Rhoda, and sometimes she practised some of the steps she'd seen the girls do, but the thought of getting on the stage and dancing was very different.

It was on Thursday that her mind was almost made up for her.

'Daisy,' called Mr Holden as she went over to the box office to hand in the tickets that she had collected and put on her wire. 'I won't be in till lunchtime on Sat'day, though well before we open. Will you be all right?'

'Yes, yes, of course.' He had been late in

before. He never told her where he was going and she wouldn't dare ask.

What if she did come in early? Who would tell him? She had tomorrow to think about it and make a decision.

On Saturday morning Daisy thought that Mary was still asleep when she slipped out of bed. She had been so excited that last night sleep had been hard to come by. Her mind was turning over and over. What if she made a fool of herself? Last night Rhoda had told her that she'd settled it with Joe and today Daisy was hopefully going to dance on the stage, but what if she fell over and embarrassed herself?

'Where you going?' asked Mary as she peered over the blankets.

'I thought you was asleep. I've got to go to work.'

Mary watched her sister get dressed. 'Why you going so early?'

'I have to.'

Mary turned over and mumbled, 'It ain't fair. I'm always on me own. I thought we could go out somewhere.'

Although Daisy felt full of guilt, she knew this might be the only opportunity she'd have. 'I'm sorry, but it's only the once. I'll take you out tomorrow. You try and think of where you'd like to go.'

When Mary didn't answer, Daisy knew she was angry. 'I'm sorry. But I really do have to go.'

'You think more of your blooming job than you do of me.'

Daisy sat back down on the bed. 'Mary, that's a rotten thing to say. I work very hard and make sure you have what I can afford. If I got the sack and had to go back in a shop, you wouldn't have new clothes.'

'They ain't new.'

'I know, but at least you've got shoes that don't let in water now.'

Mary didn't answer.

Daisy went into the other room and put the curling tongs she had bought in the market on the fire. Should she tell Mary what she was going to do? Would she mind? Or would she feel they were drifting apart? Daisy couldn't bear that, and as this might be only a one-off, she decided to keep it to herself. She stood in front of the piece of broken mirror that was wedged up on the mantelpiece. She had found the mirror years ago and her mother had been very pleased when she brought it home, then she could comb her hair and pinch her cheeks to make them red. Daisy still thought about her mother often. She had always looked nice and tried so hard to keep herself and the girls neat and clean even when they had nothing.

Mary came into the room. 'What are you doing to your hair with those things?'

'I'm trying to put some waves in.'

'Well it looks silly.'

'It's all the rage.'

'Why do you have to put them in the fire?'

'I have to warm them up.'

'You'll set your hair on fire if you ain't careful.'

'I'm careful.' Daisy knew that if she was going to see Rhoda and Joe this morning, she had to look the part. When Daisy had asked Rhoda how the girls all had waves in their hair, Rhoda had told her that they used tongs, and so Daisy had gone and bought some; she wanted to be fashionable like the other girls.

She stood looking at herself. 'What d'you think?'

'I think it looks silly all sticking up like that.'

'It'll look better when I've brushed it out.'

Mary walked back into the bedroom. Daisy knew she was angry, but she couldn't let this opportunity pass by. She had both their futures to think about, after all.

Chapter 8

DAISY WAS VERY nervous as she made her way to work, and even more so when she pushed open the door that led to the stalls. It was very dark but the stage was well lit and all the girls were standing around chatting. Daisy slowly walked down the aisle and Rhoda caught sight of her.

'Daisy, come on up here.'

Daisy made her way to the steps at the side of the stage, and as she carefully mounted them she smiled at Joe and the girls.

'So, you wonner be a dancer,' said Joe, walking round her and looking her up and down, making one or two of the girls giggle.

'I don't know, but I'd like to have a go.'

'Have you been to dancing classes before?'

Daisy shook her head.

'Well that's not a very good start, is it? Do you know your left foot from your right?'

'Yes.'

There was more giggling from the girls.

'Right, show me the time step.'

Daisy stood looking at him. 'What's that?'

'Oh dear. Rhoda, darling, what have I told you about bringing in lame ducks for me to turn into proud peacocks.'

'Don't talk such a load of tripe,' she replied. 'Give the girl a chance.'

Joe tossed his head. 'I sometimes despair at what you expect from me. Daisy, I can only give you a short while to see what you can do, as we've got to get on with this rehearsal.'

'Thank you. I understand, Mr Joe.'

Again some of the girls laughed, and Daisy wanted to die of embarrassment. What had she let herself in for? She wanted to run away and she looked over at Rhoda, who gave her the thumbs-up.

Joe clapped his hands. 'Come along, girls, we ain't got all day, and it looks like we've got to start right from the beginning with Daisy here. Now get in line and show Daisy what the time step is. Right, one two three.'

Daisy looked around bewildered as they stood in a line and began to tap their feet.

'Get on the end next to Rhoda and see if you can keep up,' yelled Joe. 'Right, girls. Straight tap, forward tap, back tap, toe tap.'

Daisy did as she was told and, holding Rhoda round the waist, began to join in, but her long skirt was making it difficult.

'Stop. Stop.' Joe walked up to Daisy. 'Have you got any shorts?' he asked.

Daisy shook her head. 'What for?'

'To wear, of course. You can't do anything in that skirt.'

'I'll lend you a pair,' said Rhoda. 'Come with me.'

Daisy was shaking with fear. She was making a right mess of this time step. She was totally out of rhythm and felt such a fool.

She followed Rhoda behind a screen. 'I can't do this. I'm wasting Mr Joe's time.'

'Don't worry; you'll soon get the hang of it.' Rhoda dived into a large bag and handed her a pair of shorts. 'Put these on.'

Daisy held them up. 'I can't wear these.'

'Why not, we're about the same size.'

'I can't show me legs off like that.'

'Why not? All of them out there are wearing shorts.' She inclined her head to where Daisy could hear the girls laughing. 'And you've seen some of the costumes we wear on stage. If you wonner be a dancer, you'll have to show 'em what you've got.'

'I don't know if I want to be a dancer.'

'You'll never know till you try. Come on, take that skirt off and put these on.'

Slowly Daisy did as she was told and stood in front of Rhoda embarrassed. Only Mary had seen her half naked like this.

Rhoda walked round her. 'D'you know, Dais, you ain't got a bad pair of pins. Come on, let's show 'em what you can do.'

Daisy slunk behind Rhoda as they went back on to the stage, but nobody took any notice of her.

'Right. Get in line again and let's see what you're made of,' said Joe.

'This is what you do,' said Rhoda, taking Daisy's hand and slowly going through the time step.

'Ready,' shouted Joe. 'Right, one two three. Tap forward . . .' He walked up and down the line looking at them while shouting out instructions.

The clattering of their feet dancing in rhythm was intoxicating, and suddenly Daisy was in step and beginning to enjoy it, despite dancing in her everyday shoes.

Joe walked up to Daisy. 'That wasn't bad for a beginner. Now we're gonner do the riff.'

'What's that?'

'Watch. Toe, heel, heel, ball.'

Daisy was concentrating on what Joe was showing her. He was very light on his feet.

'Right. Let's see if you can follow what the others do, but don't get in the way.'

For the next half-hour, Daisy tried to follow the other girls, and when she got it right, she loved it.

'Sorry, love,' said Joe, coming over to her. 'You'll have to stand out the way now, we must get on with the rehearsal.'

'Of course. I understand.'

'Stay and watch, you might be able to pick up a few steps.'

'Thank you for being so patient.'

Joe came up close to her. 'D'you know, I reckon with a bit of teaching, you could be quite good.'

Daisy blushed. 'I'm not sure about that.' She watched him walk over to the girls, then she went round the back to put her skirt back on. Rhoda followed her.

'Dais, that was wonderful. You picked that up real quick.'

'Did I? I must admit I felt a bit like an elephant and I couldn't think what was coming next.'

'You did very well. Did you enjoy it?'

'Yes I did, and Mr Joe said I was all right.'

'Well then, if he reckons you've got what it takes, you're halfway there.'

Daisy's eyes were shining. 'Do you really think so?'

'Perhaps you can come again next Sat'day.'

'I'd love to. Where did you learn to dance?'

'Went to dancing classes.'

'My mum couldn't afford such things, and besides, she always said that only loose women went on the stage.'

Rhoda laughed. 'And what did she say about the blokes?'

'They were all fancy blokes.'

She laughed again. 'Yer mum could be right there.'

For the rest of the week Daisy wanted to find out if Mr Holden was going to be around on Saturday. All week she had been practising the time step and the riff. It was coming easy now, but could she master some of the other intricate steps they did in the show? Today was Friday, and so far Mr Holden hadn't said anything. Daisy would be so disappointed if she couldn't get up on the stage. Her mind was full of it as for the past hour she had been standing in the laundry room rubbing the pillowcases up and down the scrubbing board. She wiped her hands down her sacking apron. She desperately wanted to do some more dancing. Perhaps she might even be good enough to go on the stage, but that was all wishful dreaming. She picked up the heavy bucket of washing and took it along to the drying room.

Daisy was getting ready for work when Mary came in from school full of excitement.

'Guess what? Tilly's mum's asked me to tea

termorrer. Is that all right?' Mary felt that her sister didn't really care where she was while she was at work. They might have more to eat now, and she did have shoes that didn't let in the water, but she was lonely, and every night she tried to concentrate on her reading and writing but the racket from the street and fights in the courtyard frightened her. She wished that Daisy didn't have to work every night.

'That's fine.'

'She said I could go round in the morning and spend all day with 'em, that's if I want.' Mary looked at her sister, worried she'd say no.

'That's all right.'

'You don't mind?'

'No. You go and enjoy yourself. I'll give you sixpence to get something to eat.'

'Thanks, Dais.'

'Don't get into any mischief.' Daisy was pleased her sister had a friend to play with.

'I won't.'

'On Sunday you can show me what you've done at school this week.'

Daisy checked the back of her legs to make sure her stockings were straight. It wouldn't do to have wrinkles in them. Mr Holden was very fussy that the girls should always look smart.

Saturday morning Daisy was thrilled to be standing in the foyer waiting for Rhoda and the gang to arrive. When Mr Holden had said he would be out again today she was overjoyed.

'You gonner have another go?' asked Charlie as he stood next to her.

'I hope so.'

'You looked as if you was enjoying yourself.'

'I was. Oh Charlie, it was lovely being with the girls and tapping away.'

Charlie smiled. 'I could see that.'

'You won't say anything to Mr Holden, will you?'

'Course not. Go on, they've arrived.'

Daisy rushed up to the stage and Rhoda took her to one side and handed her her shorts. Then once again she was standing in line waiting for her orders from Joe.

'I see you've come along again,' he said.

She nodded. 'I hope you don't mind.'

'Just as long as you don't get in the way.'

'I won't.'

'Good.'

For the next hour or so Daisy was joining in where she could. She was so thrilled. She knew this was where she should be.

'Right, girls, we're gonner do the Little Bo Peep number.' Joe looked around. 'Now, you've gotter get this right for when we go on to the Empire. Daisy, you go over there and watch.'

She did as she was told and watched as the girls were suddenly transformed into a troupe of professional dancers. At the end of the number she clapped. 'That was wonderful,' she said, jumping to her feet.

'I'm glad you approve,' said Joe.

Rhoda came up to her. 'I think you've made a good impression on his nibs.'

'Rhoda, this is so . . . I don't know. I've never felt so happy before. I only hope Mr Holden goes away next Sat'day and I can come again.'

'Dais, I'm sorry, but we're gonner be at the Empire for a season. I'm so excited. We won't be playing in some cinema while they change the film; we will be on a real stage, doing a proper show.'

Daisy stood and looked at her. 'Why didn't you tell me?'

'Didn't think it would be that important to you. You have lots of acts come and go.'

'We do. But I like you. You've given me a new outlook.'

'I'm sorry.'

'What should I do?'

'If you want my advice, you'll join a dance group.'

'I can't, not without you around.'

'You should, you're a natural dancer.'

Daisy tried to smile. 'Am I? Do you really think I could go on the stage?'

'Don't see why not. I'll have a word with Joe. He knows a lot of people, he might be able to help.'

'Thank you.'

'Wait and see what Joe says. Now, I must go and get something to eat. See you tonight.'

Daisy stood and watched her walk away. She had been so happy dancing, and now it could all be coming to an end. She wondered what the entertainment would be next Saturday.

That evening Mr Holden came and stood next to her as the girls were dancing.

'Rhoda was telling me that this is their last week,' Daisy said.

'That's right. I've been setting up next Sat'day's slot.'

'We gonner have another dance troupe?'

'No.' He turned and smiled at her. 'I think you'll like this. This time we're gonner have a dancing dog act.'

Daisy couldn't answer that.

Chapter 9

DAISY WAITED TILL the first house had settled down to watch the picture and Mr Holden was up with the projectionist, then quickly made her way backstage.

'Hello, Dais,' said Rhoda as she came out of the dressing room, still in the bright pink shorts and white top she had been wearing for the tap dancing number. 'What can I do for you?'

Daisy looked round nervously. 'Did you have a word with Mr Joe?'

'Yer. He reckons you should try and see a Madam Truelove. I remember her when she was just plain Jenny Clifton. She used to be a dancer before she married; now she teaches and the good news is that he thinks she could live quite near here.'

'D'you know where?'

'Joe's gonner look in the trade paper and he'll write it down for you. I hope you can afford the lessons as I really think you'll make it.'

Daisy smiled. 'Do you? Do you really?'

'I certainly do, and by the way, so does Joe, otherwise he wouldn't bother.'

Although Daisy was trying to be happy, she was upset that her friend would be leaving tonight. Rhoda was the first friend she'd ever had and she was very sorry to see her go. 'Thanks.'

'I'll try and say goodbye before we leave tonight.'

Daisy hurried down the corridor. 'You can always write to me here,' she said quickly over her shoulder. She wanted to be a dancer, but how much did this Madam Truelove charge? And would it all be a waste of money?

At the end of the evening the cinema was empty and all the lights were on. Somehow it always looked so stark and uninteresting at the end of the last performance. Cigarette butts along with sweet wrappers and apple cores littered the floor. Daisy was pleased she didn't have to do the sweeping-up in here now. It looked hard working between the rows of red plush seats. Daisy stood waiting for Rhoda. She was beginning to feel a bit down, as during the evening common sense had come to her. Daisy had enjoyed Rhoda's company so much and knew this was the life she wanted to lead, but what about Mary? She couldn't just go off all over the place and leave her.

'Hello, Daisy, here's that address.' Rhoda handed Daisy a piece of paper.

'Thank you.'

'I'm glad you come to see us off. D'you know, I reckon we could make a good pair. How about calling us the Rhoda Sisters?' She stepped forward, then very dramatically opened her arms and said, 'Make way for the dynamic Rhoda Sisters.' She laughed as she picked up her bag.

Daisy had been admiring Rhoda's very fetching navy cloche hat and her matching coat with a big fur collar. Her pointed shoes were also navy blue. 'You look very nice,' she said.

'Well you have to look the part, you never know who's waiting at the stage door. Might be some rich impresario who wants me to star in his next big show.'

'Would you leave Mr Joe and the girls?'

'Too bloody right. But I don't think that will ever happen; well, not here, not round Rotherhithe.' She grinned.

'Are you and Mr Joe, you know, walking out?'

Rhoda burst out laughing again. 'Course not.' She moved closer. 'The reason is . . .'

'Rhoda. Get your arse out here,' Joe called from the stage.

'Coming. Bye for now, Dais, and keep up with the dancing.' She kissed Daisy on both cheeks and sashayed down the corridor and out of the door.

Daisy watched her and felt really down. How she would love this sort of life.

'Everything all right, girl?' asked Charlie, coming up to her.

'Yes, just saying goodbye to Rhoda.'

'You got on all right with that lot, didn't you?' She nodded.

'Mind you, I thought that Joe was a bit how's-yer-father. Would hate a boy of mine to act like that.'

'You ain't got a son.'

'I know, but I still wouldn't like it if I did.'

'Just 'cos he's a dancer?'

'No, it's because he looks like a bit of a nancy boy.'

'What d'you mean?'

'Don't worry about it now. I'll tell you one day. Next week we're gonner have a bloody dog act. All I hope is that it's well trained. We don't wonner be going round clearing up after it, do we?'

Daisy shook her head.

'Must finish locking up, then I'll be off. See you termorrer.'

'Yes. Bye.' Daisy picked up her handbag and put the address in it, but she knew it would be in vain. She looked up at the office where she knew Mr Holden was adding up tonight's takings. What would he say if he knew she had been thinking of becoming a dancer?

When Daisy arrived home, the first thing she always did was to look in on Mary, who was fast asleep. She stood at the bedroom door and watched the little girl's steady breathing. How could she even think of becoming a dancer? She had her sister to look after. She wandered into the living room, where the kettle on the hob was gently raising its lid. She made herself a cup of tea and took the paper Rhoda had given her from her handbag.

Madam Truelove. Dance teacher of the Baby Beams troupe, 92 Carr Street. Carr Street was just off Rotherhithe New Road. She turned the paper over and sat and looked at it. Would it do any harm just to go and see this woman? Perhaps Mary might like to join her dance troupe. Once again Daisy was letting her imagination run away with her. She smiled. What if they both learnt to dance? They could become the Cooper Sisters. With this thought racing round her head, she turned out the gaslight and made her way to bed.

Mary stirred as Daisy slipped in beside her. She held her sister close. 'Looks like we could be starting a new life soon,' Daisy whispered.

Sunday morning as usual Daisy was up first. She made the tea and was sitting in front of the fire toasting some bread when Mary wandered in rubbing the sleep from her eyes.

'Hello, Mary. Do you want some toast?'

Mary nodded. 'Can we have jam on it?'

'Course we can. Get a plate and come and sit down.'

Mary took a plate from the dresser and sat next to her.

How different things are now I'm working at the cinema, thought Daisy. They had toast and jam and a few cups and plates on the dresser. 'What you doing this morning?' she asked Mary as she passed the toast to her.

'Nothing. Why?'

'Have you got any sums for me to look at?'

'No.'

'And what does your teacher have to say about you?'

'She says I'm doing all right.'

Daisy sat forward. 'How about if we go out this morning?'

'Where to?'

'I've got to go and see a lady in Carr Street.'

'What for?'

'You'll see when we get there.'

'Are we gonner go and try to find our relations?'

'No. I think I would have to go to the police station for that and I don't think they would be much help on a Sunday.'

'Oh,' was all Mary said.

Seeing how Mary looked disappoionted, Daisy added, 'We will go one day. Now, when you've finished your toast get yourself dressed and put on that hat and coat I bought you last week.'

'It itches. I'm sure it's got fleas in it.'

'Course it ain't.' Sometimes Daisy got cross with Mary; she never seemed to be satisfied with anything she bought her just lately. 'What's wrong with you?'

'I'm fed up with being on me own every night. Why can't you get a job where you're home with me?'

'I wouldn't get the money I'm earning, that's why.' Daisy didn't dare add that she loved her job. 'Remember how we had to scrimp and save when I was at the greengrocer's?'

Mary nodded but still kept her grumpy look. 'I'll go and get ready.'

'Good girl.' Would Mary like to have

dancing lessons? Well, she would find out soon enough.

When they approached 92 Carr Street, Daisy was impressed at the size of the house.

As they walked up the path Mary asked, 'What we doing here?'

'Read what it say's on that brass plate.'

'Baby Beams Dancing School.' She looked at Daisy, horrified. 'I ain't going ter no dancing school. What do I wonner come here for?'

'I thought it would be nice for us to do something together.'

'What, learn ter dance?'

'If I could dance, I could do it at the cinema, you know, like Rhoda does on a Sat'day night.'

'You gonner get up there and show off yer legs?'

'I don't know. I don't know if I can dance, or how much this woman charges. But I thought we could do it together.'

'I don't wonner learn to dance.'

'Oh come on, Mary, it could be good fun. Besides, now we're here, let's ring the bell and find out.'

Mary stood back and Daisy rang the bell.

It was a minute or two before the door flew open. 'What time do you call this?' asked the woman who had opened it.

'I'm sorry,' said Daisy, flustered. The woman was still in her long floaty nightie and she wore a matching dressing gown over it. They were in the most beautiful blue colour.

'It's Sunday, you know. A day of rest.' The woman ran her fingers through her blonde hair that looked a bit like a bird's nest.

'I am so very sorry. Come on, Mary.' Daisy turned to walk away.

'Just a minute. Now you've got me out of bed, what d'you want?'

'I work at the cinema, and Joe and Rhoda told me to come and see you as you teach people to dance.'

'Joe and Rhoda.' Her brusque voice softened. 'Where are they working now?'

'They were at the cinema, but they're finished now; we've got a dog act next week.' Daisy didn't know why she said that. Was it because she was frightened of this woman, who was head and shoulders taller than her and had a powerful presence?

'So, my old mate Rhoda sent you. It's years since I saw her. You'd better come in, otherwise I'll catch me death of cold standing here.' She stood to one side and they entered the house.

Daisy tried hard not to be seen looking all around her. The hall was magnificent. The light from the door's stained-glass window sent a myriad of colours across the tiled floor that had scatter rugs at all the doors. In front of them the stairs disappeared round a bend and were tiled the same as the hall floor. There was also a rich wooden handrail along the wall. A large vase of flowers stood on the half-table against one wall.

'Right, we'll go in here.' Madam Truelove pushed open the door to the room at the front of the house. It was a bright room with the whole of one wall covered with a mirror. The only furniture was a piano; there were no rugs on the wooden floor.

'This is me studio. Now, what's this all about?'

Daisy was nervous. She cleared her throat. 'Mr Joe gave me your address and said you might give me, and me sister here,' she added rapidly, 'dancing lessons.'

'Have you done any dancing before?'

'No. But Rhoda said I was picking it up real quick when they let me join in.' Out of the corner of her eye she saw Mary look at her.

'I see. Turn round.'

Daisy did as she was told.

'You've got the build to be a dancer. And what about you, young lady?'

'I don't wonner dance. This is all for me sister.'

'I see.'

'Madam Truelove, how much d'you charge?'

'The first lesson's free so that I can weigh up your potential. If you're any good and I want to take you on, I charge one and six an hour and I expect you to sign a contract to say that whenever I get someone who wants dancers I can send you straight away.'

'I'm not sure if I could do that.'

'Well that would be up to you. But I run a business here and a lot of people want my dancers and they have to be ready to drop everything.'

Daisy stood looking down at her feet. She felt very dejected.

'Cheer up. Let's see what your potential is

first. You may have two left feet and perform like an elephant, in which case that wouldn't be any use to me and I'd be taking your money under false pretences and you'd be wasting my time.'

'When shall I come?'

'How about tomorrow morning about ten.'

'That would be nice. Thank you.'

When they were outside, Mary turned on her. 'What d'yer wonner do this for?'

'I want to be a dancer.'

'Why?'

'Oh Mary, don't you see, I'll be able to go all over the place dancing.'

'And you'll be leaving me on me own all the time. So what yer gonner do with me then? Put me in a home?'

'No, of course not. Why don't you come with me and see if you'd like to dance?'

'I don't wonner stand on some stage prancing about in me drawers.'

'It's not like that.'

'It is.' Mary kicked a stone. 'I thought we'd always be together, just you and me. I thought you promised Mum you'd always look after me.'

Daisy stopped and held her sister tight. She felt full of guilt. What had she been thinking about? This couldn't be for her. Girls from Chapel Court didn't become dancers. 'Of course I'll look after you. It was silly of me to even think of doing this.'

Mary smiled and taking her big sister's hand, they walked home.

Chapter 10

FOR MOST OF the night Daisy lay wide awake. She knew she should have dismissed all thoughts of Madam Truelove from her mind but she couldn't. Over and over her thoughts churned. What could happen if she went to see the woman this morning? Should she go? It wouldn't hurt anyone, not just to go and see her; after all it was free, but should she lie to Mary?

As soon as it started to get light, Daisy left Mary sleeping and made her way into the other room. She made up the fire and put the kettle on the hob. Why was she feeling so disgruntled? Was it so wrong to see if she was able to do something completely different? But what if this woman told her she had the potential to become a dancer? How could she pursue it knowing that it would always be evening work and she could be asked to work a long way from here? No, she couldn't leave Mary. Besides, she lived in Chapel Court; nobody from round here did things like that. She sat on the battered sofa and watched the flames lick the sides of the blackened kettle. 'What shall I do, Mum?' she whispered out loud. 'Would it do any harm just to go and see this woman?'

After Mary left for school, Daisy began her chores but couldn't concentrate. In the end she changed her clothes, combed her hair and left the building.

Once again she was walking up the path to Madam Truelove's. The sound of someone playing the piano drifted through the window and Daisy could hear the dance teacher shouting at her pupils. She sounded very angry. Is this what I want? Daisy asked herself before ringing the bell. But it was too late to change her mind, as a young lady wearing a black dress with a spotless white apron over and a little cap at the front of her dark hair opened the door immediately.

'Are you Daisy?'

'Yes.'

'I saw you walking up the path. Come in, Madam's expecting you.'

'Thank you,' said Daisy, unsure of what to do or say next.

'Wait here.' The young lady gently knocked on the door to the studio. 'Daisy's here, Madam.' She turned to Daisy. 'She'll be out in a minute.'

'Thank you,' said Daisy again.

After a while a young lady came out followed by Madam. The young lady was wiping her eyes.

'I despair of you, Betty, I really do. I know you can do it, but you must just apply yourself and don't let that father of yours nag you. I will tell him when you're ready to go on the stage, so don't listen to him.'

'But I have to, Madam. He pays for my lessons.'

'I know that. Practise today's steps and see if you can do any better tomorrow.'

'I will.' The young lady quickly glanced at Daisy and left.

'Come in, Daisy.' Madam Truelove's face was now wreathed in smiles. Daisy was admiring her frock; it was long and very floaty with large flowers all over, and somehow she seemed to waft about. Her hair was held back with a matching band. 'I'm only hoping that you will bring a smile to my face this bright Monday morning. Now, have you got tap shoes?'

Daisy looked bewildered. 'I didn't think . . .'

'Don't worry, I always keep a few pairs here. They're in the cupboard. Find yourself a pair and make sure they fit well. And a pair of shorts while you're there; you can't dance in that skirt.'

Daisy looked at the pianist. She was an elderly lady who was wearing a floor-length lavender-coloured frock, and her white hair was held back with a matching band. She only gave Daisy a cursory glance as she scrabbled about in the cupboard filled with hats, canes and various other props. Shyly Daisy pulled on a pair of shorts under her skirt, then, turning her back, discreetly let her skirt fall to the ground and stepped out of it. She felt uneasy about showing her legs as she undid her suspenders and rolled down her stockings. After trying on different shoes, she found a pair that fitted. 'These seem all right.' She stood up and her taps made a noise on the wooden floor. She smiled and looked down at the shiny black shoes. She had tied the black ribbons in big bows like she'd seen Rhoda do.

'Right, now stand next to me and look in the mirror, don't look down at your feet. First we'll do the time step, that's the easy one, and then we'll progress from there.'

An hour later Daisy was elated. Most of the time she was able to follow Madam Truelove; a few times she got it wrong, but all the while her teacher was shouting encouragement.

A knock on the door stopped them and the maid called out that Madam's next pupil had arrived.

Madam Truelove dabbed at her face with a towel. She then held Daisy's shoulders. 'You have done exceptionally well. Joe and Rhoda were right to send you to me. This morning has been a pleasure, you are definitely a natural and I believe that after a couple of months you could be ready to go on the stage.'

Daisy was thrilled. 'Do you really think so?'

She looked at the pianist; she too was smiling.

'Now, can you come again tomorrow?'

Daisy looked at her in horror. 'No, I couldn't.'

'I'd like you to come every day.'

'I'm sorry, but I wouldn't be able to afford more than one lesson a week.'

'We will have to see what sort of arrangement we can come to. It is so rare to get someone off the streets that can actually dance.'

Daisy couldn't answer.

'She don't often say that, love,' said the woman at the piano. 'So if I was you, I'd take her up on it.'

'I don't know.'

'Did you enjoy dancing?' asked Madam.

'Yes. Yes, I did.'

'Well then. But it's up to you. With me teaching you and plenty of practice, you could have a glamorous life, meeting people who love to have a good time. You could be wearing the latest furs and fashions and taken out to be wined and dined at all the top places. That's how I met my husband. I was a dancer once; now look at all I've got.' She waved her arms about theatrically. 'Think very carefully about it. The world could be your oyster; with your looks you could knock 'em dead. But I must insist that I manage you.'

Daisy couldn't believe this woman; she was racing ahead. All Daisy had done was dance a few steps, and now Madam had her going out wearing wonderful clothes and being wined and dined. 'Can I have time to think about this?'

'Of course, but please, if you can't manage tomorrow, come back next week.' Madam kissed Daisy on both cheeks and then opened the door.

As Daisy walked back home, her mind was racing. How could so much happen in such a short time? She knew she loved dancing and that it did come easy to her, but for Madam Truelove to get so enthusiastic about it . . . Daisy smiled to herself. She must have some pretty awful students if I'm the best she's got. But what could she tell Mary? After all, she had made a promise.

That afternoon when she arrived at work she desperately wanted to talk to someone about this morning, but she didn't have anyone. If only Rhoda and Joe were still here.

'You look a bit down in the mouth,' said Charlie when she walked in.

'I really miss Rhoda.'

'I expect you do. Why don't you pop over and see 'em next Sat'day morning, They're over Lambeth way, ain't they?'

'I don't know. Where is that?'

'It ain't that far away. I reckon you can get a bus there. Ask Mr H, he'll know.'

Daisy smiled. 'Thanks, Charlie.'

The following Saturday, Daisy didn't go to Lambeth because she would have to take Mary and she would think they were going to look for their relations. Daisy wouldn't know where to start. Mary would be very angry if she knew Daisy was only going to talk to Rhoda about dancing, so she decided to take her to the market.

On Monday Daisy went along to the dance school and was greeted with open arms.

'Daisy, I'm so pleased you've come. Now, this morning we are going to run through a routine that some of my older students do on a stage up north. I have brought in the gramophone, so when you get the routine you can dance to it the same as they do.'

Daisy was bewildered. All this was happening too fast.

'Get your tap shoes on and we can begin.'

In no time Daisy was standing in front of the huge mirror following Madam Truelove's steps. The shouts of enthusiasm only made her work harder.

'Get a cane and top hat from the cupboard. Right, follow me.'

After a while, a tapping on the door brought them to a stop.

'I've never been so excited about anything in my life before,' said Madam as she dabbed at her face with a towel. 'I feel that after all these years a light is shining on me.'

Daisy smiled. She wanted to laugh at this woman who was in such a state over her dancing.

'Daisy, when can you come back again? Can you be here tomorrow?'

'No. I'm sorry. As I said, I can only just about afford to come once a week.'

'That will have to do for the time being, but you must try to come more often.'

As Daisy walked home, she knew that once a week was going to be a bit of a struggle, and although she was full of guilt at seemingly wasting their money, it was something she had to do.

Every week for the next month, Daisy went to her dancing school. Madam only changed her sixpence as she said she enjoyed teaching her so much. She even helped her buy some tap shoes and shorts. They were second hand but that didn't matter. Daisy left them at the school, as she didn't want Mary to find them. All the while her conscience was bothering her. She knew she should tell her sister, but she also knew that Mary wouldn't understand.

But Mary suspected Daisy was still going to the dancing school, and one Monday morning she came home from school as she wasn't feeling very well and wasn't surprised to find her sister wasn't home.

When Daisy did come in she looked flustered and guilty at seeing Mary sitting there. 'What you doing home?' she asked her younger sister.

'I wasn't feeling very well.'

'What's wrong with you?'

'I've got a stomach ache. Where you bin?'

'Shopping.'

'What d'you buy?'

Daisy began to get agitated. 'I didn't get anything.'

'You look ever so hot.'

'It's very warm out.'

'It ain't that warm.' Mary looked at her.

Daisy dabbed at her face. 'It is outside.'

'You've been to the dancing school again, ain't you?'

'What if I have?'

'You promised you wouldn't go again.'

'But I enjoy it.'

'I hate you. You told me a fib.' Mary went and flung herself on the bed.

Daisy went in to her. 'Why are you so against me doing this?'

Mary turned her back to her and didn't answer.

'Well if that's the way you feel.' Daisy went and sat on the sofa.

Mary knew she was being unreasonable, but she didn't want Daisy to learn to dance and leave her alone even more than she did now. She had been round the back of the cinema and seen some of the dancers leaning against the wall smoking and laughing about how they'd been out with men and after getting drunk slept with them. She didn't want that to happen to her sister, so she decided to teach her a lesson.

On Friday night when Daisy got home from the cinema, as usual she crept in to see Mary, but she wasn't in bed. Where was she? Was she out in the lav? Daisy went outside to look, but the lav was empty. She was beginning to panic. Had she come home from school? Who would she go to? Daisy couldn't remember the name of her school friend or where she lived. Tears rolled down her cheeks. She should have taken more interest in her sister. She was beside herself. Who could she go to for help? Mrs Wilson might know something; Mary was always saying what a nice lady she was and she sometimes went to see her. Daisy looked at the little clock they now possessed. It was midnight. Could she go and wake Mrs Wilson up? Mary shouldn't be out at this time of night.

Daisy put on her coat and left the building. As

she hurried to Mrs Wilson, she was beginning to get very angry with Mary. How could she behave like this? Daisy had always tried to be good to her. She brushed away her tears with her hand. They would have to have a long talk and get this sorted out.

Chapter 11

IT WAS VERY DARK round the buildings; the only sound apart from some dogs barking was the hissing from the street gas lamp. Daisy had to feel her way up the smelly stairs to Mrs Wilson's flat. Her heart was in her mouth; she was frightened. What if someone jumped out on her? She was so angry with Mary. How dare she do this to her after all they'd been through? Why can't she see that I must have a life other than work? Daisy thought. But for all her anger she still felt very guilty and worried about her. What if Mary wasn't there? What should she do then?

Gently she knocked on Mrs Wilson's door.

All That Jazz

The door was jerked open. 'What the bloody 'ell you doing banging on me door at this time o' night?' Mrs Wilson, who was wearing a coat over her dull pink winceyette nightgown, looked very surprised when she held up her candle and realised who it was. 'Daisy, what you doing 'ere? It's gorn midnight.'

Daisy knew right away that Mary wasn't there. 'It's Mary, she ain't at home. I don't know where she is.' She burst into tears.

'Come on in, love. She must be with her little friend.'

'But why didn't she tell me? I don't know where her friend lives. I'll kill her when she gets home.'

'Now you know you won't. I'll just light the gas. Sit yourself down and we'll try to work this out.' She struck a match and lit the gas mantle that made a loud popping noise then filled the room with a warm glow.

'You don't know where her friend lives, do you?' asked Daisy.

'No. You can't do anythink till the morning, and then you can go to the school, and who knows, she might even be there. Now I think you'd better settle yourself down here for the night, but first I'll make us a nice cuppa tea.'

'It's Sat'day tomorrow. I can't go to the school, it's closed.'

'I know, but the caretaker might be able to help you.'

'But what if she comes home now and I ain't there?'

'It's nearly one o clock in the morning. I shouldn't think she'll be wandering round the streets at this time o' night.'

'No. I suppose you're right.'

Daisy sat and drank the tea Mrs Wilson gave her.

'It's my fault she's staying away.'

'Now why's that? You've always got on so well together.'

'It's because I want to be a dancer.'

'Mary did tell me you was going to some woman for lessons and that she was worried that you might go away.'

'I know. She thinks I'll go on the stage and go away and leave her.'

'So what makes you wonner be a dancer?'

'I've been having lessons and my teacher says I'm very good. And I love it.' Daisy slumped back down again.

'Well, it ain't all bad to have dreams. I'll just get you a blanket.'

'Thank you, Mrs Wilson. I know Mary comes here sometimes.'

'Yes, she does. I'm sure when she gets home she'll be sorry she's upset you. She is very lonely, you know.'

'I know, but I have to go to work to keep us.'

Mrs Wilson patted her hand. 'I know that, love, and so does she.'

Mary was frightened. She didn't know where she was and it was very dark. She began to cry. Why had she got this silly idea in her head to run away? She was angry with her sister; she shouldn't have gone to those dancing lessons. Mary had been full of brave thoughts when she left this afternoon after her sister had gone to work. Daisy had always said they had relations who lived over the river but she didn't know where. She had promised that one day she would try to find them. Mary remembered Daisy saying that they might have to go to a police station to find out. When she left home, that was where she decided to go, but so far she hadn't seen one. She had walked a very long way, her legs hurt and her shoes had been rubbing and had made a blister. She wanted to cry. Earlier she had crossed over a very long bridge and the water below had lots of boats going up and down and it looked very dark and murky. She had stood there for a long while looking at all the activity below. This afternoon she had thought this was a good idea, but now it was dark and she was frightened. She shuddered. She had been out for hours and was lost. She shouldn't have been so silly but she was angry with Daisy. Why hadn't her sister told her she was going to those daft dancing lessons? The thought that had been going round in her head was, what if Daisy goes on the stage, then what will happen to me? Rene Watts had told her that as she had no parents and her sister didn't look after her she could finish up in a kids' home or a workhouse where they starved you and beat you.

Mary sat and leaned against a wall. What should she do? A horse and cart went clomping past and she jerked her head up; she had started to drop off to sleep. She mustn't sit here; she had to find someone to help her. Mary looked around. There didn't seem to be any houses round here. Out of the corner of her eye she saw something move. It was a rat. She couldn't stand rats. They had bitten some of the kids round the buildings. It started to come towards her. She screamed and ran. She didn't see or hear the motorcar that suddenly came round the corner.

Daisy lay awake for most of the night and was relieved when through the thin curtains she could see dawn breaking. She stood up and folded her blanket, filled the kettle and put it on the fire ready for when Mrs Wilson got up.

'You all right, love?' Mrs Wilson asked as she walked into the room, her long steel-grey hair that was normally in a bun hanging down her back.

'Yes thank you.'

'Don't suppose you got a lot of sleep, then?'

'No. What time d'you think I should go to the school?'

'Don't rightly know. I'd give it a while yet. Don't wonner upset the caretaker by banging on the door and waking him.' She went and took some bread from the white enamel bread bin.

'I'll cut off a slice and you can toast it.' She clutched the loaf to her bosom and began slicing through it. 'Here you are, love. Stick that on the toasting fork.' She handed Daisy a thick slice of bread.

'Thank you.' Daisy pushed the fork's prongs through the bread and held it close to the fire. 'What should I do if he can't help me?'

'Then you'll have to go to the police station.'

Daisy turned the bread over and brushed away the tears that were trickling down her cheeks. 'I dunno what I'll do if anythink's happened to her.'

'I'm sure she's all right.'

'But what if she's lying dead somewhere?'

'Now come on. I think you've been seeing too many of them there films.'

Daisy handed the browned toast to Mrs Wilson.

'I've got a bit of jam, would you like that?'

Daisy nodded. 'I'll go round the school about eight. He should be around by then.'

'Come back and tell me what he says. I'm in all day terday. Harry Thorn's coming round later. He's letting me know when the vicar can bury old Mrs Richardson. Poor dear's bin laying waiting for over a week. Bin waiting for her son to come up from the country.'

All of this was going over Daisy's head. She couldn't concentrate on what Mrs Wilson was saying as every few minutes she was looking at the clock that sat on the mantelpiece. At last she said, 'I think I'll go now. Thank you for letting me stay.'

'That's all right, love. Now don't forget, let me know what happens. And if Harry or me hear anything I'll let you know.'

'Thank you.' Daisy pulled on her coat and left.

'What shall I do?' The man was holding his head and pacing up and down.

His female companion was kneeling over the little girl lying in the road. 'Her head's injured. You must take her to the hospital.'

'It wasn't my fault, she ran out in front of me.'

'I know. I saw it. Remember?'

He clutched at her arm. 'Penny, if I do take her, you will tell them it's not my fault, won't you?'

'Of course. What was she doing round here at this time of night and all alone?'

'How the hell do I know?'

'Don't start getting annoyed with me!'

'I'm sorry. But you know how Father always goes on about my driving. What if some of his old cronies in the police get to hear about this? They're always looking for an excuse to put me down.'

'Roger, stop pacing and calm down. Besides, that's not the point at the moment; this young girl is, so come on, put her in the car.'

Reluctantly he scooped the child up in his arms and placed her on the back seat of his car. Penny sat next to her. She was worried that the little girl hadn't moved or cried out.

When Daisy arrived at the school she decided to look around before she went to the caretaker's house. Everywhere seemed very quiet. She walked round the playground. Could Mary be sleeping in one of the sheds? She pushed open a door and it creaked loudly, making her jump. She peered in, waiting for her eyes to get accustomed to the gloom.

'And what d'you think you're doing?'

She spun round. A large man stood in front of her. 'I'm sorry. I was wondering if me sister might be here.'

'And why would she be in the shed?'

'I dunno. I was just looking for her. She ain't been home all night and I thought she might be hiding here.'

'So where's yer mum and dad? They snooping around here as well?'

'No. We ain't got a mum or dad.'

'Oh, I see, so you've run away as well, then?'

'No. Me dad was killed in the war and me mum died a couple of years ago. Please, have you seen her? Her name's Mary, Mary Cooper.'

'Don't know any of the kids' names; you'd better come and see me missus, she might be able to help yer.'

Daisy followed him to the house.

'And who have we here?' asked a round, rosy-faced woman.

'Caught her snooping round the sheds.'

'I was looking for my sister. She ain't come home all night and I'm very worried about her.'

' 'Ere, ain't you the girl what used to work in the greengrocer's?'

Daisy could only nod as tears were running down her cheeks.

'You should 'ear old Ethel Martin going on about how you left her in the lurch. She can't get anyone to stay more than a week or two. You work in that new cinema, don't you?'

Again Daisy could only nod.

'Must be nice seeing all them films every night. 'Ere, d'yer get a chance ter get any free tickets?'

'No.'

'I see. Now what's this you was saying about yer sister?'

Daisy took a deep breath and tried to control her quivering voice. 'Mary Cooper, that's her name, ain't been home all night and I don't know where she is.'

'I know little Mary Cooper. Nice kid.'

'You don't know who she plays with?'

'Na.'

'She sometimes goes home with her friend, but I can't remember her friend's name.'

'Sorry, love. I can't help yer. Look, if she ain't turned up by Monday, come back and have a word with her teacher. She might know something.'

'Thank you.' Daisy turned and walked away.

'You wait till I tell old Ethel Martin I saw yer, and yer look so nice as well.'

Daisy's mind was in turmoil. What should she do now? Where could she go? If only she had someone to talk to.

'I'm afraid the young lady has a nasty bump on her head. The graze is only superficial and doesn't need stitches. I can't see any broken bones or anything like that.'

'Thank goodness. She will be all right, won't she, doctor?'

'I don't see why not. She is out cold at the moment but we will just clean up the wound and she should come round soon. Do you know her?'

'No,' said Penny. 'Unfortunately she just ran into the road and my husband couldn't avoid hitting her.'

'I see. You will have to report this.'

'Yes, I know. At the moment my husband is very shaken.'

'I can understand that.'

'I'll leave you our address and you can keep us informed of her progress.'

'I'll have to inform her next of kin.'

'I don't know anything about her. Does she have any identification on her? We could go and tell her parents. They must be very worried about her. What was she doing out on her own at this time of night?'

'I'm afraid a lot of these children are left to roam the streets while their parents are out boozing. I'll get a nurse to go through her pockets.'

Penny smiled. 'Thank you.' She walked back to the waiting room, and as soon as she opened the door Roger was on his feet.

'Well?'

'She's concussed, but no bones are broken.'

He quickly sat back down. 'Thank God for that. Do they know who she is?'

'No. The nurse is going through her pockets. I said we'd go and tell her next of kin when they give us an address.'

'Yes. Yes, of course. Thank you, darling, for being so level headed. I'm sorry, I just went to pieces.'

'I know. But everything's going to be fine.'

He stood up again and kissed her cheek. 'I don't know what I'd do without you.'

'We have to go to the police station to report this.'

'Do we have to?'

'Yes, but don't worry about it.'

Roger took his wife's arm and they left the hospital.

Chapter 12

As Daisy walked slowly back to Mrs Wilson's, she was at her wits' end. What should she do? She had to go to work later this morning, but how could she go knowing that Mary was wandering about somewhere? If she was at her friend's then heaven help her when she finally showed her face. Why was she doing this?

She told Mrs Wilson what the caretaker's wife had said and then reluctantly made her way home. Inside their rooms she sat and cried. 'Mary, please come home. I'll give up my dancing if it upsets you so much.'

When it was time for her to leave for work,

she was even more anxious. She left Mary a note and told her to come to the cinema. She knew she might not be able to concentrate, but at least this would give her something to do. Who knows, Mary might walk into the cinema later. She would know that Daisy wouldn't make a fuss, not in front of everyone.

'So yer sister ain't been home all night, then?' said Charlie after Daisy had told him what had happened.

Daisy shook her head. 'I don't know where to start looking for her.'

'And you reckon this is all 'cos you've bin having these 'ere dancing lessons?'

Daisy nodded. 'I'm so worried about her. Where can she be?' She straightened her skirt when she saw Mr Holden approaching.

'Hallo, Daisy. Everything all right?'

'Yes thank you.' How could she tell Mr Holden what had happened? He would be so cross with her for having dancing lessons.

'I shouldn't be too worried,' whispered Charlie as their boss walked away. 'I reckon she'll be home waiting for you.'

'I hope so.'

But Mary wasn't home that night. All Sunday

Daisy walked the streets looking down alleyways, going to the park, to the places she knew Mary liked. That night she paced the floor. In the morning she knew she would have to go to Mary's school and find this friend of hers.

As soon as it was light, Daisy dressed and made her way to the school. She hung around the gate waiting for the pupils and teachers to arrive.

At long last a steady stream of noisy children and adults began to come through the gates. Daisy walked up to one girl and asked her if she knew Mary Cooper; the girl shook her head.

'What class she in?' asked her friend.

'I don't know.'

' 'Ere, you work at the cinema,' said the girl. 'Me mum takes me sometimes. I like all the funny ones. It must be really lovely sitting watching those films all day.'

'Could you take me in to see the head-mistress?'

'Cor, what's this Mary done? She bin bunking in without paying?'

'No. I just need to see someone.'

'All right. Come on.' The girl led the way

across the playground and into the school. The smell of disinfectant and chalk filled the air. 'She's in that door there,' she whispered.

'Thank you.' Daisy tentatively knocked on the glass panel.

'Come,' said a voice from inside.

Daisy entered the room. In front of her, sitting behind a wide desk, was a thin-faced woman.

'Yes. What can I do for you?'

'I'm Daisy Cooper. I've come looking for me sister.'

'Who might she be? And why are you looking for her in this school?'

Daisy went into the details of the past few days. When she'd finished, the thin-faced woman said, 'You'd better sit down.'

'Can you help me find out if she has been staying with her friend?'

'Wait here.' The woman left her desk and went out of the room.

For what seemed forever, Daisy sat and waited. At long last the headmistress came back accompanied by another woman and a young girl about Mary's age. Was this her friend? Daisy quickly stood up.

'This is Miss Harris, Mary's teacher, and your

sister's friend Tilly. Tell Miss Cooper what you know, Tilly.'

Tilly shifted nervously from one foot to the other. She looked at Daisy. 'I think Mary run away 'cos you was having those silly dancing lessons and she thought you was gonner go away on the stage and put her in a home.' It was all said in a rush.

Daisy stood dumbfounded.

'I know both your parents are dead. Would you have done that?' asked the headmistress.

'No, of course not.' Daisy slumped back in the chair.

'She was very upset about it,' said Mary's teacher.

Daisy looked at Tilly. 'She wasn't with you this weekend?'

Tilly shook her head.

'Have you any idea where she went?' asked the headmistress.

Again Tilly only shook her head.

'You would tell us if you knew, wouldn't you?'

Tilly nodded at her teacher.

'I think this matter must now be put into the hands of the police,' said the headmistress.

Daisy began to cry.

'Miss Harris, take Tilly back to the class.'

Miss Harris and Tilly left.

'Where could she have gone to? Where can she be?'

'You say that you don't have any relatives she may have gone to?'

'No.'

'In that case I think you'd better go to the police and tell them what has happened. They might have some idea where she could be hiding. Please come and let us know what has happened, and tell Mary that she need not be afraid to come back to school. She won't be reprimanded.'

Daisy wiped her eyes and stood up. 'Thank you.'

'I shouldn't worry too much. Girls in Mary's position can be very insecure and possessive.'

Daisy gave a slight smile and left.

At the police station, Daisy went into all the details regarding Mary's disappearance.

'And you say you ain't got no relations?' the policeman asked her.

'No.'

'Well we ain't had any reports of young girls being found wandering the streets. Have you tried the hospitals?'

Daisy looked alarmed. 'You don't think she's been hurt?'

'Dunno. It's best you try them first before we start putting her name and description out.'

'Thank you.'

Daisy left the police station and made her way to the nearest hospital, but again there had been no sightings of her sister. For the rest of the morning she went from one hospital to another. At two o'clock she reluctantly made her way to work. She knew she had to tell Mr Holden about Mary.

Daisy hung about the foyer, and as soon as the manager walked in she said, 'Mr Holden, could I have a word with you?'

'Of course. Whatever is it? You look dreadful, are you ill?'

'No, it's something else.'

'Come to my office.'

Daisy followed him up the stairs, and after she had told him all that had happened, he asked her to sit down. 'And you say she hasn't been seen since Friday?'

Daisy was trying hard not to cry.

'No. I've been to every hospital round here and now I've got to go back to the police station and they will ask their policemen to look out for her.' Tears ran down Daisy's cheeks.

'I'm so sorry, my dear. Whatever made her do such a thing?'

Daisy crossed her fingers behind her back. 'I don't know.'

'I think you'd better go home and wait for her.'

'I'd rather not. I've left a note to tell her to come here. If I'm at home I shall be pacing and looking out for her. Here I'll have something to keep me mind off it for a little while.'

He smiled. 'Daisy.' He coughed. 'I don't know how to say this.'

She looked up, startled. What was he going to say?

'You don't think someone might have taken her?'

'What? Why?'

'There's some very funny people about and this place must seem very glamorous.'

'But why would they take Mary?'

'They could want money. The company's growing and, as I said, there are some funny people about. Sorry, that was a silly thought. Anyway if you want to go back to the police station you can go now.'

'Thank you.' Daisy hurried down the stairs, where Charlie was waiting for her. 'Well, what did he say?'

'I can go to the police station now. But I'm coming back to work, and if she should come here, hold on to her.'

'I will, love, I will. Go on, and try not to worry too much. I'm sure it will all right itself soon.'

Penny looked at the little girl. She was pale and very still, her eyes were closed, and she hadn't recovered consciousness.

'And you've no idea who she is?' she asked the doctor.

'No. The nurse has been through her clothes, and she said she doesn't think she comes from a very well-off family.'

'Her parents must be worried sick. Will there be any long-term damage when she recovers consciousness?'

'The X-rays show that nothing is broken, and her bodily functions seem to be working fine, but at this stage it's hard to say. Four days is a long while without a glimmer of movement, and we don't really know what the outcome will be.'

Penny looked at the doctor. 'Are you saying she could be . . . brain damaged?'

'I don't think so, but we can never tell.' He looked down at the child then at Penny. 'How's your husband taking this?'

'Very hard.'

'He did report it to the police, didn't he?'

Penny nodded. 'Yes. I took him there myself.' She didn't tell him that Roger had told the police that they had found her by the roadside. 'What will happen to her?'

'She will stay here till she fully recovers, and hopefully there won't be any long-term problems and she can tell us who she is and where she lives.'

'We will pay all her medical expenses.'

'I thought you might.' The doctor left the room, and Penny took the little girl's hand.

'I wish you could tell us who you are and where you live. Your parents must be at their wits' end wondering where you are. Please wake up soon. I want to see what colour your eyes are.' She brushed the child's hair from her cheek, then gently kissed it. At the door she said, 'I'll be back tomorrow.'

Outside, she walked over to Roger, who was waiting next to the car.

'Well, how is she?'

'No change.'

'Pen, you'll have to stop coming here.'

'Why?'

'It looks as if I . . .'

'Roger, stop feeling sorry for yourself. Somewhere out there is a mother and father wondering what's happened to their daughter, and all you can think of is yourself. Take me home.' Penny got in the car and they drove away in silence.

When Daisy returned to the cinema, everyone wanted to know what had happened.

'What did the coppers have ter say?' asked Charlie.

'Not a lot. They said they would tell all the officers to keep a lookout for her as they walk round, but I don't think they hold out much hope. They said she will come back when she feels like it.'

'Do you want to keep trying the hospitals?' asked Mr Holden.

'I'll go round them again tomorrow, if that's all right with you.'

'Yes. Take as long as you like. What about hospitals over the water?'

'No, she wouldn't go as far as that; besides, she don't even know what bridge she'd have to cross. We ain't ever been that far away before. She's lived in Rotherhithe all her life.'

'It was just a thought.'

'Thank you, Mr Holden.'

He smiled and walked away.

'Here, love, you had anything to eat today?' asked Charlie.

'No. The last thing I had was some tea and toast at Mrs Wilson's.'

'Right, before we start we'll go to the pie and mash shop, my treat.'

'Thank you, Charlie, but I . . .'

'Stop right there. You've got to keep yer

strength up, so come on. Keep yer coat on, and let's be off.'

In the cosy warmth of the café, Daisy sat and ate the pie and mash Charlie had bought her. Although she was hungry she wasn't really enjoying it, as all the while she was looking out of the window watching the people in the street. If only Mary would walk past, but somehow Daisy knew that wouldn't be.

Chapter 13

A S THE WEEKS WENT by, Daisy lost weight, her clothes hung on her and she looked dreadful, with black bags under her eyes through lack of sleep.

'Now you listen to me, young lady. If you don't look after yerself yer going ter be ill, then when she does come back you'll be fit fer nothing.' These past weeks Charlie had been trying hard to cheer Daisy up. Sometimes he took her out for pie and mash, and most days he brought her in a sandwich, but Daisy knew she wouldn't enjoy anything again till Mary was home safe and sound.

'I can't help it. I worry about her all the time.'

'I know that, love, but you've done yer best to try and find her.'

'It's been a month now.'

'I know. Look, why don't you go and see that dancing teacher of yours? She's bin round here enough times begging you to go back. It'll give you something to do and take yer mind off of things.'

'I couldn't do that. I wouldn't be able to concentrate. Besides, that was the cause of Mary going off in the first place.'

'I know that, but think about it. You can always give it up when she comes home.'

Daisy gave him a weak smile. 'You're a good man, Charlie.'

He turned away, embarrassed. 'It's just that I worry about yer,' he said as he walked away.

That night as Daisy made her way home she thought about what Charlie had said. He was right. Madam Truelove had been to the cinema a few times asking Daisy to go back to her. Daisy had told her the reason she couldn't, but like Charlie, Madam Truelove said it would help to take her mind off things. Daisy knew she had done all she could to find her sister, so perhaps they were right. After all, it seemed that Mary didn't want to come home.

Mary sat staring out of the window. Tears ran down her face. Who was she? Her head hurt with trying hard to remember. When she'd regained consciousness and the doctor asked her her name, she couldn't remember it. He'd told her she had been in an accident, but she couldn't remember anything about it or where she was going late at night and on her own. At first she'd panicked, then she had been angry with herself and had cried and cried, but the doctor had told her not to worry, her memory would come back. But when? For weeks now she had just sat and stared out of the window trying to remember who she was. The woman whose name was Penny came in to see her most days and she always brought her clothes and sweets. The clothes were much nicer than those she had been told she was wearing. She didn't like those; they were scruffy looking and smelt funny. Penny had told her that she and her husband had found her lying in the road and a car must have hit her. Nobody knew how she'd got there or where she came from. The doctor had said she could leave the hospital as there wasn't anything physically wrong with her, but where could she go? Once again she was filled with fear.

Everybody seemed surprised that her parents hadn't been looking for her. Who were her mum and dad?

'Rose, how are you today?' asked Penny as she came up to Mary, smiling.

'All right. Is me name really Rose?'

'I don't know. The nurses called you that when we brought you into the hospital.' Penny sat next to her and held her hand. 'Now, the doctor has told me that you can go home.'

'I know. But where can I go? Where is home? Where do I live?'

'You still don't remember?'

Mary shook her head and a tear ran down her cheek. Then the awfulness of the situation began to register and she blurted out, 'Will I finish up in the workhouse?'

'What do you know about the workhouse?'

'I don't know. It just come inter me head.'

'Well I'm sure it won't be too long before you remember who you are and where you live.'

Mary looked at her as tears filled her eyes

again. 'I am trying ever so hard, but it won't come.'

Penny stood up and held Mary close. 'Don't worry about it too much. I expect it will happen all of a sudden.'

'Look, Roger, we must help the poor girl.'

'But why?'

'Because you're the cause of this. Somewhere a mother and father must be frantic wondering where their daughter has got to.'

'So why should we bring her here? If as you say she knew about the workhouse, she must come from that kind of background where they finish up. No, I'm sorry, Pen, she's not coming here.'

Penny James stormed out of the room. She always knew her husband was selfish and a coward, but this really was the limit. She couldn't let that poor child finish up in an orphanage. She would go and see the doctor and find out if she could bring her here, but first she had to see Mrs Richardson about preparing one of the bedrooms. Penny walked up the wide staircase. The south-facing room would be the best; it was bright, and the poor child needed all the help she could give her. She could be the daughter she had always wanted, but Penny knew she had to take one step at a time, as Roger had always been so against having children. She pushed open the door, went over to the window and looked out at the lovely garden. When she married Roger ten years ago, the thought of the lifestyle he led thrilled her and she knew she wanted to be part of it, but over the years she had come to realise that going out to theatres and wild parties was all very shallow. Although she had a lovely house, it wasn't a loving home with young children running around. Rose could be a gift from heaven. Roger would be cross at first, but Penny could always get round him. She left the room and went to see Mrs Richardson.

'I can't believe you've done this, Pen,' said Roger after Penny had shown Mary her room. 'Bringing her here. You could have visited her in some orphanage.'

'Shh, keep your voice down.'

'Why? This is my house and I shall do and say

what I please. Have you heard the way she speaks? Like some cockney ragamuffin. She must come from some back alley. She could even be faking this, and who knows, we could end up being robbed or worse.'

'I think you are overreacting and being paranoid. She's a poor child who has lost her memory because you hit her with your car. When she recovers her memory she will go back home.'

'That could be years that we have to put up with her.'

Penny was finding it hard to control a smile after that statement.

Upstairs, Mary looked round the room that she had been told was to be hers. It was very nice, with pretty curtains and furniture. Did she live in a house like this? The gentle tap on the door made her jump and she rushed over to open it.

'Mrs James said for you to come down for afternoon tea.'

'All right.'

Mary liked Mrs Richardson. She was thin and wiry and had a kind face. Her grey hair was pulled back into a tight bun, and it reminded

Mary of someone she once knew. Could that be her mum?

The kitchen was bright and the back door was open, and Mary wandered over to it. She stood looking out at the sweeping lawn.

'Does anything here remind you of where you used to live, love?' asked Mrs Richardson.

Mary shook her head. 'D'you think me mum and dad's looking for me?'

'I would think so.'

Mary began to cry.

'There, there, love.' Mrs Richardson held her close and Mary buried her head in her apron that smelt of soap. 'Come and sit at the table and I'll find you a glass of lemonade and a nice cake. I made a batch only yesterday.'

Mary sat at the large deal table and wiped her eyes on the cloth Mrs Richardson gave her.

When Daisy knocked on Madam Truelove's front door, she was overwhelmed at the reception. Madam Truelove threw her arms round her and she was crushed to the woman's ample bosom.

'Daisy, my darling, you've come.'

'I thought I'd just come for a few lessons, just till Mary gets home.'

'Yes. Yes, of course.' She ushered Daisy into the studio. 'Your tap shoes and shorts are still in the cupboard, so put them on quickly. We mustn't waste time.'

Daisy did as she was told and was soon standing once more in front of the large mirror.

'Good. We will go over all you learnt before. Music please, Mrs Ward.'

Once the piano was being played, everything Daisy had learnt came back to her and she found she was following Madam's steps as if she had never stopped coming.

'Daisy, that was wonderful.'

Once again Daisy found herself being hugged.

'Tomorrow we will go through that routine I told you my Baby Beams were doing.'

'I don't know about coming tomorrow.'

'Why?'

Daisy didn't have an answer.

'I want to get you on the stage. I shall be your agent; I'll make sure you play at the best venues and get the best money.'

'Why are you doing all this for me?'

'I have been in this business for a very long while. Joe sent you here because I can spot star quality. As a businesswoman, I want a part of you.'

Daisy giggled. 'I ain't all that good, am I?'

'I wouldn't be wasting my time with you if I thought any different. Now come back tomorrow.' She kissed Daisy on both cheeks. 'Till tomorrow.'

As Daisy made her way home, she suddenly realised that she had been laughing. That was something she hadn't done in a very long while.

Chapter 14

A MONTH HAD GONE past since she'd moved in with Penny and Roger, and Mary still couldn't remember who she was – even after Penny took her to places she thought might help trigger her memory. Mary was always hopeful, but nothing ever came back to her. Who was she? Did she have any brothers or sisters? Some days she felt sad and confused and weepy when she wondered who her parents were and why they didn't come looking for her. But on others she was happy, never more so than when Penny took her out and bought her lovely clothes. Sometimes she sat and looked at the clothes they told her she had been wearing when she was taken to the hospital; the doctors were hoping they would bring back some memory, but they never did. She didn't like them, as they were old and scruffy looking; were they really hers? Mary knew that Roger thought she was a nuisance and didn't like her; he was always correcting her when she spoke and commenting on her table manners. She didn't talk like them, so where did she come from? He said it must be from the East End, but even when they took her round the East End it didn't help, she didn't recognise any of it. Would she ever remember who she was? Sometimes she could hear them arguing about her. She would then go to the kitchen and talk to Mrs Richardson.

Today Roger had taken Penny out and Mary was sitting at the kitchen table reading a book.

'So you can read all right?'

'Yes. Funny, ain't it?'

'I should say so.'

'Penny said I must have gone to school.'

'But you don't remember where?'

Mary shook her head. 'Mrs Richardson, why don't Mr Roger like me?'

'Don't rightly know. I think he's worried that Miss Penny is spending too much time with you.

They was always out 'fore you came; now she only wants to go out with you. I think he feels a bit put out.'

Mary slid off the chair and made her way up to her room. She loved Penny and she didn't want to come between them. If only she could remember who she was, then she could go back home. But where was home? She had been upset when she overheard Roger say that she could be faking it so she didn't have to go back to where she came from. Penny had got very angry and told him not to be so stupid. He then told her to remember her roots. Mary had walked away after that; she didn't want to hear any more.

Penny was surprised when Roger told her he was taking her out for lunch.

'Can Rose come as well?' had been her first reaction.

'No. This is just for us.' He kissed her cheek.

They had been driving for a while, but he wouldn't tell her where they were going.

Penny smiled. 'I wish we could have brought Rose. She would have loved this.'

'I'm sure she would, but as I said, this is just for us.'

He turned the car in to a long drive. It was then that Penny saw the sign.

'Turn the car round this instant,' she said angrily.

'This is for the best.'

'For you it might be, but not for me or Rose.'

'Penny, be sensible. How long will we have to keep her?'

'Till she recovers her memory.'

'And how long will that be?'

'I don't know, but does it matter?'

'It matters to me. It could be years. If ever.' He stopped the car in front of the large house.

'I'm not putting her into an orphanage.'

'It's not an orphanage, it's a children's home, and it's all been arranged. Now come and meet the matron, who will set your mind at rest.'

'I will not set foot in that place.'

Roger turned and took her hand. 'Please, Penny. I need you and miss you being with me.'

She snatched her hand away.

He sat back against the leather seat. 'I'm not going to give in on this, Penny. One way or another she's coming here. You can come and see her and even take her out if you wish. But she's coming here whether you like it or not.'

Penny was taken aback by his forcefulness.

'So what's it to be? Rose comes here or . . .?' He didn't finish the sentence.

'I don't believe this. What have you got against her?'

'I don't want to be reminded of her day after day. Don't you think I feel guilty about what happened? And as you are becoming more and more obsessed with her, you'll be reluctant to let her go when she does recover her memory.'

'But why can't she stay till then?'

'I'm worried that you're more interested in her than me.'

'Stop being so childish.'

'Yes, I am being childish, but you have to choose between her and me.'

'What?'

'It could mean the end of our wonderful marriage. Think about how it was, Pen.'

Penny remembered how it was when she was poor and had nothing. Roger was a sleeping partner in a large business and was very wealthy; he had given her a wonderful home and life. She had everything she ever wanted, and he did love her.

'I've never known you to be like this.'

'I've never had cause to. I want our life together back again.'

Penny sat and thought about how hard times had been before she met Roger. In many ways Rose reminded her of herself when she was her age. The way she spoke and the clothes she had been wearing all added up to a sad childhood, and she wanted to help her. Penny had left home when she was just sixteen and was living in one room with two others in a very run-down part of south London. She had met Roger at a club she had been to with another man, who treated her badly but paid her rent. Roger took her eye straight away, and after that first meeting she knew she wanted the kind of life he had. That was years ago, and she loved her lifestyle. Now it could all be taken away. Despite what she felt for Rose, she knew she had to do what Roger asked.

She got out of the car.

'I'm glad you've seen sense.'

'If it's some awful place, I won't bring her here.'

'I can assure you it's fine.'

They walked up the stone steps and rang the bell. A young girl opened the door.

Roger smiled. 'I'm Mr James, I believe we are expected.'

'Come in.'

Penny was surprised at the decor. She was expecting a Dickensian establishment, but this was very nice.

'That's Matron's office,' said the young girl, pointing to a door.

'Thank you.' Roger knocked on the door and a voice told them to come in.

The woman behind the desk stood up and held out her hand. 'Mr James, so very nice to see you again, and this must be Mrs James? Please sit down.'

Penny and Roger did as they were told.

'Now, I understand you have a young lady you wish to stay with us?'

'Yes.'

'As you can see, we are not the type of children's home that is portrayed in books.'

'How can you afford to look after children in this environment?' said Penny.

'A lot of our children are war orphans. Some

of them come from very wealthy families and unfortunately the relatives don't want the bother of bringing them up. Others come from families who work abroad and don't want to have to take the children round with them. They pay for their upkeep.'

'I see. And what happens if their money runs out?' asked Penny.

'Some go home, but I'm afraid others have to go into a state-run establishment.'

'That must be very hard for them.'

'Yes, it must be,' Matron said. 'Now, tell me about Rose.'

'Not a lot to tell really,' said Roger quickly. 'We found her at the side of her road; it appeared she had been knocked down by a motorcar. She hadn't been badly injured but she had lost her memory. We have looked after her for a while, but now we think she should mix with other children, as we don't have any of our own. Hopefully that will bring her memory back, then she can be reunited with her family, who must be worried sick about her disappearance.'

Penny looked at Roger. He had his little speech all ready. He must have been preparing for this for a while.

'I can understand that. And you are to be admired. Not many would be that concerned and willing to pay for her keep.'

'When can we bring her here?'

'Whenever you want to. She will sleep in the dormitory with the other girls and she will have schooling. They do have to help with the cleaning and in the kitchen, but that's good training for when they leave us. A lot of them go into service, though only to the best homes, you understand. We are very fussy.'

Roger stood up and held out his hand. 'Thank you, Matron. We will bring her tomorrow.'

'Very well. Goodbye. Till tomorrow.'

As soon as they got in the car, Penny turned on Roger. 'I can't believe you have done this.'

'This is best for Rose.'

'And what about when you stop paying for her keep?'

'She might not be there for very long. Not once she recovers her memory.'

'So you think you are doing the right thing?'

'I know I am. Now tomorrow you will pack up all the clothes you've bought her and we will bring her here to start a new life. Who knows, she might be with her own family next week.'

'And what if it goes on for months?'

'We will have to see about that.'

They continued the journey in silence.

The morning that Mary was put into the home, Daisy went along to her dancing class as usual, and when she walked in, to her great surprise Rhoda was waiting for her. They threw their arms around each other and Daisy cried on her friend's shoulder.

'There, there,' said Rhoda, patting her back. 'I'm so sorry I've not got in touch before. When I wrote to Jenny to ask how you were getting on, she told me about Mary going missing, and I knew I had to see you.'

Daisy wiped her eyes.

'That was only after you wrote and gave me your address,' said Jenny Truelove.

'We were busy.'

'That's no excuse. Look, why don't you go in me kitchen and make yourself a cuppa. You can catch up there.'

Daisy was surprised at Madam's sudden London accent as Rhoda took her hand and led her to the kitchen.

'You didn't write,' said Daisy.

'Before we start, I'll put the kettle on.'

Daisy looked round. 'I ain't ever been in here before. It's like something out of a book.'

'Jenny told me that she married very well.' Rhoda sat at the table next to Daisy.

'So why does she keep giving dancing lessons?'

'It's her life. You look very thin. Are you eating properly?'

Daisy gave a slight smile. 'Charlie's always trying to feed me up. He has been so kind.'

'I think everybody would want to help you.' Rhoda went over to the stove and made the tea in a delicate china teapot that had pretty mauve flowers all over it. She also put the matching china cups and saucers on the table. 'Right, the tea's made, so now you can tell me all about what happened.'

As Daisy told Rhoda the story of how Mary had disappeared, Rhoda poured out the tea. She remained silent throughout, and when Daisy had finished she reached across and held her hand.

'I'm so sorry I wasn't around for you. You see, we have been up north doing a show. Wait till I tell Joe all this.'

'So what are you doing down here?' Daisy began drinking her tea.

'We've been offered a job in a West End nightclub and I thought I'd come and see Jenny while we were rehearsing. I never did answer the first letter she sent me, or write to you; writing ain't one of me strong points. But I thought your sister would be back be now. Anyway, we open at the end of the month in time for Christmas. It's all very exciting. It's a brand-new club and we're getting good money, and you wait till you see the flat we're renting.' She grinned. 'You should see our costumes; some of 'em are a bit revealing.'

'I'm so pleased for you. You are both very good dancers.'

'And from what I gather, so are you. Jenny's been singing your praises and she wants you to go into one of her shows.'

'Yes, I know. But I can't leave the cinema. What if Mary comes back and I'm not around?'

'I can understand that. But you must think of yourself.'

'How can I?'

'I dunno. Look, I will come and see you again very soon.' Rhoda finished her tea.

'Promise.'

'I promise. We're not too far away now.' She looked at her watch. 'I must go. You know what Joe is like when we're rehearsing.'

'He hasn't changed, then?'

'No.'

'Please don't leave it so long next time. I really do need a friend to talk to.'

Rhoda stood up and held her close. 'I know you do, and I promise I will come and see you again.'

'Where are you living now?'

'I'll write it down.' She rummaged in her bag and took out a scrap of paper. She began to write her address on it. 'Don't lose it.'

'I won't.'

After Rhoda left, Daisy told Madam Truelove she didn't want to dance today.

'I can understand that. Come back tomorrow.' She kissed Daisy on both cheeks.

As Daisy walked home she felt very sad. She would love to go on the stage, but knew she had to be around for when Mary came back home.

Chapter 15

TODAY WAS SUNDAY the fourth of November, and as soon as Daisy opened her eyes she began to cry. Today Mary would be eight. For all these years she had never had the opportunity to have nice things, but this birthday Daisy had bought her a lovely silver cross and chain. She sat up in bed and looked at its little red box. 'Where are you, Mary?' she said aloud. 'Please come home. I'm so lonely without you.' She knew most people thought that her sister was dead. She had once overheard someone say that it wasn't natural for a child to just disappear off the face of the earth, and that she could be at the bottom of the Thames. She knew that some others talked about the white slave trade. 'Please, Mary, come back home. It's your birthday today and I've got you a cake. You've never had a birthday cake before.' Tears ran down her face, but deep down even Daisy knew that something terrible must have happened to her sister; she wouldn't have stayed away from her all this time.

As she lay listening to the rain pounding on the roof, she wondered what could she do with herself today. She didn't like Sundays and would be glad when the Church allowed the cinema to open on the Sabbath. But that was her life now. Work and not much play. The only highlights in her week were when the film changed and when she went to her dancing lessons. Madam Truelove wanted her to take part in a Christmas show, but that would mean giving up her job. She was turning this over and over in her mind when someone started banging on her door. Who could it be at this time in the morning? It must be Mary. She'd come home. Daisy jumped up and almost fell over her shoes in her excitement to get to the door.

'Mary! Mary!' she cried out. But her hopes were dashed when she pulled open the door and saw a young boy standing there with rain dripping off his cap. 'Yes. What d'you want?'

'I got a note here from some funny old lady. She wants yer to go to her house.'

'Why?'

'I dunno.' He handed Daisy a note and said, 'She said you'd give me a tanner.'

'What! I ain't got a tanner to give you.'

'Well, it'll 'ave ter be a thrupenny bit, then.'

'You'll get a penny and that'll have to be it.'

He looked down and kicked the ground. 'No 'arm in trying.'

'Wait here.' Daisy shut the door and looked quickly at the note. It was from Madam. She took a penny from her purse. What did Jenny want at this time in the morning? Was she ill?

Banging on the door again made her hurry to open it. 'I'm coming,' she called out, then giving him the money she closed the door and sat down to read the note properly.

Dear Daisy,
Sorry to bother you on a Sunday but one of my girls has had an accident and as the show opens on Wednesday it makes the

line-up all out. Please come and talk about
it. I really need your help.

Jenny Truelove

Daisy sat and looked at the note. She couldn't go
and dance on Wednesday. She couldn't let Mr
Holden down. Besides, that only gave her two
days to learn the routine. What should she do?
As she had nothing else to do, she decided to go
and find out more about it.

The rain had stopped by the time Daisy
arrived at Jenny's, and as usual she was hugged
as soon as the door was opened.

'What's this all about?' Daisy asked. She
could talk to Madam more like a friend now, not
just pupil and teacher.

Jenny went into great detail about how one of
her dancers had broken her leg and was unable
to perform. 'So I need you to help me out.'

'But I can't leave Mr Holden. Or learn the
steps in such a short time.'

'You can, that's what we've been doing these
past months.'

Daisy was bewildered. Half of her wanted to
take up this challenge, but she was loyal to Mr

Holden; after all, he had given her a chance and she would always be grateful for that. 'I'm sorry, but I can't.'

'Don't you want this opportunity?'

'I don't know.'

'Think it over.'

'I will.'

When Daisy left, she took the paper with Rhoda's address on from her bag. She felt she had to see her friend; she would get the bus and go and find her. She desperately needed someone to talk to.

Mary sat on the bed she had been told would be hers, hugging her small bag with her clothes in. Why had Penny sent her here? The tears trickled down her cheeks. But she knew it wasn't Penny; it had been Roger.

'Come on, Rose. We've got to go down to dinner,' said Nellie, who had brought her up to this large room with its very high ceiling. The beds that lined the walls were all covered with the same beige counterpane. Big windows that looked out on to a park had the same colour curtains.

'I don't want any dinner.'

'Well I do, and if I don't take you down I don't get any, so come on.'

Reluctantly Mary followed her.

The dining room was also very large and high, with long tables down the middle. It was very noisy, with children of all ages either sitting down or dishing out food.

A very tall, upright woman came up to her. 'Rose, I'm Miss Coleman, I'm your teacher and in charge of you. Now sit here and take note of all that goes on. You all have to take it in turn to wait on us and then do the washing-up. Other days you have to help prepare the vegetables and clean the dormitories, and you always have to make your own bed in the mornings. I warn you, Matron is very strict about everything being clean and tidy.'

Mary sat bewildered as she watched the children struggling with large bowls and pans and putting food on the plates. Some were very young and had a job to hold the things. 'Don't any of these have mums or dads?' she asked Miss Coleman.

'Some do and their circumstances make it impossible for them to stay at home. But some are unfortunate and don't have parents. You are very lucky having a benefactor paying for you to come here.'

Mary wanted to say she didn't think she was very lucky, as she didn't know if she was an orphan, but Nellie was shaking her head and looking alarmed, so she said nothing.

'Now this afternoon you will attend school. Nellie here will look after you.'

Miss Coleman knew that Mary had lost her memory, and that afternoon she gave her a few tests and was very surprised at how quickly she picked things up. 'You must have had some kind of schooling.'

Mary couldn't answer that.

After lessons Nellie told her they had some free time till tea.

'I hope tea's better than dinner,' said Mary, as Nellie led her into another large room that had books on some of the shelves round the walls.

'We only have bread and jam, but we do have some nice cake.'

'Where did all these books come from?' asked Mary.

'People give them to us,' Nellie said as they

sat down in armchairs. 'So, where you from?' she asked.

'Mr and Mrs James brought me here.'

'I know that, but before that? What happened to your mum and dad?'

'I don't know.'

'Don't talk daft. Everybody knows who their mum and dad was. My dad was killed in the war, he was an officer, and me mum is in hospital suffering from depression.'

'What's that?' asked Mary.

'She just sits and drinks all day and the staff were worried about her and me, so my grandpa sent me here in case she killed me or something.'

Mary sat and listened with wide eyes. Perhaps that was what had happened to her own mum; she was in hospital and couldn't look for her. 'Will you go home when she comes out of hospital?'

'Don't know.' Nellie smoothed down her frock. Mary could see the material was lovely and the frock was very well made.

'If you're well off, why can't you have someone to look after you and not be sent here?' she asked the other girl.

'My grandpa has a business to run and he said I would be in the way.'

In some ways Mary felt sorry for Nellie; she had a family but they didn't want her.

'So tell me, how come you finished up here?' Nellie asked again.

'I was knocked down be a car and I stayed with Miss Penny and Mr Roger for a while but then he got fed up with me and brought me here.'

'And you really don't know who you are or where you come from?'

Mary shook her head. A tear slid slowly down her face.

'Don't cry. It's not too bad here. But if they stop paying, then you get sent to the orphanage and I think that's really bad.'

Mary gave a sob. 'I wish I knew who I was.'

'Don't worry. I expect it'll all come back one day.'

But Mary wasn't so sure.

It took Daisy a while to find where Rhoda lived. The houses were very tall, with lots of windows, and still clutching the paper with the address on it, she knocked on the door. She shifted from one foot to the other for what seemed an age before she heard someone shuffling to answer the door.

'Yes?' A woman wearing a wrap-round overall, her hair hidden by a scarf, stood and looked at Daisy. 'Who d'yer want?'

'Does Rhoda live here?'

She took the cigarette from her mouth and shouted, 'Joe. Rhoda. There's someone here to see yer.'

Joe appeared at the top of the stairs, and for a moment he just stood and looked at Daisy. Then he rushed down the stairs and grabbed her and held her close. 'Daisy. Daisy. It's so lovely to see you.' He kissed her cheek. 'Rhoda, get yer arse down here and come and see who's called to see us.'

Rhoda stood at the top of the stairs and yelled out, 'Daisy! Me old mate. How are you?' She clattered down the bare stairs wearing only a flimsy dressing gown that parted as she ran down, showing off her shapely legs. A multi-coloured scarf was tied round her hair.

Someone shouted out, 'Keep the bleeding noise down, can't yer? Some of us are trying to sleep.'

Rhoda grinned. 'Come on up to our flat.'

Daisy followed her up the stairs, with Joe coming up behind.

'Put the kettle on, Joe,' said Rhoda.

Daisy was surprised he did as she asked without a word of protest.

'So, to what do we owe this visit?' asked Rhoda.

Daisy went into the details of how one of Jenny's girls had broken her leg and she wanted Daisy to take her place.

'So why don't you?' asked Joe, putting the tea on the table.

'I can't let Mr Holden down.'

'I can understand that,' said Rhoda. 'But it's a shame to waste such an opportunity.'

'You know you are a very good dancer, don't you?' said Joe. 'I'd willingly have you in my team any day. We've got some right elephants with us at the moment, and now we're going to be appearing at this new nightclub, well, all I can say is that you'd go down a storm, ain't I right, Rhod?'

'You certainly would. Oh Dais, it's very glamorous. We open the week before Christmas and the boss wants it to be perfect. We've been busy rehearsing. Kenny is a bit of a wide boy, but as long as you keep away from his wandering hands it's fine.'

'Don't put the poor gel off before she starts.'

'What d'you mean.'

'I'm asking you to come and join us,' said Joe.

'What! I can't believe this, the offer of two jobs in one day.'

'Daisy, please say yes. You can stay here with Joe and me; as you can see, we've got a settee you can sleep on. Please, Dais.'

'I don't know.'

'Rhoda, take Daisy and let her have a look round the place; perhaps that'll help her to make up her mind.'

'We're ever so lucky,' said Rhoda as she took Daisy into a bedroom. Daisy noted there was only one single bed, and it was a tangled mess where Rhoda had just jumped out of. 'We've got two bedrooms; that's Joe's,' she added as they passed another door. 'Then there's the front room and the kitchenette.'

Daisy was taken back. 'Can you afford all this?'

'Well, me and Joe share, so that makes it easier, and besides, we're getting very good money.'

They wandered back into the front room, and this time Daisy noted that besides the settee and armchair, there was also a small table with chairs pushed underneath. On the table was a lace runner with a cut-glass bowl in the middle. 'This is a very nice place.'

Joe was sitting at the table and looked up from his newspaper. 'All you've got to do is think about it. You can start after Christmas if you like.'

'Joe, why are you offering me this?'

He folded the newspaper. 'Like Jenny Truelove I can see a good dancer, and like her I want you on my team. You're very pretty, and although you work half the night, the rewards are good.'

Daisy sat bewildered. 'I don't know what to say.'

'If you go with Jenny you'll have to sign a contract and she'll tie it up so tight you won't be able to shit without telling her, but with us, though you'll have to sign a contract of course, it's very flexible. Ain't that right, Rhod?'

Rhoda nodded.

'So, what d'yer say?'

'I don't know. What if Mary comes back? I'd have to stay at home then.'

'We would cross that bridge if and when it happens.'

Sadly Daisy looked down at her hands. 'It's Mary's birthday today.' A tear ran down her face.

Rhoda jumped up and held her friend tight. 'Oh Dais, what can I say?'

'I'm sorry, Daisy,' said Joe, looking genuinely upset. 'I wouldn't hurt you or put you under any pressure.'

'Can I think about this?'

'Sure. But I'd love you to come and work at the GG Club.'

'GG? It sounds very horsy.'

Joe laughed. 'No. GG stands for gin and girls.'

Daisy's mind was in turmoil as she sat and half listened to them telling her about the nightclub. What should she do? She knew then that she wouldn't go and dance for Jenny Truelove, but this new proposal sounded wonderful and she had till after Christmas to think about it.

'Talking about Christmas, what are you doing for the big day?' asked Rhoda, bringing her back.

'Ain't even thought about it. I'll be working all Christmas Eve, but as for the day ...' She shrugged.

'Well that's settled. You must come to the nightclub Christmas Eve, then stay here the night and spend the day with us. That way you'll meet the other girls and Mr Kenny, the boss.'

'That's a good idea, Rhod,' said Joe.

Daisy stood. 'Thank you both so much. As soon as I finish on Christmas Eve I'll come and see you; can't say I fancy being all on me own.'

'I'll just write down the address and how you get there,' said Joe.

Daisy took the paper and smiled. 'Now I'd better get out of your way. And you can get dressed,' she said, looking at Rhoda.

'She always walks about half naked on Sundays.'

'No I don't, you cheeky bugger. It's just that I like to relax.'

'I'll be going anyway. I've got a lot to think about.'

Rhoda and Joe both kissed her cheek.

'Bye, Daisy. Look forward to seeing you at the club. And don't worry, I'll get a table all fixed up for you.'

As Daisy made her way home, a watery sun was trying very hard to come out. She looked up. Without Mary her life had been very dark, but today she could see that there could be a light at the end of the long tunnel. But what about Mary? Was she all right? Daisy knew she would never be truly happy till she found her sister.

Chapter 16

ALTHOUGH DAISY KNEW she had upset Jenny
by not wanting to dance in her show, she
also knew she had done the right thing, and so
on Christmas Eve she was very excited. For the
first time ever she was going out with her
friends. She had told Charlie about her forth-
coming trip to the nightclub with Rhoda.

She changed from her uniform to a bright red
floaty frock and black winkle-picker shoes she'd
bought from the second-hand stall at the market.
The shoes pinched a bit but they didn't look too
scuffed. The frock was a bit short and must have
been made for a much smaller girl – it was a bit
daring for her – but she didn't care. She was

going out and was determined to have a good time.

Charlie and Daisy stood in the foyer waiting for Mr Holden to give them their wages.

'I'm ever so excited,' Daisy said, clutching her bag.

'That Rhoda's good 'en, so don't worry, she'll look after yer. You just make sure you have a good time.'

Daisy hadn't told him about the job offer; she thought she would wait till she'd seen where Joe and Rhoda worked and how difficult their routine was before she made up her mind.

'I must say, you look very nice,' said Charlie. 'Turn round.'

Daisy did as she was told. 'You don't think it's a bit daring, me showing me legs like this?'

He laughed. 'Course not. And if you don't mind me saying, they're a very nice pair of legs.'

Daisy blushed and was still giggling as Mr Holden came down the stairs.

'I must say you look charming, Daisy. Off somewhere nice?'

'Thank you. I'm going to the nightclub where Rhoda works. You remember Rhoda, she was a dancer here.'

'Yes. Of course. Well, have a good time and here's your wages. Don't spend them all tonight.'

'No, I won't. Thank you.'

Mr Holden handed over the wage packet. 'I've put in a little extra; I must say, I'm always pleased with you two.'

'Thanks, boss,' said Charlie.

'Don't know what I'd do without you both. I can always rely on you. You ain't let me down so far, so let's hope that come next year, when we can open on Sunday, we'll have more punters coming in.'

Daisy looked away; she didn't want her face to reveal that she might not be here when that happened.

'And just you wait till we get the films they're calling the talkies. They're all the rage in America.'

Daisy looked amazed. 'Talking pictures?'

'Yep. I've read all about 'em.'

'Well that'll be a turn-up for the books,' said Charlie.

'Anyway. I mustn't keep you. Merry Christmas, and I'll see you the day after tomorrow.'

'Bye,' they said together.

'I was hoping we wouldn't have any films on Boxing Day. I would have liked to stay with Rhoda a bit longer.'

'It's the business we're in, love. Bye, have a good time tonight, and Merry Christmas.' Charlie kissed her cheek. 'I'll see you Wednesday.'

'Merry Christmas,' said Daisy as she watched him walk away. Then she picked up her bag and made her way to the nightclub. Somehow she knew this was going to be a night to remember.

Mary was also looking forward to Christmas; tonight at midnight they were going to church. Yesterday she had been very excited when Penny gave her a parcel to put underneath the tree that had been standing in the hall. The parcel had felt very soft, so Mary guessed it could be a nice frock. The label said it was for Rose, but she knew it wasn't her real name and she was still trying so hard to remember what that was. She and Nellie had gone through many names but she didn't recognise any of them. Every day for the past week Mary had stood and looked at the tree. She didn't ever remember seeing anything as beautiful as this before. And the miniature nativity scene fascinated her. The baby Jesus, the three kings and the animals in the stable was something she knew she hadn't seen before; she was convinced that something as beautiful as this would have stayed in her mind.

When Nellie asked her what her Christmases were like before she came here, she said she didn't know.

'You said you never went to church?'

Mary shook her head.

'And you never had a tree and presents?'

'I don't think so.'

'It's funny how you can remember some things but not others.'

Mary didn't answer; she was trying hard to think.

Daisy stood in the cloakroom waiting to be taken to her table. The young girl who had taken her coat looked at it with disgust, and that made Daisy feel cheap. She put it on a coat hanger next to some very expensive fur coats. Daisy noted there was a saucer with money in it that she guessed were tips, but she wasn't going to give the girl a tip; not after the way she had

looked at her and held her coat like it was going
to bite her.

'Are you the friend of Joe and Rhoda?' asked
a good-looking young man in an evening suit.

'Yes. How did you guess?'

'Joe told me to look out for a pretty girl on her
own.'

'I bet he didn't say that.'

'He did. This way, miss. He's nice bloke, that
Joe.'

Daisy smiled, and when he led her into the
nightclub it took all her self-control not to cry out
with joy. She had never been in such a lovely
place before. It was breathtakingly beautiful. In
the foyer was a huge Christmas tree decorated
with twinkling lights and baubles. She wanted to
stay and admire the tree, but the young man was
off and she had to follow him very closely; she
didn't want to lose him.

The lights in the nightclub were very dim,
and she was terrified she would fall over something or someone's feet. Dotted round the edge
of the dance floor were small tables, each with a
crisp white cloth that went to the floor and a
round lamp. A dance band was playing on the
small stage and a lot of couples were dancing.

The young man led her to a table at the side; she was pleased to see it was tucked away. He pulled out a chair.

'Sit yourself here. You've missed the first show, but the next starts a bit later on. Do you want a drink?'

'I don't know. I've never been in a place like this before.'

He gave her a warm smile and his eyes twinkled. 'Well you can't sit here all night without a drink. I'll send over a cocktail.'

'What's that?'

'It's all the rage.'

Daisy smiled. 'All right then. Thank you.'

She sat back and watched the young man move towards the bar. He was so nice and hadn't made her feel like a nobody, for that was what she was, despite the glamorous surroundings. She felt very self-conscious and out of place in her second-hand frock. The women were beautifully dressed and their jewellery sparkled when it caught the light. Most of them were drinking and smoking, their cigarettes in long holders, and they looked very elegant even if some of them were a little loud. The men were all wearing evening suits with black bow ties like the one Mr Holden wore when there was a special do on.

A waiter was at her side almost at once. 'Here's your drink, miss.' He put a fancy glass with a wide top on the table. It had a cherry on a stick in it.

'Thank you.' Daisy began to panic. How did you drink it? And what did you do with the cherry and the stick? She looked about her and noted that the other women toyed with the stick for a while and then popped the cherry in their mouth. After putting the stick in the ashtray, they sipped the drink. She did the same and took a small sip. The smell and the taste almost took her breath away, but she decided it was very nice and took another sip. Tonight she was going in to enjoy herself.

It was very late when all the older children were marching in twos from the church, and there was a lot of giggling, but Mary was quietly going over the wonderful spectacle she had seen this evening. The church had a lovely high ceiling and pretty coloured windows and many pictures of Jesus looking down at them. For weeks they had been learning carols, but the singing sounded so much better with the organ and a proper choir than the tinny piano at the home, and the vicar in his robes told them the story of the first Christmas when Joseph and Mary's son Jesus was born in a stable. It sounded far more exciting than when Miss Coleman told it to the children. Mary had sat open mouthed. It was something she knew she had never seen before. She knew she would never have forgotten something so very special.

Nellie was holding her hand and Mary was deep in thought as they walked along. It was the name Mary that had intrigued her so much. Other than stories, where had she heard it before? There was something about that name today that seemed to captivate her interest. Could it be possible that it had been her name?

'I can't wait till tomorrow when we can open our presents,' said Nellie, interrupting her thoughts.

There were many gaily wrapped presents under the tree now and they reached up into the branches. Mary knew that the very large parcel against the wall was from Nellie's grandfather, and there was also one from her mother. 'Do you know what you've got?' asked Mary.

'No, but I'm hoping it's a bicycle.'

'A bicycle?'

'Can you ride one?'

'Don't know.'

'You can have a go if you like.'

Mary smiled. She didn't ever remember a Christmas like this. She wished she was with Penny, but she knew that would never be, not now. But what kind of Christmases had she had in the past? And did her mum and dad miss her? It had been a long while now and still nobody had come looking for her. A tear trickled down her cheek and she quickly brushed it away. She mustn't be sad; after all, this was the day baby Jesus was born. But when had she been born? Penny had decided that her birthday was going to be the day they found her. And so now her birthday was the twenty-third of July.

Chapter 17

DAISY JUST WANTED to get up and dance, the music and the atmosphere were so intoxicating. When the music stopped there was a drum roll and the dancers slowly cleared the floor. All the lights were dimmed and a large man, immaculate in his evening suit, walked to the centre. His black hair was slicked down and he had a flushed face. A spotlight was on him, and as he raised his hand for silence a diamond ring glinted on his little finger.

'For all you latecomers, welcome to the GG Club. As you know, this club has only been open just over a week, and tonight we have something very special for you.'

All That Jazz

There were loud whoops of delight and banging on tables.

'You've been drinking the gin; now it's time to meet the girls again.'

Daisy sat up. This was what she'd been waiting for. When the four girls came on, Rhoda was at the end. They were wearing very short frocks covered with silver fringe that sparkled and moved with every step they took. They had tight-fitting silver cloche caps and the music was very fast. Daisy sat entranced. She didn't recognise any of the steps. The girls left to the sound of loud applause and whistles. Next came a comedian who told some very rude jokes. The band started again and from the side came the girls dressed as Father Christmas, with very short red skirts showing their red knickers. They high-kicked their way across the floor and Daisy sat enthralled as she watched Rhoda go through a very complicated routine. This time she recognised some of the steps – the ever-present time step and the riff – but there were quite a few she didn't know. Then the girls broke away and wandered round the room singing to the punters. When Rhoda came up to her, suddenly the spotlight was on them and Daisy smiled.

Once again they left to loud applause, then it was time for people to dance again.

The big man who had made the announcements came up to Daisy and sat at her table. He clicked his fingers and a waiter hurried over. 'Whisky for me, and for the young lady?' He looked at Daisy.

'I don't know.'

'I can see you've had a cocktail.' He turned to the waiter. 'Bring her another one.'

'Thank you,' said Daisy politely.

'So, you're a friend of Joe and Rhoda's?'

'Yes.'

'Great dancers.'

'Yes, they are.'

'By the way, I'm Kenny. I own this place and I understand from them that you also dance.'

'I go to a dancing school.'

'Would you like to work here?'

'I don't know.'

The waiter put the drinks on the table.

'Well, according to young Joe, you've got what it takes and you're quite a looker, which helps.' He leaned forward. 'And the pay's good.' He sat back and lit a large cigar.

Daisy noted he had a gold cigarette lighter.

She was beginning to feel very ill at ease. She didn't know how to talk to someone with such a large personality.

'I'm gonner make this the best club in London.'

People walked past and patted him on the back.

'Great place this, Kenny,' someone said.

'Glad you're enjoying it,' he replied with a grin, puffing away on his large cigar.

He looked round the room and, still wearing a huge grin, gave some people a wave. After a while he looked at his watch. 'It's nearly midnight; got to wish the punters a Merry Christmas. I'll talk to you again, so think about what I said.'

He raised his glass and downed his drink, then walked up to the bandleader and whispered something to him. The band finished the number, then there was a drum roll and Mr Kenny walked into the middle of the dance floor with the spotlight on him once again.

'Merry Christmas, everybody!' he yelled.

Daisy, like everybody else in the room, jumped to her feet as balloons fell from the ceiling. People were kissing each other and Joe and Rhoda, who was wearing a lovely long green frock, pushed their way through the crowd filling the floor. Rhoda grabbed Daisy.

'Merry Christmas.' She held Daisy tight and kissed her cheek.

Then Joe did the same, but he kissed her lips long and hard and Daisy felt an unexpected tingle. 'I'm so pleased you came,' he whispered in her ear.

This was something Daisy had never felt before. She was light hearted with drink and the atmophere. She'd never thought about Joe in that way before and she was taken aback. Did he have feelings for her? She quickly dismissed the idea; Joe belonged to her friend Rhoda.

Joe and Rhoda were whisked away into the crowd. The young man who had showed her to her table was pushing his way through the throng kissing all the women. He came up to Daisy and, taking her in his arms, kissed her moist lips. Daisy was even more bewildered when Mr Kenny made his way towards her and kissed her on both cheeks. As they moved on, she sat down, giddy with excitement. She had always known theatre folk were very emotional, but this had surprised her. And who was that young man, and why had he come over to her? She sat and watched him go round the room. He was very good looking. He had dark, smouldering film-star looks and was tall and slim. When he looked over at Daisy and smiled, she smiled back.

The band started up again, and once more the floor was filled with people dancing.

It was four o'clock in the morning. The band had left the stage and only a few people were still sitting at the tables. When Rhoda and Joe came out in their everyday clothes, they sat down with Daisy.

'Did you enjoy the show?' asked Joe.

'Yes, I did. Rhoda, you were wonderful.'

'That's down to Joe's choreography.'

'They were very fast routines.'

'He certainly makes us work.' Rhoda touched his cheek.

'Here comes Kenny,' said Joe, looking over Rhoda's shoulder.

'You were wonderful tonight, Rhoda.' Kenny kissed her cheek.

'Thank you.'

He snapped his fingers, and once again a waiter was at his side. 'Bring us a bottle of champagne.'

The waiter scurried off.

'Do you like champagne?' he asked Daisy.

She giggled. 'I don't know.' She had already had three cocktails and felt very happy.

The champagne was brought to the table and Kenny poured out four glasses. 'Merry Christmas, everybody.'

'Merry Christmas,' they said together.

'So, where do you live?' Kenny asked Daisy.

'Rotherhithe.' Daisy giggled as the bubbles tickled her nose.

'I don't know it that well, but I think me family come from round there. You're not going back there tonight, are you?'

'No. I'm staying with Rhoda and Joe.'

'That's all right then.'

The young man who had showed Daisy to the table and had kissed her came up to them. 'Mr Kenny, you want me to take the takings to the office?'

'Na. Come and sit with us. Grab another chair and a glass and have a drink. By the way, this is Daisy.'

'Hello, Daisy,' the young man said, smiling as he pushed a chair next to Daisy.

'And Daisy, this is Tom, me right-hand man.'

'Hello,' said Daisy. He was indeed a very handsome man.

Daisy's mind was in a whirl as she had another glass of champagne. She could hear the laughter and conversation, but didn't really know what was going on.

'Daisy. Daisy.' Someone was shaking her. 'Come on. Time to go home.'

She was pulled to her feet and Rhoda was putting her coat on her.

'Joe, grab her arm. Thanks, Kenny. See you Thursday.'

Kenny kissed Rhoda's cheek. 'Can you manage?' he asked.

'Yer, she's only little, I'll put her over me shoulder,' said Joe.

'Tom's outside with me car.'

'Thanks.'

Between Joe and Rhoda they got Daisy into the back seat of the car.

'Is she always like this?' asked Tom, who was in the driving seat and looking over his shoulder.

'No,' said Rhoda indignantly. 'I don't suppose she's ever had a drink in her life before.'

Joe had his arm round Daisy, holding her up.

Tom smiled as he turned back to face the front. He thought Daisy was a beauty who he would definitely like to get to know better. But he had noted the way the boss had looked at her earlier this evening when they were sitting together talking. It could spell trouble if the boss liked what he saw.

When Mary opened her eyes on Christmas morning, most of the girls were already up and dressed.

'Come on, sleepy-head,' said Nellie. 'It'll soon be time for breakfast, then we can open our presents.' She pulled the blankets off Mary.

Mary didn't feel as happy as most of the girls; she was wondering if her parents were thinking of her and wanted her back home. Slowly a tear ran down her face.

Nellie sat on her bed. 'Don't cry. I'll share some of my presents with you.'

Mary brushed the tear away with the flat of

her hand. 'It ain't that, I was just wondering if me mum and dad miss me.'

Nellie put her arms round her friend and hugged her. 'I bet they do. Now come on, don't be sad. I'm sure that one day you'll remember who you are, then think of the time you'll have.'

But Mary wasn't so sure. Why would they have waited so long to try and find her?

After breakfast they were all seated in the large hall and the matron began distributing the presents. Mary was surprised when she received two. One was a frock from Penny, and the other, which had her name on the label, said it was from a well-wisher. She quickly opened it, and inside was a hand-made doll.

She looked at Nellie. 'Who would send me this?'

'The church find out who's an orphan and sends along some things the ladies make.'

'But how do they know about me?'

'Matron tells them. Look what my mother's sent me.' She handed Mary a book full of pictures of flowers.

'It's beautiful.'

'It's all right. But I like my bicycle best. After dinner I'll let you have a ride.'

'I don't think I can ride.'

'Well, we shall see.' Nellie laughed. 'And if you fall off and bang your head, who knows? You might get your memory back.'

Mary stared at her.

'What you looking at me like that for?'

'Do you think I could get my memory back if I banged my head?'

'I don't know.'

Mary suddenly felt happier. Perhaps this was the answer.

'Rose, is everything all right?' asked Miss Coleman.

'Yes thank you, miss. Nellie said I can have a ride on her bicycle after dinner.'

'I don't think so. It's pouring with rain and Matron won't let you go out in that.'

Mary looked out of the window at the rain coming down. She prayed it would clear soon, and then she could put her plan into action.

When Daisy opened her eyes she was lying on a sofa. For a moment or two she wondered where she was.

'Wake up, sleepy-head,' said Joe, who was

standing over her and holding out a cup of tea. 'And how's your head this morning?'

'What happened? How did I get here?'

'You all right?'

She nodded and her head felt as if it would fall off.

'I think you had a little bit too much to drink.'

'So how did I get here?'

'We came home in Kenny's car.'

Daisy blushed. 'Was I silly?' She had seen too many films not to know how silly people could be when they'd had too much to drink.

'No, you just fell asleep.'

Daisy sat up and was relieved to see that she was still dressed. 'Is Rhoda up?'

'She's downstairs in the bathroom. You can go down there when she comes back up.'

'Thank you so much, Mr Joe.'

He laughed. 'Just call me Joe. By the way, I think you made a hit with Kenny last night. He was most impressed with you.'

'Why? I didn't say that much to him.'

'It was your looks.'

She laughed. 'He must need glasses.'

'Don't put yourself down, Daisy, you are lovely.'

Daisy looked into her cup. She didn't know what to say. She wasn't used to such compliments, especially from Joe.

'If you decide to work with us, I'll have a word with Kenny. He wants his club to be the talk of the town.' Joe sat next to her. 'D'you know, he went to America to find out what the latest dances are. You know that number with the shiny dresses, well that's called the Charleston.'

'It was very fast.'

'Then there's the Black Bottom and loads more. I'm very excited about them.'

'How did he bring them from America?'

'Sheet music, records and film. He took us to see a film about them and then we stayed behind while they showed it again. I went a few more times and gradually picked up most of the steps. They call the music jazz. It's so exciting.'

'You are very clever.'

He laughed. 'Anyway,' he said, standing up. 'Merry Christmas.' He bent down and kissed her cheek.

'Merry Christmas,' she said softly.

*

All That Jazz

It was late in the evening when Daisy made her way home. She'd had a wonderful day and last night was something she would never forget. She had made up her mind that this was something she really wanted to do. Joe said she could join their group, and he would make all the arrangements with Kenny. He and Rhoda had said she could stay with them till she got herself sorted out. All she had to do now was tell Mr Holden and Jenny.

When she pushed the door to their rooms open guilt filled her. What sort of Christmas had Mary had? She sat on the bed and cried. How could she be happy while her sister was on her own somewhere? And would she ever find her?

Chapter 18

1924

As Daisy walked home from the market on New Year's Eve, she knew that 1924 was going to be very different for her. Yesterday she had been to see Joe and Rhoda and told them that she wanted to join their troupe. They had wanted her to come back tonight and be with them to see the New Year in at the club, but as much as she wanted to, she knew she had to go to work.

On Christmas Eve the club had been so exciting, and it was then that she knew she was desperate for some excitement in her life. When she told Joe and Rhoda her decision they had hugged her and she found she liked being hugged by Joe. Somehow it felt right being in his arms, although she felt guilty about doing this in front of Rhoda. Then she remembered how Charlie had told her that he thought Joe was more likely to prefer men to women. At first she wasn't sure what he meant till he had spelt it out to her and left her confused. She really didn't think that Joe could be like that, especially as he had kissed her the other night.

When she got back to Chapel Court and closed the door, she sat on her bed and thought about the big decision she had made. Was she making the right move? What about Mary? What sort of life was she leading? She must be really happy for her to have completely disowned Daisy, especially after all they had been to each other. But could she be dead? Daisy didn't want to think about that. She wiped away a tear with the back of her hand. If only Mary would write or contact her, just to tell her she was safe, but this must be the way she wanted it. Despite being unhappy at not finding her sister, Daisy knew the time had come for her to move on.

Joe had told her he would have a word with Kenny, but he couldn't see that there would be any problems, as the dancers were his domain.

Daisy's mood swings were becoming very dramatic: one minute she was happy and laughing about her future; the next she was downcast at what she would be leaving behind. Once she began at the GG Club she was going to stay with Joe and Rhoda till she got some money together for a couple of rooms of her own. Today she was feeling depressed, as this afternoon she was going to tell Mr Holden she was leaving the cinema. But first she had to go and see Jenny.

When Daisy told her that she wouldn't be coming to her dance classes any more, Jenny was upset.

'Mind you, I'm not surprised Joe's snapped you up. You certainly have what it takes. I shall be sorry to lose you.' She hugged Daisy tight and said, 'If you ever want to come and work with my Babes, you know you'll always be welcome.'

After the exchange of kisses and promises, Daisy hurried to work, her thoughts in turmoil.

That afternoon Daisy stood nervously waiting for the manager. As soon as he walked in she said, 'Mr Holden, could I speak to you?'

'Of course, Daisy, what is it?'

She gave a nervous cough. She had already told Charlie she was leaving and he'd been very upset but told her he could understand. He had also promised that if Mary ever did come looking for her, he would personally bring her to Daisy. She had been very touched at that.

Noting her discomfort, Mr Holden asked, 'Would you rather come up to the office than talk here in the foyer?'

She nodded, and when he went up the stairs she followed.

'Right,' he said, sitting behind his desk, 'what's the problem?'

'There's no problem. I must tell you that I have loved working for you, but I am going to leave.'

'What? Why?'

'I've been having dancing lessons for some time now, and I've been offered a job with Joe and Rhoda.'

'I see.' He steepled his fingers. 'And when do you intend to start this new venture?'

'I thought after I'd given you a week's notice.' Daisy had her own fingers crossed behind her back. She wasn't even sure if he wanted more than a week's notice.

'I see,' he repeated. 'Well, you must have been into this with Rhoda and Joe. Are you sure it's what you want?'

She nodded.

'What about your sister?'

'I still haven't heard anything. It's been nearly six months now.'

'Yes, it is a long while. I must say I have really enjoyed having you work for me. You're a good worker and always ready to help. I really will miss you. So will Charlie.'

Daisy swallowed hard. 'Thank you. And I'll miss coming here. I'll always be grateful for all you've done for me these past years. I've loved working here.'

He smiled. 'It's been a pleasure. Now get downstairs and tell Charlie to let 'em in.'

'Thank you,' said Daisy again as she left the office and hurried down the stairs.

Next week her new life would begin.

Today was New Year's Day 1924, and as Daisy moved slowly round her two rooms her thoughts were tumbling about. Had she done the right thing? Would she be happy working in a club? She began putting a few things into a cardboard box; not that she had much she wanted to keep. She had been very careful with her money since her mother died and only bought a few extras. She folded Mary's clothes and put them in a paper bag. She did wonder why she was keeping them, as Mary would have grown out of them by now, and besides, Daisy would soon have enough money to buy her new things. But how would Mary react to her new life? Would she be upset at being left for most of the night? After all, she had been angry at being left just in the evenings. Where would they live? They wouldn't be able to stay with Joe and Rhoda. Was she doing the right thing? Once again the practicalities were taking over and she was filled with doubt and guilt.

She held one of Mary's frocks to her cheek, and the smell of it reminded her of her sister. Tears rolled down her face. Should she be leaving this place? If only she could find out where Mary was.

Sunday the sixth of January was bitterly cold. As Daisy stood in her room and looked around for the last time, she began to cry. So much had happened here, but she knew she had to move on. Mr Holden had been very nice and said she could leave at the end of the week. He'd also given her an extra two pounds and told her she would always be welcome to come back if she changed her mind. Charlie had held her tight and told her to keep in touch, and promised that if he ever heard anything about Mary he would come to see her as quick as he could. Even the cleaner gave her a hug, as did the girl in the ticket kiosk. In many ways Daisy was sorry to leave them, but she knew her future lay in dancing. It was something she wanted to do more than anything else.

She sat on the bus with her cardboard box on her lap on the way to her new life.

Mary sat in the library and looked out of the window. Snow was falling. She would have loved to go out and play snowballs or make a snowman like she had seen in the books she had read. She couldn't remember ever playing snowballs or making a snowman. Had she lived somewhere it never snowed? She smoothed down the skirt of the new blue wool dress that Penny had given her for Christmas. Today Penny was coming to see her, and Mary knew she had to look her best.

She sat up when the door opened and Penny walked in. Mary rushed over to her and held her close.

'How are you?' asked Penny, holding Mary's hand as they made their way to a sofa.

'I'm all right.'

'I see you're wearing your new dress.'

Mary nodded.

'Do you like it?'

Again Mary only nodded.

'You're very quiet today. Is anything wrong?'

'Miss Penny, Nellie said I could have a ride on her new bicycle.'

'That's nice of her. Can you ride a bicycle?'

'I don't know. Matron said we've got to wait for better weather.' She stopped and looked at her hands. 'If I fall off and bang my head, d'you think it will bring my memory back?'

'What! Who told you that?'

'It was just something me and Nellie thought could happen.'

'Well don't you ever think of doing anything so stupid as that. You could do yourself a very serious injury and you could even die.'

Tears ran down Mary's face. 'All I want is to know who I am.'

Penny held her close and patted her hair. 'There, there. Of course you do.' It broke her heart to see Rose so unhappy, and she knew then that somehow she had to persuade Roger to let her bring the little girl home again.

'I'm sorry, Pen, but no.' Roger looked up from the newspaper he was reading.

'Please, Roger, she is so unhappy there.'

Roger put the paper down on a small glass table next to his large armchair. 'By the way, I forgot to mention that we have to go to Germany for a few weeks.'

'What?'

'I have to go and see some business acquaintances.'

'Why do you need me?'

'It always helps to have a pretty woman on your arm.'

'For how long?'

226

'I don't know, it could be a couple of weeks or longer.'

'I won't go.'

'I think you will, and don't forget we are having dinner with Martha and William tomorrow night.'

'Do we have to?'

'Yes. Besides, I thought you liked Martha's company.'

'She's all right.'

'So stop looking like a spoilt child.'

'What do you expect? Are you prepared to forget Rose?'

'So far I have let you have your own way with that child, but now I'm going be firm about it.'

'You haven't answered my question. Remember, it was you that hit her.'

'And I'm trying to put it all behind me.'

Penny knew it was pointless talking to Roger. He had changed since Rose came into their lives. He had always let her have her own way before, but was he jealous of that poor child? She stormed out of the room, knowing she would have to do as she was told. But what about Rose? Would her husband still pay for her upkeep? The thought of the little girl finishing up in an orphanage really upset her. After all, it was Roger's fault she had lost her memory.

She threw herself on the bed and cried. She really loved that sad little girl, but she knew she wouldn't go against Roger's wishes.

Penny knew she looked good as she walked up the stone steps to Martha and William Tunbridge's large house. Roger had told her so and had made a fuss of her as she tried to get ready. He also gave her a beautiful gold rope necklace and kissed her neck as he fastened it for her, whispering that she was the loveliest person who had ever walked into his life.

Light kisses were exchanged when the door was opened and they made their way into the drawing room for drinks.

As usual Martha looked elegant in a matronly way. Her mauve gown matched her eyes perfectly and her grey hair was as usual beautifully coiffured. William always looked smart and was a pillar of society.

'And where's young Harry this evening?' asked Roger, not that he was really interested in their son.

'He's in bed. He has a very important piano exam tomorrow,' said Martha, smiling.

After the usual chatter about business, the weather and how they had spent their Christmases, Martha's maid told them dinner was ready to be served.

'You look a little piqued, my dear Penny. Is everything all right?' asked Martha.

Penny looked at Roger, who frowned at her. 'I'm fine. It's just that we're going to Germany soon and I'm concerned it might be cold.'

'I shouldn't worry too much about that,' said William. 'The hotels are very warm and the wine is delicious.'

'And it could always be a good excuse to get a new fur coat and hat,' said Martha, smiling.

Penny smiled back and Roger raised his glass to her.

While the men were having their port, Penny and her hostess moved into the drawing room. Over coffee Martha began to press her to find out what was really worrying her.

'Are you pregnant, my dear?'

'No, Roger doesn't want children.'

'What a pity. Who will he leave his estate to?'

Penny shrugged. 'A dogs' home, I expect.'

Martha laughed. 'My God, I hope not. Just think of all the poor children that could do with a decent home.'

Penny knew that Martha Tunbridge was noted for her good deeds and charity work, but didn't know exactly what she did.

She sat forward. 'Do you have anything to do with the Haven children's home?'

'Not a lot. What do you know about that place?'

Penny sat back. 'Just that someone I know has a child in there.'

'Well they are well looked after, that is till their benefactor stops paying, then I'm afraid they have go to one of the institutions run purely on charity, and that's a big shock for some of those poor children, I can tell you.'

Laughter from outside the door told them the men were coming to join them.

Later that night, as they were leaving, Penny whispered to Martha, 'Can I come and see you sometime?'

'Any time,' she answered, very intrigued at what Penny James wanted.

Chapter 19

LATER THAT AFTERNOON Daisy went along to the club with Rhoda and Joe. When they went through the back door and she was taken backstage it wasn't as glamorous as she thought it would be. Rhoda changed into her rehearsal clothes and started to do some warming-up exercises.

Joe pulled back a curtain to reveal a rail of frocks. 'These are the outfits the girls wear at the moment.'

They were shiny, with lots of beads and sequins, if a little sparse.

Joe noted Daisy's look of surprise. 'Kenny wants his customers to get their money's worth, and that means showing plenty of flesh. Do you have any problems with that?'

'No,' she said shyly, but some of those were even less than what the girls wore on Christmas Eve. And she knew that Joe would see a lot more of her now.

'Also we have to have a change of costumes and dance steps every couple of weeks, not that the punters notice the steps, just as long as you're wearing something a bit revealing.' He smiled; he had a boyish grin.

Since Christmas Eve, Daisy had begun to think about Joe differently. She knew she was just another dancer to him, but she began to notice so much about him. She could see that he had lovely blue eyes. He was slightly taller than her, and with his unruly dark hair that was always falling over his eyes, he was very handsome, slim and agile.

'I'll take you along to our dressmaker and see if she can fit you up with some costumes.'

Daisy was suddenly worried. 'I can't go on just yet, I don't know the steps.'

'And Joe wouldn't expect you to, would you?' asked Rhoda, straightening up.

'Course not. Helen will want to measure you,

and she'll also give you some rehearsal clothes. Have you got any tap shoes?'

'They're only second-hand.'

'We can't have that, I'll take you along to the costumiers who supply us with shoes, feathers and all the other props we use.'

Daisy was beginning to feel bewildered.

'Don't look so worried,' said Rhoda as she bent to touch her toes again.

'Will I have to pay for all of these?'

Joe laughed. 'No, of course not. As I told you, Kenny wants to make this the best club in London, and to do that he knows he has to spend money.'

'He is very good to us,' said Rhoda.

'I ain't had anything new since me dad died.'

'When was that, Dais?' asked Rhoda.

'The Somme.'

'I'm so sorry. Would you like to come and meet some of the house staff?' asked Joe.

'See you later,' said Rhoda as Daisy followed him.

The large room looked so different with the big lights on and no customers. Waiters were laying spotless white cloths on the tables and the barmen were busy polishing glasses. There was a lot of laughing and shouting over the noise coming from the band that was busy rehearsing. Everybody looked so different in their everyday clothes. After introducing her to some of the men whose names she couldn't remember, Joe took her arm and guided her out to see the cloakroom girl. Daisy glared at her when she saw her reaction to Joe.

'Hello there, handsome. You gonner take me out soon?'

This was the girl who had taken Daisy's coat and treated it like an old rag.

'Sally, this is Daisy,' said Joe, ignoring that remark. 'She's joining my girls.'

'So you're a dancer?'

'Yes,' said Daisy confidently.

'When you gonner start?'

'As soon as I master the dances.' Daisy knew she wasn't nearly as pretty as Sally, who was a slim, dark-haired beauty whose dark eyes flashed a warning at her, but she wasn't going to let this little madam walk all over her; after all, she was a dancer.

When they returned to the rehearsal room, the three other dancers had arrived and Daisy was introduced to them. She was aware they all had the very latest bobbed hair. Thelma was tall and her blonde hair was almost white; she reminded Daisy of the film star Vilma Banky. Rene was also tall but dark. June was blonde too, and with Rhoda's copper-coloured hair they complemented each other. They were all tall, slim and lovely. Although Daisy was as tall as them, her confidence was beginning to drain away; now she felt very mousy, old fashioned and out of place.

The door opened and Tom, the good-looking man who had showed her to her table when she first came to the club, walked in. 'Hello there, Daisy. It is Daisy?'

Daisy nodded, impressed he'd got her name right.

'And did you have a hangover after I took you home?' He gave her a beaming smile.

Daisy blushed and quickly looked at Joe.

'No, she didn't. What is it you want, Tom?'

'If Daisy is working for Kenny, I need to know a few particulars. You know what a stickler he is for keeping the books shipshape.'

'It's OK, Daisy, I'll come up with you to the office. He'll only want to know where you're staying and get you to sign a contract.'

'Thank you, Joe.'

Daisy stood to one side as Joe clapped his hands and told the girls to get into line. 'You too, Daisy.'

Daisy went to speak, but Rhoda whispered loudly, 'Just do as he says.'

'Right, we're gonner do the Charleston number again. Last night you were very sloppy. I want clear-cut moves. D'you understand?'

A murmur of 'Yes, Joe' came from the girls.

Daisy stood petrified. She didn't know how to do the Charleston.

'Right, Daisy, this is how it goes.' Joe began dancing. 'Come on, all of you, join in.'

Daisy quickly began to follow Joe. At first she got in a bit of a muddle, but it wasn't long before she was swinging her legs and arms in time with the others.

'Great, that's great.' Joe came and grabbed her shoulders. 'I knew you could do it. Now cool down, then we'll go up and sort things out with Kenny.'

Penny had been in Germany for three weeks now; she was cold, miserable and lonely. Most days Roger was at meetings and at night they dined alone. He had never been involved with his business so much before. Why was he doing this now? Was it just to keep her away from Rose?

That evening she was sitting waiting for him to return when the phone rang.

'Mr James's suite. Mrs James speaking.'

'Penny, darling, I shall be a little late this evening. Why don't you go down and start without me?'

'How long will you be?'

'I've no idea.'

'No, I'll wait for you.'

'Please yourself. We can always have room service if I'm that late.'

'OK.'

'Bye, darling.' The phone went dead.

Penny kicked of her shoes and sat back on the chaise longue. Somehow she knew this was going to be a long evening. After a while she looked up Martha Tunbridge's number and dialled the operator for a connection. She had to talk to someone.

*

Mary was getting very low; she had had one letter from Penny telling her she was in Germany. She and Nellie looked that up in the atlas and could see it was a long way away.

'D'you think she'll come back?' asked Nellie.

Mary shrugged.

'I'd love to go abroad,' said Nellie. 'My dad went all round the world. Him and my mother even went to New York on a big ship.'

'Where's New York?'

'America, silly.'

'Why didn't they take you?'

'I was only a baby.'

Mary listened to Nellie talking about her family and the places they had been, but she didn't want to talk as she was beginning to get worried. What if Penny never came back? What if Roger stopped paying for her? She knew the only place she would be going would be the orphanage.

A week later Mary was called to the matron's office.

She held on to Nellie's hand. 'D'you think I'm gonner be sent away?'

'Of course not. She might just want to see you.'

'But why?'

'I don't know. Now come on, it doesn't do to keep Matron waiting.'

They hurried along the corridor and Mary gently tapped on the door.

'Come in.'

Mary went in and left Nellie outside.

'Rose, this is Mrs Tunbridge. She has a message from Mrs James.'

Mary felt her world collapse. She knew then that she was going to be sent to the orphanage.

'Hello there, Rose.' Mrs Tunbridge stood up and held out her gloved hand; she smelled lovely. Mary gazed at her. She was wearing the most beautiful blue hat she had ever seen, matching her coat, but it was the fox fur draped over her shoulder that held Mary's gaze; he had little white teeth that held his tail. Mrs Tunbridge sat down again. 'Penny James told me you were a pretty girl, and she wasn't wrong.'

Mary's mind was in turmoil. What did this woman want?

Matron cleared her throat. 'Mrs Tunbridge said she wanted to see you as it might be a little while before Mrs James gets back from Germany and she didn't want you to feel . . .' She stopped and looked at Mrs Tunbridge, who finished the sentence.

'Neglected.' She smiled at Mary. 'She asked me to bring you a few things.' She pointed to a parcel on Matron's desk. 'It's only some under clothes, as she thought the weather might be a little cold. I think she is feeling the cold herself in Germany. Now I must be off. I do hope I will see you again.' She held Mary's shoulders and gently kissed her cheek, leaving Mary feeling utterly bewildered.

After Mrs Tunbridge had left, Matron said, 'Don't worry about these, I'll get the housemaid to sort them out for you.'

Mary stood for a moment before she realised she was being dismissed, and then hurried out to find Nellie.

'So she brought you some underwear. Why?'

'I don't know.'

'Seems a funny thing to bring you.'

'Do you think she was telling me that Penny won't ever come back and see me again?'

'Wouldn't like to say.'

As they walked down the corridor to the dining room, Mary's mind was turning over and over. Would Penny ever come back?

After settling Martha Tunbridge in the car her driver asked, 'Is everything all right, Ma'am?'

'I don't know.'

'Do you want me to take you somewhere?'

'No. Just home.'

As they drove through the Surrey country-side, Martha's thoughts were on Rose. When she had received the phone call from Germany, she knew that there must be more to this child than what Penny had told her. She had a feeling that Roger was responsible for the child losing her memory, but how? Had he somehow been involved in the accident? She had come to the conclusion that Penny was worried that he might stop sending money to the home; she had asked if Martha would take some new clothes and reassure the child that she was still very fond of her. Martha had been intrigued. She wanted to see this child, and now she had seen what a sad little girl she was. Not to have any idea of where you came from or who your parents were must be heartbreaking, and she could see why Penny was concerned for her, but why didn't she stand up to Roger? She hadn't known Penny for very long; was there more to her than she had led everyone to believe?

For over a month Daisy had gone to the club every day and she was still staying with Rhoda and Joe. She loved Sunday evenings when they didn't work and just sat around talking and playing cards.

'It's lovely to have someone to talk to and get tea for,' said Daisy as she began to lay the table.

'You know you don't have to do this,' said Joe as he took the knives and forks from her.

'I want to. I will always be grateful to you for letting me stay here, but I really should be thinking of getting my own room somewhere soon.'

'We keep telling you you don't have to; that is, all the while you don't mind sleeping on the sofa,' said Rhoda, who was busy painting her nails.

'I don't mind it at all. But you don't want me under your feet all the time.'

'You're not under our feet. Besides, here we can keep an eye on you.'

Daisy blushed. She was pleased that Joe took an interest in her. She had made a wonderful discovery recently: Rhoda and Joe were brother and sister. She'd been so relieved and now didn't feel guilty for liking Joe. If only he would show her some affection she really would be over the moon and then all her dreams would come true. Every night as she settled herself down on the sofa she thought about Joe in the other room, but he had never given her any reason to believe it was anything more than a working relationship.

She went to rehearsals every day and worked hard, determined not to let them down. It was only this morning that Joe had said that tonight she was ready to go out front. Now she was standing nervously with the other girls waiting for the band to start the music for their entrance. Her mouth was dry, her palms were sweating and she thought she was going to be sick. Although she had done the dance many times before, suddenly she couldn't remember the steps. Would she let everybody down? The red skirt she was wearing just about covered her; it was very short, and like the others, it revealed matching knickers. The white blouse just about covered her bosoms. She could hear Mr Kenny making the announcement, their music started, and everything fell into place. They linked arms and moved off, kicking their legs high in the air as they proceeded to the centre of the room. The spotlight lit them up and the customers cheered. Daisy's nerves disappeared and she forgot all her fears and inhibitions. This was it. This was where she wanted to be.

When they came off, Joe hugged her. 'You were great, just as I said you would be. Did you enjoy it?'

Daisy hugged herself and danced a little jig. 'It was wonderful. I loved it. Thank you both so much for believing in me.' First she kissed Rhoda then Joe. It was just a friendly kiss, but she would have liked it to be more.

'Wait till four in the morning when your feet are killing you and you're dead tired, then you might not think it's so great,' said Thelma as she sat in front of the dressing table.

Daisy ignored her. No one was going to take this moment away from her.

A banging on the door made the girls hurriedly pull their dressing gowns on.

'Who is it?' called out Rhoda.

Daisy had been told not to open the door to anyone in between shows, as some of the punters tried to sneak in and see the girls as they changed and then made a fuss when they were asked to leave. And some of them looked like very hard men and could turn nasty.

'It's only me, Rhoda.'

Rhoda smiled. 'OK, Kenny. Come on in.'

He walked in and hugged Rhoda. 'You were wonderful tonight. And so were you, young Daisy. Keep up the good work, girls.'

When the door shut, the girls burst out laughing.

'D'you know, I reckon he fancies you, Rho,' said June, 'and if you play your cards right I reckon you could be the next Mrs Kenny.'

'I don't think so.'

'He might not be much to look at, but he's got a lot of dosh and, well, you can put up with anything if the money's there.'

Daisy looked at Rhoda; she knew that she liked the man, the way she talked about him when they were at home.

Sitting here laughing and talking to these girls, her fellow dancers, Daisy suddenly thought how quickly her life had changed. She still felt guilty, though, when her thoughts went to Mary. Where was her little sister?

Chapter 20

A MONTH AFTER MRS Tunbridge came to see Mary, the little girl was told to go to Matron's office. She knew she hadn't done anything wrong, so she guessed something was going to happen to her. 'D'you think I'm gonner be sent away?' she asked Nellie.

'No.'

'But I ain't had a letter from Penny for ever such a long while.'

'Perhaps that Mrs Tunbridge has come to see you again. I think she took a liking to you. She might be going to adopt you.'

'I don't want to be adopted.'

'Why not? She seems a nice lady.'

'She can't adopt me 'cos I ain't an orphan, and besides, I want ter find me own mum and dad.'

'Of course you do. Now come on, cheer up.'

But Mary couldn't find anything to be cheerful about as she and Nellie held hands and walked down the long corridor together. Unusually, Nellie was very quiet. Did she know something and wasn't telling her friend?

When Mary walked into Matron's office, Miss Coleman was standing next to Matron's desk. She looked very down and said quickly, 'Rose, Matron has some news for you.'

Matron cleared her throat. 'I'm afraid Mr James has written to me and told me that he can no longer pay for your upkeep here.'

Mary felt her knees go weak. 'Why?'

'He didn't give me a reason.'

'He is all right?'

'Yes, as far as I know.'

'And Penny, Mrs James?'

Matron nodded.

Miss Coleman thought what a charming girl Rose was to worry about someone who was going to take her away from this environment and put her God only knows where.

'When have I got to go?'

'I have arranged for Miss Coleman here to take you tomorrow.'

'Tomorrow!' Mary burst into tears. 'I don't want to go. I don't want to leave Nellie.'

'I'm sorry,' said Matron. 'But I have no other choice. You'll settle down, I'm sure, and make new friends.'

Mary wasn't listening. She didn't want to leave here. What if she never saw Penny again? Would she ever find out who she really was?

Nellie sat on the bed watching Mary put her few things into a brown paper bag.

'You can write to me when you get settled, then perhaps one day I'll be able to come and see you.'

Mary's tears plopped down on to the bag, making a big wet stain. 'I might not be allowed to write letters.'

'Course you will.'

'If Penny ever comes here looking for me, you will tell her where I've gone, won't you?'

'I can't if you don't give me your address.'

'Miss Coleman is coming with me. She can tell you the address.'

Nellie brightened up. 'All right. And I'll write to you and send you a book.'

Mary brushed her tears away with the flat of her hand and tried hard to smile. She hugged Nellie close to her. 'I do like you. You're my bestest friend ever.'

'And I promise that one day I'll come and find you, then we can go out and have a good time.'

Mary nodded. She knew this was something they were always saying, that as soon as they grew up they would go off together and find an exciting job somewhere, perhaps even travel the world. But both knew that would never happen.

On a cold Monday morning in March, Mary and Miss Coleman set off to the orphanage that was going to be Mary's new home.

'Have you been on a train before?' Miss Coleman asked her as they sat in the waiting room at the station.

Mary shook her head. 'I don't remember.'

Miss Coleman smiled at her and tapped the back of her hand. 'I'm sure that one day something will happen and bring back all your memories.'

'I have tried ever so hard to remember. I would love to know who I am and if me mum and dad are still looking for me. I do wonder if I have any brothers or sisters. I'd like a big sister, but I don't really like boys; they're noisy and rough.'

'It must be very hard for you. You are a very bright girl, and you must promise me that if you do ever remember who you are, you will come and tell me.'

'I promise.'

The train suddenly appeared down the track and Mary sat terrified. She held on tightly to Miss Coleman's hand, trembling. 'I've only seen pictures in books of trains. I didn't know they was so big and noisy. Have we got ter get on that?'

Miss Coleman smiled. 'Don't worry, it'll be all right. It's good fun and exciting to go on a train.'

Mary wasn't so sure. How could it be good fun if it was taking her away from the two people she loved most, Penny and Nellie? Would she ever see them again? She felt so alone and abandoned. All she wanted was for someone to love her.

*

When they left the countryside behind, Mary didn't like the look of all the buildings; they looked ugly.

The train drew to a stop and Miss Coleman said, 'Gather up your things, Rose, this is our station, this is where we get off.'

Mary hadn't liked being on the train. She was frightened, it was dirty and noisy, and when she looked out of the window she got a sooty smut in her eye and it stung, adding to her misery. Gently Miss Coleman had twirled the corner of her handkerchief and removed the soot.

They walked out of the station, and all around them were tall, drab and dirty-looking buildings.

'Where are we?' asked Mary.

'London.'

'Where's the orphanage?'

'Not too far away.'

People were rushing past them, their heads bent against the wind that had sprung up. Mary shivered as rubbish was blown all round her feet. They went down an alley, between tall redbrick buildings with tiny windows, and Mary suddenly stopped.

'Come on, Rose, we don't want to be out in this cold for too long.'

Mary looked at Miss Coleman with a blank expression.

'What is it?'

'I think I've been here before.'

'What? When?'

'I don't know, but I just feel that somehow, I've seen buildings like this before.' She turned and looked all about her.

Miss Coleman shuddered as she looked up. This was south of the river and a terrible part of London, with its docks, warehouses and large rundown buildings. Did Rose really come from round here? Did she once live in one of these dwellings? Her accent told her that she could have. 'Come along, let's get to the home.' She took hold of Mary's hand. Would being here bring the child's memory back? She really did hope so. Then she could be reunited with her family.

The weeks went by. Daisy loved working at the club, and when her thoughts strayed from Mary for a brief while, she was happy. She began buying new clothes. The brown cloche hat matched the fur collar on her beige coat and the brown pointed shoes, handbag and gloves finished off her outfit. She felt like a million dollars as she walked into the club.

'Wow, Daisy,' said Tom, who was talking to Sally. 'You look really great.'

'Thank you.'

'I love your coat,' said Sally.

'It's certainly a lot better than the one I was wearing when I first came here.'

'Yer, that was a bit of an old rag.'

'You'll have all the old boys fighting to take you out,' said Tom, grinning. 'I'll have to make sure I get there first.'

Daisy blushed. 'I don't see how clothes can make that much difference.' She noticed that Sally looked daggers at her.

Daisy continued to walk to the rehearsal room. She knew the time was coming for her to find a place of her own, as the more she thought of Joe in the next room, the more she knew she was falling in love with him. He had never given her any reason to make her think he felt the same way, only that first kiss. Was she looking too deeply for a reason to be wanted and loved? With Joe it was strictly business, and he praised the other girls as much as her.

'I'm thinking of trying to look for rooms,' Daisy said to June one day after rehearsals when they were busy painting their toenails.

'Why's that?'

'I just feel I should be on me own. Don't get me wrong, I love being with Rhoda and Joe, but I'd like me own room. Any ideas where I could start looking?'

'Dunno. You could try the papers.'

'I'll get one tonight before we start.'

'You've got to make sure you've got a good landlady; not all of 'em like you coming home at four o'clock and sleeping in all morning.'

'No, I suppose not.'

'Here, why don't you ask Sally?'

'What, Sally in the cloakroom?'

'She's got a couple of rooms and I know a while back she was wanting someone to help out with the rent.'

'No, I couldn't; besides, she don't like me.'

'She don't like any of us. She's jealous 'cos we can dance, and I expect we earn a bit more than her, but it's worth a try.'

'She must get good tips.'

'Daresay she does, but don't forget all the staff

has to share them and she's still just a cloakroom attendant.'

Daisy sat back and admired her handiwork; she was also giving some thought to talking to Sally. Although she didn't have a lot to say to her, in some ways it would be easier to go and ask her rather than traipse round the street looking for digs.

That evening while they were having something to eat before starting work, Daisy said to Joe and Rhoda, 'I'm gonner start looking for rooms. I thought I'd better tell you before you hear it from someone else.'

Joe looked up. 'Why? I thought you liked being with us.'

'I do. But you don't need me hanging round you all day then working with you half the night.'

'Daisy, has someone said something?' asked Rhoda.

'No. Why should they?'

'It's just that I think they think Joe has more time for you than the others.'

Daisy blushed.

'I don't,' said Joe quickly. 'It's just that Daisy is a better dancer than that lot put together and takes orders without a fuss, and I want to use her potential to the full.'

Rhoda burst out laughing. 'What a right load of old claptrap. It's because you don't want Tom sniffing round her. You know what he's like; he'll whisk her away and she'll be up the spout before you can say Jack Robinson, then you'll be your best dancer short.'

Daisy sat dumbfounded.

'I must admit, that does have something to do with it after that thing with Amy.'

Daisy couldn't believe this conversation as she looked from one to the other. Was Joe jealous of Tom? She had never given him any reason to be. 'What happened to Amy?' she asked.

'She was one of my dancers, and when we came here she met Tom and fell for him hook line and sinker, but after a few weeks he gave her the brush-off and the poor girl jumped off a bridge.'

'Joe, you can't really say it was his fault. She was a bit unstable and a drunk, so don't listen to him, Daisy.'

'As far as I'm concerned he was to blame for her drinking, and I don't want to lose another good dancer.'

So that was all Daisy was to Joe, just another dancer. 'Me moving out has nothing to do with Tom.'

'Well, that's all right then. I'm just going to make sure the lighting is right; the spot was waving about all over the place last night.'

'You don't want to take too much notice of what Joe says. So, where do you intend to live?' asked Rhoda as Joe left.

'I don't know. It has to be near the club.'

'It can be a bit pricey round here.'

'June did say that Sally was looking for someone to share. I might ask her.'

'You wonner watch her, she can be a bit of a cow at times.'

Daisy gathered up the empty paper bags and walked over to the sink. 'Rhoda, has Joe ever had a girlfriend?'

'Na. Dancing has been his life ever since he was a kid. When Dad walked out on Mum he used to go round the people waiting in line to go into the music halls and dance for a few pennies. He was very good. A dance teacher took him on and, as they say, the rest is history. Then I joined him and we've been together ever since.'

'What about you? Have you ever been in love?'

Rhoda laughed. 'A couple of times, but the blokes don't hang around for long when they find out what hours I work. So I tell you now, make sure the bloke you find is in this business.'

Daisy smiled. 'I will.'

'Right, now come on, let's get ready. We've a long night in front of us.'

Daisy knew then that she had a goal to make Joe realise she was much more than just another dancer, but she had to tread very carefully.

Chapter 21

WHEN MARY WALKED into the drab building and looked about her, she had a very peculiar feeling. She knew that this was to be her home from now on, but it wasn't only that, there was something else that she couldn't explain. She gripped Miss Coleman's hand tightly. All the children she had passed looked sad and dirty. She didn't want to stay here.

'All right, Rose?' asked Miss Coleman.

'I don't like it here,' she whispered.

'It won't seem so bad after you settle in.'

'They all look so scruffy.'

'I expect it's their work clothes.' But Miss Coleman also had her doubts. The children did look neglected and their eyes had a faraway look in them. She didn't want to leave Rose. 'When we see the person in charge, they'll make you feel better.' She knew this wasn't true, but it was the only words of comfort she could offer this poor child.

The woman who called them into the sparse office was tall, skinny and upright. She was dressed all in black, her hair hidden under a tight-fitting white cap, emphasising her sharp features. Miss Coleman could see there wasn't any compassion in this woman's cold darting eyes. She sat behind her desk but didn't offer a seat to Miss Coleman.

'This is Rose,' said Miss Coleman with a smile. 'I'm afraid she doesn't have a surname as she lost her memory around nine months ago.' She could feel Mary's hand shaking.

'I see,' came the reply.

Mary shifted from one foot to the other.

'So where has she been all this time?'

'After her accident a couple looked after her, then she was brought to the Haven, but after a while we were told that the money wasn't going to be paid any more for her upkeep.'

'Well, she will find things a little different

here, but if she accepts that this place is run through charity and we don't have money from private sources, she will fit in.'

Mary wanted to shout out, this is me, I'm here and I don't want to fit in, but she knew this would be hopeless.

'You can go now, Miss . . .'

'Miss Coleman. Thank you.'

Mary looked up at Miss Coleman with wide pleading eyes. She didn't want her to go and hung on to her hand. Miss Coleman bent down and hugged her.

'Please tell Nellie where I am,' whispered Mary as her tears began to fall.

'I will.' She pushed her gently away. 'Now be a good girl.'

Mary nodded furiously. 'Bye.' She brushed her tears away with the flat of her hand as she watched Miss Coleman leave the room.

Miss Coleman was upset, and when she was outside she looked up at the tiny windows. She had never been here before. Why had Matron sent Rose here? Had Mr James told her to send her right away and this was the furthest place Matron knew? She would have to try and get in touch with Mrs James or Mrs Tunbridge. She couldn't let Rose spend years and years in such a miserable place. She hurried along to the railway station. As soon as she could she would try and find their addresses. Nellie might even have them. She had more of a spring in her step as she hurried along, now that she had a purpose.

'Now come along, we don't stand for all that nonsense here. My name is Miss Fielding.' The woman rang the large brass bell that squatted on her desk, and a short woman waddled in.

'Yes?'

'Norman, take this child and get her sorted out, then bring her clothes back here.'

'Yes,' said the woman again, then turned to Mary. 'Come on.'

Mary followed her out of the room. Why were they going to take her clothes? What was her fate now? And how could she run away?

For the first week Mary could only cry, she was so unhappy. She was given a coarse grey dress to wear and boots that were too big for her and rubbed her heels, making them sore.

The short woman, whose name was Miss Norman, was in charge of the girls, and she told

Mary not to make a fuss. 'You wonner be grateful you've got a pair of boots. Some kids what come 'ere ain't ever had boots on their feet before. Besides, you'll grow into 'em. And fer Christ's sake stop that bloody snivelling and wailing, yer gitting on me nerves.'

The food was awful. Every morning they had a bowl of porridge that was full of lumps. At first Mary didn't eat it, but since lunch consisted of just a small slice of bread and marg, and the meal at night was mostly slops with a few vegetables, she soon became hungry and knew she had to eat whatever was put in front of her. She was so unhappy.

When she was given the job of helping look after the toddlers, it made her feel better. These poor little mites looked so sad, with their running red eyes and sores round their mouths, and they seemed to be permanently wet and smelly.

Most of the other girls kept themselves to themselves, so Mary quickly learnt to keep her thoughts to herself. At times she felt she was in prison. All she wanted to do was remember who she was and go home.

She was staring out of one of the small

windows when she suddenly felt odd. What was it? Her head began hurting and her eyes went out of focus and she couldn't see. What was happening to her? She staggered out of the room.

'Rose, what d'yer think yer doing?' shouted Miss Norman. 'Get back in ter those kids.'

Mary turned and looked at her, then she slumped to the floor.

When she opened her eyes she was on her bed. 'Where am I?'

'You all right?'

Mary knew she was at the home for destitute children. She sat up. 'Yes thank you. What happened to me?'

'You passed out. You shouldn't be ser fussy about what you eat. Now come on, get back to the kids.'

Mary slid off the bed that just had a thin mattress and one blanket, and made her way back downstairs to the nursery. When she went into the room again she went over to the window. There was something familiar about the building opposite. She knew she had seen buildings like this before, and when it was dark a man would light the gas lamps with a long pole. Where was it? When she tried to remember, it hurt her head.

Daisy was deep in thought as she walked to work.

'You found a room yet?' June asked her as they met on the way to the club. Daisy had been thinking about her sister and their mother, as she often did when she was alone.

'No. I don't really like to ask Sally. And those in the papers are a bit too much rent.'

'Don't worry about living with Sally, she's all right. A bit messy, but then you're such a tidy cow that she'd probably welcome you with open arms, just as long as you don't try and pinch her fellers.'

'I wouldn't do that. Is she going out with Tom?'

'I think she'd like to, but he's got other ambitions. He's looking for a very rich widow.' June laughed. 'Just like I'm looking for a very rich husband, but there's not much chance of that.'

'I thought she had a soft spot for Joe.'

'She might have done at first, but he ain't

interested in anything but dancing. Now come on, to work. Joe's a right old slave-driver.' She pushed open the door that led to the foyer of the club. 'Hello, Sally, all right then?'

'Mustn't grumble.' Sally went back to sorting her tickets out for tonight.

Daisy thought once again about Sally and her room; she knew that soon she had to make the break. She hung back till June had left the foyer. 'Sally, June said you was looking for someone to take a room where you live. Is that right?'

'Could be. Why?'

'I'm thinking of moving out of Rhoda's.'

'Why?'

'No reason. I think they need to be on their own, that's all.'

'Yer, I suppose it can be a bit much working with 'em all night and then seeing 'em all day.'

'So are you thinking of letting out a room?'

'Come round in the morning. Not too early, mind. I'll write the address down and give it to you later.'

*

It was almost lunchtime when Daisy left Rhoda's. She'd told them she was off to try and get a handbag to match her new black shoes. She didn't want to say anything till she was settled.

Sally didn't live that far from the club, but in the opposite direction from Rhoda and Joe. Daisy was very surprised at the neat block of flats, so different from Chapel Court, and as she studied the list of tenants' names on the wall in the porch, she could see that many seemed to live alone.

Sally lived on the second floor, and she was still wearing her pink frilly dressing gown and looking very bleary eyed when she opened the door. 'Oh, it's you. You'd better come in.'

'This is very nice,' said Daisy, looking around. It wasn't very tidy or spacious but it had a large window that overlooked the street below.

'Sit yourself down.'

As Daisy sat on the brown rexine armchair she wanted to ask how Sally had got such a nice place furnished, and how she had so far managed to pay the rent, which by the look of it must be quite a lot, but hopefully she would find all that out later.

'I might at well tell yer right away. Me and me dad used to live here, but he died a while back.'

Daisy went to speak but Sally held up her hand. 'I took on the lease. It's a bit pricey, but as it's got two bedrooms I thought if I could get someone to stay, then all me troubles would be over. You see I didn't want to leave here.'

Daisy could see that anybody would like to live here.

Sally took a cigarette from the packet on the table and offered Daisy one.

Daisy shook her head. 'I don't smoke.'

'Well that's one thing in yer favour, so you won't be pinching me fags.' She lit her cigarette. 'I used to have one of the barmen from the club staying, but he turned out to be a right shit, bloody untidy and a dirty sod, and never paid his rent on time. He got the push before you started, I think he took some money and that don't go down very well with Kenny, I can tell you. D'you fancy a cuppa, my mouth feels like the bottom of a bird cage.'

'Yes please.' Despite her first misgivings, Daisy was beginning to warm to Sally.

'This is the kitchenette,' called Sally. 'Come and look.'

It was just off the room they had been in, and was very small.

'It ain't very big, but it did me and me dad.'

'It's very nice.' Daisy was comparing it with Chapel Court again and the space they had had there.

'It could do with a tidy-up. But I don't bother till Sunday.'

In Daisy's mind's eye she could see herself here washing up and cooking, and she dared to ask, 'What sort of rent did you want?'

'You ain't seen the bedroom yet. That's a bit of a mess. After Stan walked out I just left it. Wait till I've done the tea, then we'll go and have a look.'

Daisy really wanted to know if she could afford it before she got herself enthusiastic.

Sally carried the tray back into the sitting room. 'I'll want a pound a week.'

Daisy almost let out a yell of joy; she could easily afford that.

'And you'll have to pay for yer food and gas.'

Daisy tried to keep her voice under control. 'I think that would be all right,' she said steadily. Obviously Sally didn't know how much Daisy earned; it must be a lot more than her, but then again she was a dancer. She sat up. 'When can I move in?'

'Bloody hell, you don't waste any time, do yer?'

'No point in hanging about.'

'No, suppose not. There is one other thing.'

Daisy held her breath.

'We'd better make some kind of pact. If I bring a bloke home for the night you don't look surprised in the morning. OK?'

Daisy nodded.

'And the same goes for you, but don't make too much noise when you're at it.'

Daisy only smiled.

'Right, now come and see your room.'

Daisy stood in the doorway. Sally was right, it was a mess. Dirty washing all over the floor, and it definitely smelled.

'It's worse than I thought,' said Sally, puffing away at her cigarette.

'I'll open a window. It looks worse than it is, it won't take too much to get it sorted out,' said Daisy, trying hard not to show too much enthusiasm.

'So, d'you wonner give it a go?'

Daisy nodded.

'Right then, Daisy, what's yer surname? Just so that I can give you a rent book. Got ter keep it all kosher.'

'Cooper.' Daisy was surprised that Sally wanted to be businesslike.

'Right then, Daisy Cooper, welcome.' Sally held out her hand and gave Daisy a warm smile.

This was it. Daisy felt she had moved up in the world. Chapel Court, the greengrocer's and the cinema seemed a lifetime away. But what about Mary? Had she been as lucky? Daisy still believed she was alive. Whoever she was with must be very nice to her to keep her away from her sister all this time, or had Mary been ashamed of where they lived and who they were? If she came back now, she and Daisy could easily share the bedroom.

Daisy left Sally feeling very happy. At least she'd have a home for Mary to come back to – if she ever did come back . . .

Chapter 22

IT WAS A WARM June night, and as the girls danced the Charleston, the Black Bottom and other fast numbers, they thought they would melt under the hot lights and the smoky atmosphere. When they came off after their first slot, Joe was waiting for them, and he didn't look very happy as they made their way into their dressing room.

'You was a bit sloppy tonight.'

'But Joe, it's so hot,' said Thelma in her little-girl voice as she dabbed at her damp forehead.

'You are all paid to do a job, so just do it. And make sure you pick your feet up next time out.'

'What's got into him?' asked Rene as she ran

her fingers through her dark bobbed hair. 'Me hair's soaking wet. I thought we did all right.'

'He's just a bit grumpy, that's all,' said Rhoda. She sat at the dressing table and, after holding a towel to her face, began to repair her make-up.

Daisy sat next to her. Rhoda continued looking in the mirror and adjusted the long feather in her hair band. Daisy glanced at her and, making sure no one could overhear, whispered, 'Is anything wrong?'

Rhoda quickly looked round and in a quiet voice said, 'I think he feels that his flock might be drifting away and it's going to be hard to find new good dancers.'

'Who's leaving?'

'No one, but with you going and living with Sally, well ... He reckons anything can happen.'

'I'm only living away, not going and working somewhere else.'

'Shh, keep your voice down.'

Daisy sat back. Did Joe think that much of her that he missed her being around all day? If so, why didn't he say something? 'Well if you ask me, I think he's being daft and it's not fair to take it out on the others.'

Rhoda shrugged and looked back into the mirror.

Daisy was concerned. Should she have a word with Joe? She didn't want him to be upset. After all, she'd only moved out. She would wait till they finished tonight and then try and get him on his own before Rhoda joined him. She smiled to herself. This could be it; this could be when he declared his love for her.

For the rest of the night she danced like she had wings on her feet.

'Joe, wait.' Daisy was pleased to see he was alone and she ran after him as he left the club.

He stopped. 'Yes, what is it?'

'Can I have a word?'

'What about?'

Daisy looked behind her. She didn't want any of the others to see her talking to him. 'Joe, don't be cross just because I'm living with Sally. I know you think she has lots of blokes there, but she don't, honest.'

'How do you know, you've only been there a

couple of weeks. She's probably on her best behaviour.'

'Why are you so angry with me?'

'I'm not angry with you.'

'Rhoda said she thought you was annoyed because I'd . . .' Daisy didn't know what to say. How could she tell him she thought he loved her and missed her? 'It doesn't matter. And Joe, I will never leave you.'

'That's nice to know; now I must go. See you tomorrow.'

'Bye.' She stood and watched him disappear round the corner. He didn't even give her his usual friendly goodbye kiss on the cheek. She went back into the club to wait for Sally.

'Hello, Daisy, everything all right?'

'Yes thank you, Mr Kenny.'

'You look a bit down.'

She smiled at him. 'I must be tired. It's been very warm dancing tonight.'

'It certainly has. You waiting for Sally?'

She nodded.

'She won't be long. Just giving Tom her tips to put away. See you tomorrow. Good night.'

'Good night.' As she watched Kenny get into his car, she leant back against the wall.

'You still waiting? Thought you would have gone home be now,' said Sally as she came out laughing with Tom.

'I'm sorry, I didn't realise you were . . .'

'Don't worry, Dais, I'm only gonner walk her home.' Tom held his hands up. 'No hanky-panky, I promise.'

'It's none of my business what you do.'

'Who's rattled your cage tonight?' asked Sally.

'No one, it's just that it's so hot.'

'That's true,' said Tom.

'Look, I'll walk on ahead.'

'You don't have to,' said Tom. 'Has Joe been giving you a hard time?'

'No. Why should he?'

'I think our Daisy has got a soft spot for Joe,' said Sally.

'No I haven't.' She was pleased it was dark and they couldn't see her blush.

'You don't wonner hang round waiting for him,' said Tom.

'Why? Not that I want to in that way,' she said hurriedly. 'He's my boss and dance teacher.'

Sally burst out laughing. 'He's my boss and dance teacher,' she said, mimicking Daisy. 'Look, love, he's like all blokes, they're only on this earth to get what they can, and if a better-looking and better dancer comes along, well then I'm afraid it's goodbye, little Daisy.'

'Don't say that,' said Tom. 'Don't destroy all her dreams.'

'Do you mind?' Daisy suddenly said loudly. 'This is me you're talking about. And anyway, Tom, why didn't you take Mr Kenny home instead of hanging round here and making a nuisance of yourself?'

Tom laughed. 'He had a date. Now stop being silly and let me walk you both home. I won't even ask to come in for a nightcap.'

Daisy walked the rest of the way in silence. She shouldn't get cross with them. They didn't mean any harm, and she was grateful for their friendship.

The following lunchtime Sally slowly emerged from her bedroom.

'Tea's made,' said Daisy. She began to pour it out. 'Look, I'm sorry about last night, if I got in the way with Tom bringing you home.'

'Why do you always have to be so bloody cheerful in the mornings?'

'Sorry.'

'And don't keep saying sorry.'

Daisy went to say it again but quickly stopped herself.

'In any case, Tom wasn't gonner bring me home, it was just that Kenny said he was driving himself and Tom said he'd walk with me. After all, he does live this way as well. So there wasn't anything in it, more's the pity.'

'But there might have been if I hadn't butted in.'

'I don't think so. Just going to the lav, I'll have another cuppa later.'

Daisy watched her leave the room. Should she tell Tom how Sally felt about him? No, perhaps not. She didn't want to interfere.

Penny James had been back in England a few months now and she was worried at not hearing from Rose. She had written to her care of the Haven and so far she hadn't had any letters answered or returned. She knew Roger had had Rose sent to another home, but he had assured her it was very similar to the Haven, and every time she asked him why she had been moved, he told her it was because the Haven had had a lot of new children, and because Rose was older and used to life in an institution she could cope with the change. She did ask him to take her there, but he was always busy. She also asked him a few times if everything was all right and whether he was still sending money to the home. He said that perhaps Rose's memory had returned and she had found her parents and was too busy.

'She would have let me know if she'd remembered who she was,' said Penny.

'I don't think so. Not if she came from a rough area and was ashamed of them.'

'Roger, do you know something and are keeping it from me?'

'Now why would I do that?'

'I don't even know where she is. Could we go to the Haven and get her address? I want to see her.'

'I don't think that would be very wise.'

Penny knew she wasn't going to get anywhere with Roger, so she decided to write to Mrs Tunbridge. She could use the excuse that she wanted to make sure Martha had taken the clothes for Rose, and find out if she knew anything about her.

Penny was very surprised by the answer to her letter.

Dear Mrs James,
I feel I have to write and tell you of the terrible
place your poor ward Rose has been sent to
since you stopped the payment for her. A Miss
Coleman has informed me that she has written
to you but I don't think you got her letter. If you
did, you may have chosen to ignore it. I am
going to try and find that poor child, as she
doesn't deserve this kind of treatment.
Yours sincerely,
Martha Tunbridge

Penny sat looking at the short note in complete shock. She had never received a letter from Miss Coleman. She would go and see Martha Tunbridge as soon as she could and find out where Rose was.

The following day Penny waited till Roger had left for the office. He seemed to be spending more and more time away from home since they returned from Germany. Why was he suddenly taking more of an interest in his business?

'If Mr James comes home, just tell him I'm going to see Mrs Tunbridge,' she called to Mrs Richardson as she pulled on her expensive leather gloves.

'Right you are.'

Penny walked along to the taxi rank and took a cab to the Tunbridges' house. She was determined to get to the bottom of this.

'Penny,' said Martha as she opened the door.

'I got your letter.'

'I gather that. Come in.'

Penny was shown into the expensively decorated parlour.

'I must tell you I had no idea what had happened to Rose.'

'Please sit down. Would you like some tea?'

'Perhaps later. First I must know where she is.'

'All I can tell you is that Miss Coleman from the Haven wrote to you, and when she didn't receive a reply, in desperation she wrote to me. Apparently Rose has been put into a dreadful place in London. It was because you stopped sending the money.'

Penny looked sad. 'Poor Rose. I had no idea.

Roger told me he was still paying but that she had to be moved.'

'Did he say why?'

'Something to do with new children arriving. Do you think he has been keeping letters from me?'

'I don't know.'

'Please tell me where she is.'

Martha went to the bureau and began writing down Rose's address. 'I have written to her but so far I haven't received a reply, so I have been thinking about going to see her.' She smiled. 'She is such a lovely, well-behaved child, and so pretty.'

'Yes, she is. I'd like to come with you.'

'Are you sure Mr James will allow you?'

'I like to think I can do what I like.' Within reason, she added silently, and if Roger approves.

'I can get my driver to take us there. What day would suit you?'

'As soon as possible. I don't want Rose to think I've forgotten her any longer.'

'Would Friday be suitable?'

'Yes. What time?'

'About one o'clock.'

'That will be fine. It will give me time to get some new clothes for her. I expect she's grown out of most of what she had.'

Martha Tunbridge smiled. 'That's settled, then. Shall we have tea now?'

Penny nodded as her host pulled the cord at the side of the fireplace. All that was going through her mind was the hope that Roger would be out on Friday.

Chapter 23

ON FRIDAY MORNING AT breakfast, Penny was having difficulty keeping her excitement under control.

Roger looked over the newspaper he was reading. 'Are you all right? You look a little flushed.'

'I'm fine, thank you.'

'Are you doing anything special today, dear?' he asked as he took a slice of toast from the rack and began buttering it.

'Yes, as a matter of fact I'm going shopping with Martha Tunbridge. I did tell you.'

'So you did, but don't overdo it. It just slipped my mind; I seem to have so much to think about these days.'

'Roger, is there a problem with the business?'

'No, of course not. It's just that I like to show Father I'm keeping a close eye on things.

'I do worry about you. You would tell me if there was anything wrong, wouldn't you?'

He smiled at her. 'Of course, my dear. Now, do you want some money?'

'No thank you. I can always put anything I buy on your account.'

'Of course.' He dabbed at the corners of his mouth with his napkin and stood up. 'Now I must be off. Enjoy yourself.'

'I will.'

He kissed her cheek and left.

Penny jumped up and stood at the window, waiting for him to drive away. Full of anticipation, she rushed upstairs to get ready. She was going to see Rose. She really did love that little girl, but was it also guilt that made her feel this way? After all, it was Roger's fault the poor girl was in this state. He always drove too fast.

Martha Tunbridge was ready and waiting for her and soon they were being driven to the address

Martha had. Despite Penny's eagerness to see Rose, she was very worried. Martha had told her that she had written to Rose, but so far hadn't received a reply.

'Do you think she is allowed to write?'

'I don't know, but we shall soon find out.'

They were driving along the south of the Thames.

'You did say it was Bermondsey way, ma'am?'

'Yes, Johnson. According to Miss Coleman's letter. It doesn't look a very nice area, does it?'

Penny was also looking out of the window. It was very run down, and so many dirty, thin children stood staring at them, and that worried her. Some of the children didn't even have shoes on their feet, and their mothers were standing on their doorsteps with their arms akimbo, talking, but stopped as they drove past and watched them silently with dark-ringed eyes.

Martha patted Penny's hand. 'Don't worry. I'm sure the place she is in is fine.'

But Penny wasn't so sure.

The driver stopped the car outside a large redbrick building with tiny windows. 'I think this is it, ma'am. Do you want me to come in with you?'

'No thank you, Johnson.'

Penny would have felt a lot safer if Johnson was with them.

The front door was on the street and Martha rang the bell. After a short while a young girl opened the door.

'Hello, young lady. I wonder if you could take me to see whoever is in charge?' Martha asked sweetly.

'Wait 'ere.' She shut the door.

'She didn't look very well dressed, did she?' said Penny, looking up at the building.

'Perhaps she's just a hired help.'

After a moment or two the door opened again. 'Miss Fielding said who are yer and what d'yer want?'

'My name is Mrs Tunbridge and I've come to see Rose.'

Penny was admiring the way Martha was so calm and authoritative.

The girl didn't say anything; just stepped back and closed the door again.

'Sometimes those in charge can be right little dictators. Power goes to their heads, you know.'

'So you've met people like this before?'

'In the voluntary work I do, yes, you do come across them. You would make a good worker.'

'I don't think I could. I would get too upset and involved.'

'Yes, I must admit that some things I see do upset me.'

The door opened again. 'Come in.'

They followed the girl along a corridor, and the smell of boiled cabbage and disinfectant was overpowering. The walls were institutional green with cream tiles, and quite a number of the tiles were chipped and stained. Their shoes echoed on the floor that was also tiled, but these were well worn and nondescript in colour. Despite it being bright outside, this place was very dark and gloomy, the only light coming through tiny windows set high up on one wall.

The girl stopped outside a large oak door. 'That's Miss Fielding's room.'

Martha knocked and walked in before being invited.

The tall, thin woman seated behind her desk quickly looked up.

'Good morning,' said Martha brightly.

'I understand you are here about the child named Rose?'

'Yes. Could we see her?'

Penny looked around. This was a dreadful place. How dare Roger let that lovely little girl be sent here.

Miss Fielding looked at a letter on her desk. 'Did you want to take her away?'

Penny went to speak but Martha quickly put out her hand to silence her.

'Would that be a problem?' Martha asked.

'We would have to get permission. But we do like to see our children properly housed.' She gave them a thin-lipped smile.

'I can understand that.' Martha was also smiling.

Miss Fielding rang the bell on her desk and the door was opened immediately by the girl they had first met. 'Iris, go and get Rose.'

Iris must have been waiting outside the door. 'Which Rose is that, miss?' she asked.

'The one with no surname.'

'Oh, 'er.' She turned and scampered away.

Penny shifted her weight from one foot to the other. They hadn't been invited to sit down.

'Do you have many children here?' asked Martha.

'More than enough to feed and look after,' came the curt reply, as Miss Fielding continued writing. 'After all, we are a charity and have to take whatever money we're given.'

'Rose hasn't got her memory back yet, then?' asked Penny, anxious for something to say.

'No, we would soon send her packing if we knew where she came from. We can't afford to keep children that have a home, no matter what it's like.'

There was a timid knock on the door.

'Come,' called Miss Fielding.

The door opened and for a moment Mary stood and looked at Penny, then she ran into her open arms and holding on to her cried pitifully.

Penny held her close and kissed her hair.

'You come to take me back?'

'I wish I could,' said Penny.

Mary stepped back. 'So what d'yer want coming here then?'

'I wanted to see how you were.' Penny was looking at Mary's ill-fitting dull grey frock; it was much too big for her. 'Where are the clothes I gave you?'

'They're not allowed to look different from anybody else,' said Miss Fielding.

'I've brought you some new ones.' Penny looked at Miss Fielding. 'Can she wear these?'

'No. I'll take them in case she ever goes away.'

Penny was holding on to Mary's hand. 'You look very thin. Are you keeping well?'

Mary nodded and wiped the tears from her cheeks. 'Hello,' she said to Martha Tunbridge.

'Hello, my dear. And how are you?'

Mary looked at Miss Fielding before saying, 'All right.'

Martha also looked at Miss Fielding. 'Is it possible we could go to another room?'

'No. You must stay here.'

'We would like a little privacy.'

'No. You want to think yourselves lucky I let you see her. I don't have to, you know.'

'Yes. I am aware of the rules. I do a lot of social work.'

Miss Fielding sat up and narrowed her eyes. 'Do you have any say in how we get our money?'

'I'm afraid not.'

'Pity.' She went back to her writing.

'Why can't I come and live with you?'

'I wish you could, but I'm afraid Roger won't agree.'

Mary looked at Martha. 'Could I come and live with you?'

'Rose, stop that at once, otherwise you will be sent to your room. These people have come to see how you are. What sort of impression will they take away if they think you are unhappy?'

'I am unhappy.'

'That's it. You ladies must go now.'

'But . . .' said Penny.

Martha took her arm. 'Come along, dear. We must do as we are told.'

Mary threw herself at Penny and sobbed, 'Will you come and see me again?'

'Of course. Now you be a good girl.'

'I'll try.'

'Come along, Penny,' said Martha, noting the look of anger on Miss Fielding's face. She bent and kissed Mary's cheek. 'Bye, little one.'

'Bye,' sobbed Mary as she watch them leave the room.

As soon as the door closed, Miss Fielding was round her desk, and grabbing Mary's arms, she shook her so hard that her teeth rattled. Then with an open hand she smacked Mary's face. 'How dare you? How dare you tell them you are unhappy?'

The force of the blow had made Mary's head reel, and she felt for the door behind her to lean against. She was trying hard not to cry but her face stung. She rubbed her cheek. She hated this woman and this place and she knew she had to find a way of running away. Run away. Why had she thought of that? Was this something she had done before? If so, who had she run away from? She was trying so hard to think, she wasn't listening to what Miss Fielding was saying.

'Did you hear me?'

Mary looked up.

'I said you can go to your room and miss your dinner.'

Mary didn't care. Something told her that she had run away from someone before. Was it a wicked dad or mum? Had they hit her? She had to try hard to think.

'How could Roger let Rose be sent to a place like that?'

Martha held her friend's hand. 'Try not to get too upset.'

'It's wicked. I'm not going to let her stay there.'

'I'm afraid there's not a lot you can do about it unless you have income of your own.'

'No, I don't. I know what that child is going through.'

Martha raised one eyebrow, but didn't ask any questions. She knew she would be told all in good time. 'Now come along and dry those tears.'

Penny took a handkerchief from her bag and dabbed at her face. 'Do you think I'm being silly?'

'No, I don't.'

'I must try and find a way of bringing Rose home.'

'I don't think that will be possible if, as you say, Roger is so against it.'

'I shall try and think of something. Martha, next week is the day we found her, and that's the date I have given her for a birthday.'

'We must send her a card and a present.'

'Do you think she'll get them?'

'I don't know. But we must not give up.'

Penny dabbed at her eyes again. 'I don't want to go home just yet. Could we go for a coffee or some lunch?'

'I think that is a very good idea. Johnson, you do know where to go?'

'Certainly, ma'am.'

Chapter 24

IT WAS FOUR THIRTY in the morning, and the edges of the sky were just beginning to lighten as once again Sally, Tom and Daisy walked home together. They were happy and burst into song and Daisy did a little dance along the way.

When she stopped and fell into step with them Tom said, 'You girls were good tonight.'

'Thank you,' she said, full of pride. 'I love these jazzy numbers.'

'I wish I could see you,' said Sally. 'I manage to have a quick peep now and again, but you can bet yer bottom dollar someone will want their coat or shoes just as I leave me little box.'

'So Mr Kenny's not wanting you to drive him

home again tonight then?' Daisy asked Tom.

'He's definitely got a lady friend. You should have smelled him tonight; talk about overpowering,' said Tom.

'Do we know who she is?' asked Sally.

'No. She might be one of the cigarette girls.'

'Would have thought he would have gone for someone with a bit more class,' said Sally.

'She might be a punter, but I keep looking and I ain't seen any posh dame hanging about.'

'She might be waiting at her flat,' said Sally.

'D'you know, I hadn't thought of that,' said Tom.

'This all sounds very interesting,' said Daisy.

'Anyway, don't let's worry about him. What you two doing tomorrow?'

Daisy giggled. 'I think you mean today.'

'Well, all right then, if you must nit-pick. Today?'

'Sleeping till midday at least,' said Sally.

'That leaves the afternoon and evening.'

'Nothing, why?' Sally was suddenly taking an interest in what Tom was saying.

'How about we all go to Southend?'

'Southend?' repeated Daisy. 'I ain't ever been there.'

'It's great. Mind you, if the tide's out you have a long way to walk for a paddle,' said Sally.

'How do we get there?'

'On the train,' said Sally. 'Ain't you ever been on a train?'

'Only when I was a little kid.'

'So, how about it?' said Tom quickly, as he could see that for some reason Daisy looked embarrassed. 'You two could do up a picnic.'

'I thought there might be a catch.'

'Come on, Sal, it could be fun, but are you sure you want me with you, Tom?'

'I should say so. Think of all the envious looks I'll get when I walk along the pier with two gorgeous-looking girls on me arm.'

'I ain't got nothing to wear,' said Sally.

'Nothing to wear? You should see her wardrobe, it's bursting.'

'But not with the right sort o' things. I quite fancy those beach pyjamas, they look really good when you're parading along the prom.'

'Sal, we're going to Southend, not the South of France,' Tom laughed as he stopped outside their block of flats. 'Right, here we are. I'll pick you both up about one, is that all right?'

'That's fine,' said Daisy.

Tom kissed both of their cheeks. 'See you later.' He gave them a wave as he walked on.

'That sounds ever so exciting,' said Daisy in a loud whisper as they mounted the stairs. They always tried to be quiet when they got home.

'S'pose it could be.'

As Tom continued home he couldn't help thinking about Daisy. Sally's all right for a bit of fun, he thought to himself, but I wouldn't want to be tied to her for life. But with Daisy, well that's very different. She is so innocent and she don't know just how lovely she is. No wonder Joe warned me off, but is that because he wants her for himself? Tom knew Joe held him responsible for Amy's death. He still felt guilty about that. If he'd realised what a state Amy was in that night, perhaps he could have helped her, but she had been a drunk and unstable, and he knew there was little he could have done to change what happened. Tom mused to himself. Was it just hands off Daisy because I don't want to lose another dancer? Or did Joe secretly have other motives? Tom knew only one thing: he was very fond of Daisy

Cooper and he was determined to somehow make her his own.

Despite only having a few hours' sleep, Daisy was up at ten. She had been too excited to stay in bed, and as soon as she was awake she got up and began to make some sandwiches for the picnic. Today was going to be so different; she had so much to look forward to. For one thing she was going on a train. She could just about remember when before the war her dad took her on a train. She couldn't recall where they went – it was in the country somewhere – but that had been the only time she'd been on a train. She was also looking forward to the picnic lunch. She remembered when, on bright sunny days, she, her mother and Mary had taken their slices of bread and jam to the park. They couldn't afford lemonade and only had drinking water from the fountain using those metal cups that hung on chains. It was surprising how little things could start her reflecting on those far-off happy days. Did Mary remember how it was?

As she buttered the bread, Daisy's thoughts went to how her life had changed since she became a dancer. It didn't seem possible that she could be so happy, but also so sad. She was beginning to accept that she would never see Mary again. Daisy thought her sister must really be happy with her new way of life. If only she had written to her or somehow got a message to her so they could share their joy, then both their lives would be complete. She tried to picture how Mary must have grown. I expect she's really lovely looking now, with those wonderful eyes, she thought. Her own eyes filled with tears as she began slicing the cheese.

Daisy sighed. She knew she had to throw off her melancholy mood. Today she was going to see the sea for the first time; this was something she'd always wanted to do.

Sally came into the room. 'Don't tell me, you've done the sandwiches and made a pot of tea. Honestly, I don't know where you get your energy from. Dancing all night and up at the crack of dawn.'

'You can hardly call ten o'clock the crack of dawn.'

'It is ter me.' Sally took a packet of cigarettes

off the mantelpiece. 'All right, don't nag. One of these would do you the world of good.'

'Not if I want to keep me breath for these new dances that are all the rage.'

'Yer, I suppose these do make you wheeze a bit. Is there any tea left in that pot?'

'I'll make you a fresh one if you like.'

'Na, that'll do.'

It was almost one o'clock. Tom looked in the mirror and began slicking down his straight dark hair. His new brown and white shoes went well with his grey flannels, and his crisp white shirt just finished it off. He wouldn't wear a tie; the open-necked shirt looked fine. He wanted to look as casual as he could. He wanted to impress Daisy and show her that he could look just as good out of evening clothes. If only he could prove to her that he liked her. He knew she thought he wanted Sally. Daisy was a very private person and he knew nothing about her background. She fascinated him and he desperately wanted to find out more about her. All he knew was that she was a wonderful dancer and very beautiful. And that he loved her.

He picked up his keys and cigarettes and looked round his flat. If he wanted to bring her back here at some time, he would have to start thinking about cleaning it up. He shut the door and was on his way, whistling the catchy tune to the Charleston as he walked along, conjuring up images of Daisy dancing in her short skirt and kicking her legs. He knew she was the girl for him.

In the dressing room the following afternoon Daisy couldn't wait for Rhoda to come in so she could tell her what a wonderful time she had had yesterday.

'I've never seen the sea before. It's so big.'

Rhoda laughed. 'Was the tide in?'

'Yes, and Sally and me had a lovely time splashing about. Even Tom rolled his trousers up and paddled. You should have seen him with a knotted handkerchief on his head.'

'Sounds as if you had a good time,' said Rhoda.

'We did.'

'I'm really glad for you, Dais.'

'You should have seen some of the wonderful things the women were wearing. Beach pyjamas with matching hats. Sally said they're all the rage, and they look really glamorous.'

'Wouldn't have thought Southend would be a place to dress up for,' said June.

'When we go again, me and Sally are getting some of those hats and pyjamas.'

'I dunno where you get the energy from,' said June.

'I think I'm just beginning to live my childhood.'

Rhoda gave June a withering look. 'Just remember, not everybody was blessed with a family.'

'Sorry,' said June sheepishly. It was only the girls who knew about Daisy's background and Mary, her lost sister.

'That's all right,' said Daisy cheerfully.

Joe came into the room. 'Next week we're going to do a new number, so I want you in here on Sunday afternoon.'

'But Joe,' protested June, 'it's the only day we get off.'

'I know that.'

'Slave-driver,' said Rene.

'Sorry if it stops any of you going out,' he said, looking at Daisy. And with that he left the room.

Daisy looked at Rhoda. 'Why is he doing this?'
She only shrugged.

'We could easily learn a new dance in the mornings like we've always done,' said Thelma.

Daisy was worried that he was doing it because she'd been out with Tom and Sally. But why?

It wasn't till she was waiting to go back on stage that evening that she managed to speak to Tom.

'Did you tell Joe we went out yesterday?' she asked him.

'Sure did, and you should have seen his face, it was like thunder.'

'Why?'

'Why did I tell him, or why was he annoyed?'

'Both.'

'I told him to get his back up. After all, he don't like anybody going out with his girls.'

'But didn't you tell him Sally was with us?'

'No. Didn't see it was necessary.'

'Oh Tom, you know what he thinks about you.'

'I know. Daisy, we must do it again sometime before the weather turns.'

'I doubt it. We've got to work next Sunday afternoon.'

'What?'

'Shh, keep your voice down.'

'He can't make you do that.'

'He can and he has.'

'I'll have a word with him.'

Daisy grabbed Tom's arm. 'No, please don't. Besides, Rhoda might get him to change his mind, and I don't want him to be more annoyed with me for the girls' sake. After all, I owe everything to him.'

'You owe him nothing.'

'Yes I do, Tom.' Daisy could hear the band warming up for their number. 'I've got to go.'

'Look, tell me about it some time.'

But she hurried away, the brightly coloured feathers she was wearing on her head bobbing up and down.

Chapter 25

MARTHA TUNBRIDGE WAS looking out of her drawing-room window to the fields beyond the sweep of lawn where her son Harry was riding his horse. At ten years old he was becoming a very handsome young man with his tousled blond hair falling over his bright hazel eyes. He was so talented, passing many piano exams. Her thoughts strayed to that poor child Rose; she hadn't been able to get her out of her mind since she saw her a month ago. She'd looked so distressed the first time she'd seen her at the Haven. It was so wrong of Roger James to let that child be sent to this new home. And why didn't Penny stand up to her husband? What made her so wary of him?

Martha turned when she heard the door open and smiled as William walked into the room.

'And how was your day, dear?' he asked as he gently kissed her cheek.

'Much the same as usual. Just look at young Harry. He'll be attending gymkhanas soon.'

'Yes, he certainly can ride. I only wish I could keep up with him.'

She lightly touched his cheek. 'You were good in your day, my love.'

He took her hand and kissed it. 'I know, and I wouldn't have pulled through without your love and attention.'

'Well that's all in the past. I'll get Mrs Aimes to bring in the tea.' Martha pulled on the cord at the side of the fireplace. She watched her husband lower himself down into his pale green tapestry armchair that stood looking out over the garden and remembered how six years ago he had fought for his life after the riding accident when his horse threw him. He was unconscious for hours, broke his leg in two places and punctured a lung. It took him a long while to recover and he had never ridden again. Martha didn't want Harry to ride, but her husband insisted, saying that it was part of being a country gentleman.

The gentle tap on the door brought her back and she turned to smile at her housekeeper. 'Thank you, Mrs Aimes,' she said, taking the tray and placing it on the small table. She poured out the tea and handed her husband a cup. 'William,' she said, sitting opposite him, 'I've been thinking about that poor child Rose, you know, the one that's been put into that terrible home.'

He smiled. 'How could I forget? You've been talking about her ever since you got back from that dreadful place. I could never understand why Roger stopped the payments for the other home.'

'The Haven. He must have had a reason.' Penny had asked her not to tell William too much about how they had found Rose. Once again the thought that went through Martha's mind was, was Roger responsible for Rose's accident?

'Is Roger in some kind of trouble?' William asked.

'I don't know. Penny has never said.'

'Well I suppose that's his business. So what about this child?'

'I feel so sorry for her, and I've been thinking . . .'

William placed the delicate bone-china cup and saucer on the table next to him.

'What have you got in mind?'

Martha sat forward. 'Could we adopt her?'

'I hardly think so.'

Martha sat back and a look of disappointment swept across her face.

'You see, my dear, you can't adopt anyone who could possibly still have a family.'

As William was a lawyer, Martha was aware he knew what he was talking about. 'Is there no way we could look after her?'

'I could look into it, but are you sure you want to take on something like this? We know nothing about this child and we could end up with her till she marries.'

'I'm sure you would learn to love her.'

'I'm sure I would, but suppose in time she recovers her memory and wants to leave us? I know you, my dear, you would be heart-broken.'

'But I would be happy for her if she got her memory back.'

'Let me look into this.'

Martha jumped up and kissed his cheek. 'I knew I could rely on you.'

'Please don't build your hopes up too high.'

Smiling, she picked up the tray of tea things. 'I won't, I promise. I'll just take these out to Mrs Aimes.'

'Remember, you must think about Harry. What would his reaction be to someone else seeking your affection?'

As Martha left the room, she felt very happy. She knew that William would help her as much as he could, but what about Harry? Would he feel put out if Rose did become part of their family?

Daisy was hoping Tom would be walking home with them that night, then she could try and explain why she didn't want to upset Joe over having to work on Sunday.

'You're very quiet tonight,' said Sally as the two of them sauntered along.

'We've got to work on Sunday afternoon.'

'What! I was hoping we could go to Southend again. What's brought this on?'

'Joe wants to us learn a new routine.'

'He's a bloody slave-driver. You ain't had to work on a Sunday before when you've done a new routine.'

'No, we always do it in the late mornings, and sometimes if he ain't very pleased with us we go on till the early afternoon.'

'What do the other girls have to say about it?'

'They ain't very happy.'

'I bet they ain't.'

'Look, you and Tom go to Southend. You don't want me hanging round you all the time.'

'I like having you around, but I wouldn't mind being alone all day with Tom.'

Daisy smiled. 'Good, so you and Tom go.'

'We'll see what he's got to say about it. Beside, I can't do sandwiches as good as you.'

'Don't worry, I'll do 'em for you.'

When Daisy was in bed that night, she went over what had been discussed. She really did want to go with them. Why was Joe doing this? Why didn't he want her to go out with Sally and Tom? If it was because he had feelings for her, why couldn't he just tell her, and she wouldn't go along with Sally and Tom ever again. After all, it wasn't fair on the other girls.

DEE WILLIAMS

*

At the end of the show the girls were changing. The knock on the dressing-room door made them grab their wraps, and Rhoda yelled out, 'Come in!' When the door opened Rhoda said, 'Hello, Tom. What can we do for you?'

'Hello, Rhoda. Daisy, could I have a quick word?'

'Now what you been up to?' asked June.

As Daisy went to the door she turned and shrugged, saying, 'Don't ask me.'

'Come outside a minute,' said Tom.

'What is it?'

'So it is true? Sally's just told me you've definitely got to work Sunday afternoon.'

' 'Fraid so.'

'The bastard.'

'I beg your pardon.'

'I'm sorry, I shouldn't have said that. But why's he doing this?'

'I think to stop me going out.'

'He can't do that.'

'But he has.'

Tom moved away from the door. 'Is this because he thinks you and me are . . . you know, walking out together?'

314

Daisy laughed.

'What's so funny about that?'

'He should know that it's Sally who's after you. And I know you like her. I'll tell him he's got nothing to worry about.'

Tom held her arm. 'But what if he has?'

Daisy looked at him in shock. The smile left her face. 'What?'

It was just at that moment that Joe turned the corner and Tom quickly let go of Daisy's arm.

'What's going on?'

'Nothing, Joe,' said Daisy. 'Tom was just wondering why we had to work Sunday afternoon, as him and Sally are going to Southend and wanted me to go along as well.'

'You've got to work.' He walked into the dressing room without bothering to knock.

'I'd better go. Will I see you on the way home tonight?' Daisy asked.

'No. I've got to take Kenny home.'

'Oh.'

'But don't worry, I'll try and get to see you sometime. I might come round in the morning, if that's all right?'

Daisy nodded.

'It won't be too early. And Daisy, perhaps we

could go for a coffee or something. I need to talk to you.'

'All right.'

When everybody had left, Daisy was still sitting waiting for Sally. Slowly she took off her make-up. What was it Tom wanted to say to her? She had a good idea but she had to tell him she was in love with Joe.

She had been disappointed that she wouldn't be going to Southend, as she needed to be with friends at the moment and not think about the past. As she sat in front of the large mirror she thought about last year. It didn't seem possible that it was a year ago that Mary had disappeared. Where was she? Was she happy? A tear trickled down her cheek. So much had happened in her life, but what about her sister? Was she still alive? She pushed her make-up aside, put her head down and cried.

Chapter 26

AFTER HER TALK with William, Martha Tunbridge sent a letter to Miss Fielding asking if she could visit Rose again.

When Penny and Roger came to dinner a few weeks later and the men were having their port and cigars, she told Penny what she was hoping to do.

'You mean to say that you are going to bring Rose here, to live?'

'I would like to, but I am waiting for Miss Fielding to answer my letter. It's been a month since I wrote to her.'

'Do you think you'll be allowed to have her?'

'William has looked into it, and as long as we

report to some authority or another he seems to think it will be fine.'

'What does Harry have to say about it?'

'We haven't told him yet. No point till we are know for sure that we can have her.'

'Will you adopt her?'

'No, we can't, but I hope we can make her very happy.'

'You are making me feel so ashamed.'

Martha gently touched her hand. 'I don't want you to feel like that, my dear. It's just that it really upset me seeing her in that place. She looked such a forlorn, lost little girl, and you know you will be welcome to come and visit her whenever you want to.'

'I don't think Roger would be too happy about that.'

'I shouldn't say this, but does he have to know?'

'I suppose not.'

'Penny. I don't mean to pry, but do you and Roger have some kind of problem?'

'Not really.' She looked towards the closed door. 'I told you how I met Roger, and I suppose in some ways I was a bit like Rose, homeless and without friends. Now and again he reminds me that I had nothing when he married me and I should be grateful. He does love me,' she added hastily. 'But I'll always be thankful to him for what I've got and I don't like to upset him.' She couldn't tell Martha that she had once hung about in expensive bars in the hope of finding a rich man who could give her everything she'd ever wanted. That was how she had met Roger.

'I understand.' She might understand, but Martha didn't approve of Roger having such a hold on his wife.

'Do you know, it's over a year since we found Rose.' Penny looked at her hands. 'I hope you don't think I'm being silly, but as she still doesn't know who she is or who her parents are, I have always felt that perhaps we should mark that day we found her as her birthday.'

'What a wonderful idea. If she still hasn't recovered her memory next year, we will do that.'

The laughter outside told them that the men were coming in.

'I'll let you know how things turn out with Miss Fielding,' Martha said quickly.

Penny smiled. 'Thank you.'

*

Daisy was pleased to see that Tom was late. She had left Sally in bed and decided not to tell her she was meeting Tom, as it might give out the wrong message. She would tell her later, when she found out what it was that was so important. As she walked up the road a little way, Tom turned the corner. He kissed her cheek and they went into the Lyons corner house.

'I did wonder if you'd come,' he said, looking nervous.

'I said I would. Now what is it you want to talk about?'

He took her arm. 'Let's wait till we're seated.'

Daisy laughed. 'You're making it sound ever so mysterious.' She wanted to keep this light hearted.

He only smiled at her and, taking her hand, followed the nippy as they were escorted to a table.

Daisy was slowly stirring her coffee when Tom suddenly spoke.

'Daisy, I think I'm in love with you.'

She looked up. 'No, you can't be.'

'Why? You're a lovely person who will go out of her way to help anyone, and I love everything about you. From the first moment I saw you at the club I thought you were a stunner. Daisy, I have never felt this way about anyone else. I want you to marry me. Please say you will.'

Daisy laughed nervously. 'I always thought you wanted a rich widow. And what about Sally?'

'Daisy, I want you.'

As she went to put her hand to her mouth, Daisy caught it on the spoon and spilt coffee all over her blouse. 'Now look what you've made me do.' Tears filled her eyes; she was flattered at the proposal but angry at spilling the coffee.

Tom jumped up and dabbed at her with his handkerchief. 'I'm so sorry.'

'It wasn't your fault.'

'I'll get you another.'

'No. Thanks all the same. Oh Tom, I can't marry you.'

'Why not?'

'For one thing we're friends.' She looked at the handkerchief she was clutching in her hand and said softly, 'And for another, I love Joe.'

'Joe! I see.'

'Shh, keep your voice down.'

'And has he told you what his feelings are for you?'

She shook her head.

'So you could spend your life waiting for someone who hasn't got the guts to tell you his feelings, that's of course if he does have any.'

'Don't be hard on him. He don't know how I feel.'

'But Daisy, I love you.'

'Tom, I'm very flattered, but . . .'

'Please say you could learn to love me.'

Daisy smiled at him. He was so sweet and sincere.

Tom reached across the table and held her hand. She looked into his sad eyes.

'Sally loves you, you know. It's her you should be asking to marry you.'

'I don't think so. I don't love her. We work together, and since her dad died she needs a shoulder to cry on now and again, that's all.'

Daisy sat back. She cared about Tom as a friend, but this had come completely out of the blue.

'Daisy, please take a few weeks to think this over.'

'A few weeks to make up my mind about the rest of my life?'

'Sorry. I didn't mean it to sound like that.'

Daisy looked at her watch. 'I'll have to go. I've got to change me blouse.'

'Please don't be angry about what I've just said.'

'I'm not angry. But now you know how I feel about Joe.'

'Yes. But remember, I'll be the one who'll be waiting for you.'

She stood up. 'Thanks for the coffee. I'll see you at the club.'

'Let's walk back together.'

'Tom, please don't tell anyone what we have discussed this morning.'

'No. Don't worry, your secret's safe with me.' He smiled sadly. 'That's of course unless you change your mind.'

As they walked back silently together, Daisy's thoughts were in turmoil. She was very fond of Tom and was sorry that she had upset him, but she couldn't ignore Sally. She knew Sally loved Tom, and Daisy wanted them all to be good friends. Besides, she loved Joe. She would dance for Joe till she was old and couldn't keep up. But she had lost her sister through her dancing. Daisy looked at the date on the news stand. Next Tuesday, the fourth of November, would be

Mary's ninth birthday. She had never told Tom or Sally about her missing sister. The other dancers knew, but they didn't have anything to do with them. Perhaps she should tell Tom about Mary. He was a good friend, and maybe he would help her find her sister.

Martha had invited Penny for lunch and was busy telling her about her meeting with Miss Fielding.

'So you will be able to take her away from that dreadful place?'

'Yes, once all the paperwork has been completed. She seemed pleased to see her go when she knew that my husband was a solicitor.'

'Did you see Rose? How did she look?'

'No, I didn't see her as the dragon, Miss Fielding, said she didn't want to upset her now she's settled in, just in case it didn't happen.'

'This is so good of you.' Penny looked around. 'I know she'll be very happy here. Have you told Harry?'

'Yes, and he is also looking forward to having someone to play with. I really feel I am doing something worthwhile for once in my very privileged life.'

'But what if her memory returns? Will you be prepared to give her up.'

'Of course, but as we don't know where she came from, it has got to be better for her to stay here till that time comes.'

Penny was worried. Would Martha Tunbridge have too much of a hold over Rose? She looked away. She was filled with guilt. It was all Roger's fault that this poor child had been pushed from pillar to post, but perhaps everything would work out fine for her after all. 'Will she be here in time for Christmas?' she asked.

'I hope so. I have got so much planned. And of course you are always welcome to come and see her.'

'Thank you.' Penny smiled. 'I shall look forward to that.'

Chapter 27

MARY HAD BEEN very frightened when she was taken to the washroom and, after having a wash, given her old clothes to put on. Where was she going? She asked Miss Norman what was going to happen to her, but all she would say was to wait and see. The pretty frock Penny had bought her a while back was now very short and a bit tight. Mary knew something was going to happen and she felt sick with fear.

Miss Norman took her along to Miss Fielding. 'She's cleaned up all right.'

'Thank you, Norman.'

It was then that Mary saw Mrs Tunbridge. She gave her a beaming smile.

'Hello, Rose.'

'Hello.' Mary's mind was going round in circles. What did this lady want? Was she going to send her somewhere else? Tears began to slide down her cheeks. She looked at Miss Fielding. 'Where am I going?'

'You are coming home with me,' said Mrs Tunbridge.

Mary sniffed. 'With you?'

'Yes. Would you like that?'

'Yes please.' She brushed the tears away with her hand. 'But why?'

'I will tell you all about it when we get home.'

Home. That sounded a magical word to Mary, and once again the tears fell, but these were tears of happiness. She ran over to Martha Tunbridge and threw her arms round her. 'Thank you. Thank you so much.'

'Come along,' said Mrs Tunbridge. She turned to Miss Fielding. 'And thank you.'

For the first time Miss Fielding smiled. 'It was our pleasure. And Rose. Be a good girl.'

'I will.'

'Merry Christmas,' said Miss Fielding.

'Merry Christmas,' they both replied.

Mary put on her coat, that was also far too

small for her, and walked out into the weak winter sunshine. Somehow she felt her luck was about to change at last and this could be a wonderful Christmas.

Smiling, Martha took hold of her hand and led her towards the car.

'Is that yours?'

'Yes, and this is Johnson. Say hello.'

Mary looked under her long lashes and said shyly, 'Hello.'

'Hello, miss. Welcome to the Tunbridge household.' He was holding the car door open.

Mary giggled. 'Thank you.'

'In you get, young lady,' said Martha. 'Then we can be off.'

Mary settled back in the lovely soft brown leather seat. She wanted to cry she was so happy, but why was this woman doing this for her? 'Are you just taking me to your house for Christmas?' she asked.

'No.' Martha patted her hand. 'You are going to stay with me and my husband.'

'But why?'

'I didn't like you staying in that place.'

'I didn't like it that much either. Does Penny know what you've done?'

'Yes she does, and I expect she'll be round to see you soon.'

'What about Mr Roger? He don't like me.'

'We won't worry too much about Roger.'

'What about your man?'

Martha smiled. 'Mr Tunbridge is very much looking forward to meeting you. And so is my son.'

'You've got a son?'

'Yes.'

'How old is he?'

'Ten. You don't know how old you are, do you?'

Mary shook her head.

'I think you and Harry are about the same age and I'm sure you'll get on.'

Mary hoped so, but some of the boys in the homes could be very rough. 'Does he speak posh like you?'

Martha laughed and she could see that Johnson was smiling. 'I think he must, but don't worry about it, he's a good boy.'

When they pulled into the long drive of the Tunbridge household, Mary sat back stunned. It was the most beautiful house she had ever seen. 'Is that your house?'

'Yes, it is.'

'It's just like out of a picture book.'

Martha smiled. 'I suppose it is, but for us it's home and I hope it will be yours as well.'

The steps leading up to the front door were wide and Mary followed Martha out of the car when Johnson opened the door.

The front door burst open and for a moment or two a young boy stood at the top of the steps. His hair had flopped over his eyes; he pushed it back as he ran down to greet them.

'Hello, Mama.' Martha bent to kiss his cheek, then he turned to Mary and said, 'My name's Harry. What's yours?'

'Rose.' She looked up at Martha.

'Don't worry, Harry knows all about the accident and how you lost your memory.'

'It must be very odd not being able to remember anything,' he said as they went inside.

'Yes it is.' Mary stopped.

'What is it?' asked Martha.

Mary looked around her. The hall was large and warm. A log fire burned brightly, with Christmas decorations hanging from one side of the room to the other. Mary stood and looked around her. 'This is the bestest place I have ever been in.'

Harry began to laugh.

'Wot's ser funny,' she said.

'The way you speak.'

Mary's face flushed. 'I'm sorry. Mr Roger was always telling me off for not talking proper.'

'That's all right, my dear,' said Martha. 'Harry, don't be so rude.'

'Sorry,' he said sheepishly.

'It's all right,' said Mary. 'My friend Nellie at the other place used to take the mick out of how I spoke, but I will try and talk proper.'

'Now come on, children. Rose, take off your hat and coat, and let's go and introduce you to Mrs Aimes, then we can all have tea.'

Mary followed them into the vast kitchen with a big deal table in the centre.

'Mrs Aimes, this is Rose. She has come to live with us.'

Mary wanted to curtsy. She felt she had died and gone to heaven. Was this all a dream? Would she wake up?

'I've made a nice sponge cake, and if you like you can both sit here in the warm and have a slice of it.'

'Thank you,' said Harry, scrambling up to the table.

'When you two have finished I'll take you up and show you your room, Rose,' said Martha. 'I have got you some new clothes. I hope you like them.'

Once again tears ran down Mary's cheeks.

'What is it? Is something wrong?'

Mary shook her head. 'Thank you. No one has ever been this kind to me.'

Martha held her close. 'I'm sure they have at some time.'

Harry slid off his chair. 'You can play with my toys if you like.'

Mary gave him a watery smile. 'Thank you.'

When she entered the room that was to be hers, Mary rushed to the window. 'Is that all your garden?' she asked, pointing to the vast lawn.

'Yes, and in the summer it looks lovely, it's a blaze of colour. Now these are your clothes in the wardrobe, and your underwear and socks are in your chest of drawers.'

Mary sat on the bed that had a pink counterpane that matched the curtains. 'Why are you doing all this for me?'

Martha sat next to her. 'I was blessed with

being born into a wealthy family and so was William, my husband. After Harry was born we couldn't have any more children and I always wanted a daughter. I do a lot of charitable work, and then when I heard that you had been sent to that dreadful place, I made up my mind that I would look after you.'

'But what if I get my memory back and me real mum and dad want me back?'

'Then your place will be to go home with them.'

Mary thought about that. She knew her house would never be as grand as this. 'Thank you ever so much.' She threw her arms round Martha, and laughing together they fell back on the bed. 'What shall I call you?'

'I don't know. I haven't really thought about that. What would you like to call me?'

'Dunno. I'd like to call you my fairy godmother, but that's a bit of a mouthful.'

Martha laughed. 'And you can hardly call me a fairy. What about Auntie Martha?'

'That sounds nice.'

'And you can call my husband Uncle William.'

'All right. When does he get home?' To Mary that word sounded so wonderful.

'About six.'

'Will he like me?'

'Of course he will.' Martha held her close. 'He's really looking forward to meeting you.'

'Mr Roger didn't like me.'

'William is very different to Roger.' These were the only words of comfort she could offer. 'Now, I'll run you a bath and you can put on one of your new dresses.' Martha stood up and took Mary's hand. 'The bathroom is along there,' she said, pointing to the end of the landing. 'And after dinner this evening we will have fun getting the tree decorated. It's in the drawing room all potted ready and waiting for you.'

Mary reached up and pulled on Martha's arm. Her big eyes were sparkling. 'Thank you.'

Martha bent down and kissed her cheek. 'And thank you.'

Mary hung on to her neck and held her tight.

Martha Tunbridge was very happy. But would it all end one day?

Daisy didn't want to leave Sally on Christmas morning, but Sally had told her that Tom was coming round for dinner and they'd probably have a drink or two and play cards.

'So you go off and enjoy yourself.'

After breakfast they exchanged presents. Daisy had bought Sally a pair of doeskin gloves and Sally had bought her a scarf.

Sally was admiring her gloves. 'These must have cost you a few bob.'

'I earn more than you, and it's because I enjoy living here. I'll always be grateful to you for taking me in.'

Sally laughed. 'Just as long as yer pays yer rent and keeps the place tidy, that's all I ask.'

Daisy was going to spend the day with Joe and Rhoda, but she felt a little sad at not seeing Tom over Christmas. After all, he was a good friend.

'I can't believe so much has happened this past year,' she said, straightening her paper hat as she helped Rhoda clear the table after dinner.

'There certainly have been a few changes,' said Rhoda. 'Do you ever think about your sister now?'

'All the time. I was thinking of going back to the cinema, just to make sure nobody's seen her.'

'I'm sure that Charlie would have let you know.'

'But what if he's lost me address?'

'I think he would have found you.'

'Yes, I suppose so.'

After the washing-up, they sat and talked, and Daisy noted that Joe was unusually quiet. Normally he would be telling her about the new dance routine he was planning, but when she asked if anything was wrong, he just said he was tired. Daisy did worry that he was feeling under the weather. After all, he never stopped working.

It was during the evening, when they were playing cards, that Rhoda dropped her bombshell.

'Daisy, I can't keep this to myself any longer. You are the first to know – after Joe, of course – that I'm getting married.'

Daisy dropped her cards. 'Who to?'

'Kenny.'

'You're gonner marry Mr Kenny?'

Rhoda, who had a big grin plastered across her face, nodded.

'When?'

'Next year.'

'What can I say?'

'You could congratulate me.'

'Course I will.' She rushed round the table and held Rhoda tight, knocking her paper hat askew. 'I'm so happy for you.'

'Thanks.'

Daisy sat back down. 'So you're the mystery woman Mr Kenny was taking out?'

Rhoda grinned. 'Is that what they're saying?'

'Only Tom and Sally. And what have you got to say about this, Joe?'

'What d'you think? We've had some right old rows over it, I can tell you. Silly cow, throwing her career away just like that.'

'It's my life and I can do what I like.' Rhoda sat forward, her cheeks flushed with excitement. 'Kenny is going to buy us a lovely house and I don't have to kick me legs in the air every night.'

'But I thought you loved dancing,' said Daisy, completely taken aback.

'I do. But let's face it, I ain't getting any younger and we all have to give up in the end.'

'So when's the big day going to be?'

'We ain't sure yet, could be in June.'

'I can't get over this. You've certainly kept it very quiet. I didn't even know you were going out with Mr Kenny.'

'We tried to be discreet.'

'You really are a dark horse,' said Daisy, smiling. 'I think everybody will be very surprised. As I said, we did wonder who Mr Kenny was seeing when he didn't want Tom to drive him home.'

'Well now you know. Joe, I think this calls for a drink. Kenny is going to announce it tomorrow night and we're having a get-together when the club closes.'

'Will you carry on working for now?'

'Till I get married. That'll give Joe time to find another dancer.'

'Of course.'

Joe put a glass of wine in front of Daisy.

'To Rhoda and Mr Kenny,' she said, raising her glass. 'I hope you'll both be very happy.'

'Thanks. I know I will.'

Daisy looked at Joe. How would he manage without Rhoda? Could this spur him on to think about marriage himself? She surely hoped so.

Chapter 28

As Mary lay in bed on Christmas night, she closed her eyes, then very slowly opened them. She was frightened that this was all a dream and she would wake up and be back in that horrible home. But she was still in the prettiest room she had ever seen. Not even the pictures in the books that she was always comparing things with were anything like this. She sat up and looked at the window that had pretty flowered curtains; beyond she knew was the lovely garden. This was even better than living with Penny; at least Uncle William liked her. Over her dressing-table mirror hung her bright-coloured ribbons. On the dressing table there was the new brush and comb set that had been one of her Christmas presents. She was thinking that today had been the best day of her life, not that she knew what her life had been like before July last year. But she knew it could never have been like this. Auntie Martha and Uncle William had made her so happy. Harry was such good fun and Mrs Aimes had cooked the best dinner she'd ever had. Everybody said she must have come from a cockney family by the way she talked. Although she was tired and was having difficulty keeping her eyes open, she was trying to relive every single minute of today. From the moment she opened her eyes this morning to find toys and clothes at the bottom of her bed, till now. She couldn't believe how everybody seemed to go out of their way to make her happy. So many times during the day she had just stood and let everything flow over her. She had smiled so much her cheeks hurt. She really couldn't take it all in. Her world was complete, her clothes and toys were just wonderful and she truly loved Harry.

'She is such a delightful little girl,' said William as they were preparing for bed.

Martha had smiled so much during the

day that, like Mary, her jaw ached. The house had become full of laughter as the children played. 'You approve of her, then?' said Martha, sitting at her dressing table and brushing her long hair while talking to her husband in the mirror.

William came up behind her and, lifting her hair, kissed her slender neck. 'As I said, she is delightful and I've never seen Harry looking so happy.'

'Or being so noisy.'

'Yes, he did get a bit boisterous at times.'

'What a wonderful Christmas this has been.'

'And it's all thanks to you, my dear.'

Martha was still smiling. She knew it was selfish but she didn't want Rose to ever get her memory back. Now her family was complete.

William climbed into bed. 'What have you got in store for us tomorrow?'

Martha walked towards the bed. 'I haven't anything planned. Did you have something in mind?'

'Not really. I suppose we could go for a walk through the woods.'

'That would be wonderful. It would give

Rose a chance to wear her new boots and cloak.'

William laughed. 'Now come to bed.'

Martha turned and looked at him. 'William, what should we do about her schooling?'

'I don't know. Hadn't given that much thought.'

'We can't send her to school like Harry, not to stay all week and only come home at weekends, not after what she's been through.'

'I agree, it would seem a bit unfair, but would Harry object to Rose being here with you all week while he's away?'

'I don't know.'

'I'll have a word with him tomorrow and get his reaction.'

As she got in beside her husband she cuddled up to him and kissed his cheek. 'Thank you, my darling.'

'Whatever for?'

'Letting me bring Rose into our home.'

'It's good to see Harry laughing and not sitting with his nose in a book or looking out of the window waiting till the weather improves and he can go out on his beloved horse.' He was also thinking of what would happen if Rose's memory returned. Would she want to leave them? It would break Martha's heart if she did. 'Good night, love.'

'Good night,' said Martha, still smiling.

Friday evening it was work as usual, and when Daisy and the others looked through the strips of sparkly curtain that were the background of the stage where the musicians sat, they were amazed to see that the club was so full.

'Would have thought they'd had enough to drink over Christmas,' said Rene.

'It is Friday night, and I expect some of 'em still have the Christmas spirit. So watch yourselves, girls,' said Rhoda. 'Don't let 'em pinch your arses or anything else they fancy grabbing.'

'Looks like standing room only out there,' said Joe as he pushed past her. 'Right, Daisy, straighten up your headband. Now I want you girls to give it all you've got, no sloppy step changes. Even if the punters don't notice, remember I will.'

Their music started and they were off once again into the glare of the spotlights, high-kicking in rhythm just as they had practised over and over again. After the Charleston and the Black Bottom they left the floor with loud applause and stamping feet accompanying them.

'Sounds like a very appreciative bunch out there,' said Rhoda.

'That's good. Pr'aps it'll cheer Joe up; he's getting to be a right old misery-guts. What upset him over Christmas, Rhoda?' asked June.

Daisy quickly looked over at Rhoda as they sat in front of the mirrors repairing their make-up.

'Dunno,' said Rhoda casually.

Daisy knew she was going to announce her engagement after they closed tonight, but it seemed that Joe still hadn't come to terms with the idea.

Hours later, when they were back in the dressing room getting changed to go home, Rhoda said, 'I'd like you all to hang around for a little while. Mr Kenny has something to tell you.'

June sat back down with a bump. Her face was ashen. 'Is he gonner close the club?'

'No,' said Rhoda, beaming.

'Thank Gawd for that. Me mum would have

forty fits if I stopped bringing home me wages.'

'We ain't gonner have a cut in wages, are we?' asked Rene.

'No.' Rhoda laughed just as Kenny walked in.

He kissed her cheek. 'Come on, girls. Let's go into the club.'

Once they were in there, Daisy could see that Tom and Sally, as well as all the other staff, had joined them.

'Right. Everybody grab a glass of champers,' said Kenny.

They all did as they were told.

'Now,' he said, 'raise your glasses to the woman who's gonner make me very happy. My future wife, Rhoda.'

There was a gasp from everybody, then they said, 'To Rhoda.'

'You kept that quiet, boss,' said Tom.

'It don't do to let you lot know what me intentions are.'

The dancing girls all crowded round a beaming Rhoda, wishing her good luck and asking when the wedding would be?

'We're hoping for a June wedding, and I'd like you all to be me bridesmaids.'

Tom came up to Daisy. 'You didn't look very surprised.'

'I was told over Christmas.'

'And did it spur him into making any mad promises?' Tom pointed his glass towards Joe.

'No.'

'Daisy, please don't forget my offer still stands.'

Just then the band started up again and one of the young waiters grabbed Daisy.

'Always wanted ter dance with you. I watch you every night. You're the best, you know,' he said as he whisked her round the floor.

Daisy looked over at Tom just as Sally went up to him and dragged him on to the dance floor. She began thinking about this afternoon, when she'd returned to the flat after spending the night with Rhoda and Joe. It looked a tip.

'What's been going on here?' she had asked Sally, who had still been in her dressing gown. Daisy had continued to walk round the room picking up clothes, cushions, dirty glasses and ashtrays.

Sally grinned. 'Me and Tom.'

'So what did . . .' Daisy stopped herself. She didn't want to know what they'd got up to.

'Tom stopped the night.'

'That was nice for you.'

Sally was still grinning. 'Yes, it was.'

But why did Daisy feel a little bit jealous?

'I expect he'll tell you all about it later. By the way, did you have a nice time?'

'Yes I did, thank you.'

Sally sat on the sofa and lit a cigarette. 'D'you know, I've really got it bad over Tom.'

'That's all right. Just as long as he feels the same way about you.'

'That's it, he don't. I know there's someone else, but I don't know who she is and he won't say. When I find out, I'll scratch her eyes out.'

Daisy shuddered. 'That's a bit drastic. Besides, how d'you know it's a girl?'

Sally threw her head back and laughed. 'Here, you don't think . . . Na. I can tell yer he's all man and he likes the women. I'd better go and get ready for work.'

'Daisy. Daisy, are you listening to me?' The waiter was kissing her neck and whispering in her ear.'

'Sorry. What did you say?'

'You was in your own little dream world then. Is it me dancing or me sweet talk?'

'No, sorry. I think it was the shock of the announcement.'

'Yer, it was a bit of a shock. What I was saying was, could I take you out one Sunday?'

Daisy smiled at the lad. 'It's very kind of you to ask me, but I'm usually too tired.'

'That's not what Tom says.'

'What has Tom being saying about me?'

'Nothing, just that you and him went to Southend in the summer.'

'Yes, we did. That was just a one-off, and we went with Sally. They're a couple, you know?' Daisy knew she had to start another rumour to squash the one that must have been circulating. 'Look at 'em now.'

When they glanced over at Tom and Sally dancing, they could see that her arms were wound round his neck.

As they walked home, Tom, who was a little the worse for drink, had his arms round both girls' waists. 'Great night. Fancy old Kenny and Rhoda getting hitched. They certainly kept that quiet.'

Sally, who had also had more than a few

drinks, was having a job walking, and giggled.

'Does it make you think of wedding bells, then, Tom?'

'Could do.' He looked at Daisy.

'What about you, Dais?' said Sally. 'Still dreaming of riding, or should I say dancing, orf inter the sunset with old Joe?'

Daisy laughed. 'He's got to ask me first.'

'I dunno why you hang around waiting for him,' said Tom. 'There's plenty out there that'd have you.'

'You know our Dais, dancing is the be all and end all for her, so it's gotter be another dancer. Right, here we are. You coming up for a nightcap, Tom?'

He looked at Daisy as she made her way up the steps to their front door. 'I don't think so,' he said. 'See you both tomorrow. Come and give us a kiss good night, then, Dais.'

She hesitated for a moment or two, then thought she had better do as they did every time he walked home with them and came back down the steps. She gave him a quick peck, then ran back up the steps.

'Right, my turn,' said Sally.

Sally was all over Tom, but Daisy could see

that he had his eyes open and was looking at her. She went inside and leant against the door. What was wrong with her? What was it? Why did she feel jealous when it was Joe she loved?

Chapter 29

1925

SATURDAY THE SIXTH of June was the day that Rhoda married Kenny. It was a big formal affair and the dancing girls were her brides-maids in a delicate shade of blue. Joe gave his sister away and the reception was held at the club. After the speeches the band played and the drink flowed.

The drink had made Daisy brave, and as she danced with Joe she asked him, 'Are you happy living all alone now that Rhoda's gone?'

'It suits me.'

Daisy moved closer. 'You don't fancy getting hitched, then?'

'No. Too interested in me work to worry about getting a wife.'

'What if she was a dancer?'

He laughed. 'You see the way I bully you lot, so who'd want me?'

'I would,' she whispered just as the band's drummer got going with a drum solo and everybody stopped dancing to watch him. She wasn't sure if Joe had heard her, and as she stood with her arm round him, she knew this was the time she had to make her feelings for him known.

The applause for the drummer was thunderous, and then the dancing started once again.

'Joe, can I talk to you for a moment?'

'Course.' He manoeuvred her towards the bar. 'Here, you ain't thinking of getting hitched, are you?' he asked, looking at her with a frown. 'Only I don't want to lose another dancer.'

'Is that all I am to you? Just another dancer?'

'You're the best.' He took a glass of champagne from off the counter and then, after downing it, offered Daisy one.

She shook her head, and he took another glass.

'Not seen you knock 'em back so quick before.'

'Ain't lost me sister before.'

'You haven't lost her,' Daisy said angrily. 'She's just got married, that's all.' She looked down. It was she who had lost a sister.

'Sorry, that was a bit insensitive of me.'

'Yes, it was. Beside, you've got a new dancer.'

'She's gonner need a lot of knocking into shape. Anyway, what did you want to talk about?'

'Joe, if you want someone to look after you, I'd be more than willing.'

He laughed. 'What? You wonner be me housekeeper?'

'I'd like to be a lot more than that.'

'Daisy Cooper, I'm surprised at you. You mean to say you'd like to live with me?'

She nodded. She had got this far and now she had to say it all at the risk of being laughed at. 'You see, Joe, I'm in love with you.'

'What?' he yelled, and a lot of people turned and stared at him.

Daisy looked away.

Joe gave everyone a friendly wave and they grinned and returned to what they were doing; all except Tom. He was watching them very closely. What were they talking about? He could see that Daisy was looking very uncomfortable.

A drum roll caused everybody to stop chatting and look at Kenny, who was standing on the stage.

'Right, everybody. We're off. Got a long drive and I don't wonner be too tired for tonight.'

There was loud laughter and stamping of feet. Daisy looked at Joe, who was scowling.

'Now my beautiful lady wife will throw her bouquet when we leave, so everybody outside.'

His car had tin cans and old boots tied to the bumper and JUST MARRIED scrawled across the back.

Rhoda came up to Joe and hugged him, then did the same to Daisy. 'I'm gonner miss you two,' she said.

'Not as much as we'll miss you,' said Daisy.

'See you when you get back,' said Joe.

'Ain't you gonner wish me good luck?' Rhoda asked her brother.

'You don't need it, you've got all you've ever wanted.'

'Come on, love,' said Kenny, taking her hand.

'Try and catch me flowers,' said Rhoda to Daisy as she walked away.

Daisy wanted to ask what was the point. 'That

wasn't very nice,' she said to Joe as they all stood round the car.

He ignored her remark and said, 'You'd better go and try to catch the flowers.'

Daisy wanted to say it wouldn't be worth it, as it seemed that Joe wasn't the marrying kind.

Rhoda threw her bouquet and Sally caught it, giving out great whoops of joy. Hanging on to Tom's arm, she looked up at him, her eyes full of love. Daisy looked away.

With everybody waving and cheering, the happy couple drove off.

'Right, come on, everyone, we've got a lot of champers to down,' said Tom.

Everybody followed him back into the club and the band started up again. Daisy looked around for Joe, but he wasn't anywhere to be seen. Should she go outside and find him? Would it look as though she was throwing herself at him?

Outside, Joe was leaning against the wall. How could he tell Daisy that he didn't love her? She was such a sweet, innocent kid, but he had no room in his life for a wife. He was very fond of

Daisy and would hate to see her hurt; after all, she was still living in hope of finding her sister one of these days. He ground his cigarette out with his foot and made his way back into the club. He would have a few more glasses of champagne and to hell with the consequences.

Daisy was being swept off her feet dancing with the waiters and bar staff. When the young one who had told her he thought she was the best dancer came up to her, he was so drunk he could hardly stand.

'Steady on there,' said Daisy. 'I think you've had a drop too much.'

'It's only 'cos I've got to tell you something and the drink gives me courage.'

She smiled. 'I know the feeling. Now what do you want to tell me?'

'I love you, Daisy, and I want you to marry me.'

'What?' He held her so tight she could hardly breathe.

'Look, I'm gonner get down on me knees and ask you to marry me.' With that he fell to his knees in the middle of the dance floor and everybody stopped dancing to look at them.

'Get up,' said Daisy angrily, then looked around and tried to smile at everybody.

'Not till you say you'll marry me.'

'Stop being such an idiot.'

'I love you, Daisy,' he shouted.

It was at that moment that Tom pushed his way through the throng, dragged the boy to his feet and propelled him out of the room into the cloakroom, with Daisy following close behind.

'Just what d'you think you're playing at?' demanded Tom.

'I want Daisy to marry me,' the young waiter said pathetically.

'You and everybody else. Now stop being such a fool. Go and put your head under the tap.'

'But Tom . . .'

'Just go.'

'Don't be too hard on him,' said Daisy as the boy made his way to the gents.

'Don't like to see the staff make fools of themselves,' said Tom, closing the door.

'It's the drink.'

'I know. Now are you all right?'

'Yes thanks. By the way, what did you mean when you said that everybody wants to marry me?'

'Well you know how I feel about you.'

Daisy looked at him. 'Sally caught the bouquet.'

'I know, and I think she feels that could be an omen.'

'But you don't?'

Tom went to move closer when the door burst open and Sally walked in. 'This is very cosy, you two hiding out in me own little cloakroom.'

'It's not like that,' laughed Daisy.

'We just brought young Paul in here to cool him down,' said Tom.

'I see.' Sally looked at Daisy. 'That was quite a show, him getting on his knees. Caused a right laugh, I can tell you. He's gonner have a job to live that one down. Come on, Tom, let's go and have a dance.'

'See you later,' said Daisy as they left. She sat on the chair. She felt so confused. Why couldn't it have been Joe that wanted to marry her? Was she clutching at straws? As she sat there, she remembered what Charlie had told her when Joe and Rhoda had first started dancing at the cinema. Did Joe prefer men to women? She had never felt brave enough to ask Rhoda about it. She knew how people felt about men who didn't like women, and she knew it was something people didn't admit to. After all, it was against the law. Was this why Joe didn't want to marry her?

Her thoughts went to the old days and Mary. If only she could find her. Tomorrow was Sunday. She would go and see Charlie and Mr Holden. Despite all her promises she had never been back to see them, and she wouldn't be where she was now if it hadn't been for Mr Holden giving her the chance to work in the cinema. She slid off her chair and went and joined the merrymaking. She would worry about Joe another day.

Chapter 30

THE SAME DAY that Rhoda got married, Mary was standing on the gate watching Harry galloping round the field on his horse. Although she loved her school, she loved the weekends best when Harry was home from school. He brought the horse to a stop beside her and pushed his blond hair out of his eyes. 'That was great. Are you sure you don't want to have a go?'

She shook her head. 'He frightens the life out of me.'

'You can always get up behind me.' Harry dismounted and, patting the horse's head, said, 'There's nothing to be frightened of, he's as good as gold. Here, give him a sugar lump.'

Again Mary shook her head. 'He's so big.'

Harry laughed. 'I wouldn't let you fall, you know that. I don't know why you're so frightened of him. Everything else you have a go at.'

'I know.'

'That's what I like about you. You're not like other girls, you're always willing to join in.'

Mary smiled. 'Don't forget, everything is new to me.'

'I know, but you're still a good sport.'

Mary liked Harry. They were good friends, but there was no way she was going to get on that horse. It was a long way up.

'Come on, we'll walk back to the stable. It must be almost lunchtime and you can tell me how school was this week.'

Mary smiled. 'It was good. My teacher said I was very bright when we did sums . . . I mean arithmetic.'

Harry laughed. 'Of course she doesn't really know you. I could tell her different.'

'Whatever you say you won't stop me from feeling happy.'

'Why?'

'The sun's shining and I'm here living with

you and Auntie Martha and Uncle William.'

They walked along slowly, laughing and talking all the while.

'D'you know, Rose, you've made Mama very happy. We hope in some ways that you never remember who you are. It would upset her so much if you went away.'

'In some ways I don't want to remember who I really am.' Mary looked down. She knew that she could never have had such a wonderful life as she was having now. She thought of that dreadful home she was in. She would always be grateful to Martha and William for taking her into their house, and she truly loved them.

The day after the wedding, Daisy went to see Mr Holden and Charlie. It was only a month ago that she had told Sally and Tom all about Mary and why she'd left home. It had made her feel very low. They had been shocked that Mary was still missing.

'And you still carried on dancing?' Sally had asked.

'I wasn't dancing at the time, but then when Joe offered me this job I just had to take it. I'd spent weeks looking for her, but she must have found somewhere to live and must be very happy, as she has never bothered to get in contact with me.'

At the time Tom had been very sympathetic and offered to go back to the cinema with her, but she declined, as she knew this was something she had to do on her own. She said she was waiting for the better weather. Although they knew she came from the other side of the river, she didn't want Tom or Sally to see the slum she had lived in.

That afternoon she told Sally of her intentions.

'D'you want me to come with you?' asked Sally.

Daisy smiled. She was touched by Sally's concern. 'Thanks all the same, but this is something I want to do on me own.'

'Please yourself. That was great yesterday.' Sally looked at the bouquet that was in a vase in the middle of the table. 'I wonder if it's really true that when you catch a bride's flowers you could be the next one to get married.'

'Dunno. Is that what you want?'

She nodded. 'And I'd love it to be Tom. I

really like him. What about Joe? Would you like to marry him?'

'I don't think Joe is the marrying kind.'

Sally grinned. 'Well they do say he used to have a boyfriend.'

'Did he? I've not heard that.' Daisy tried to appear indifferent.

'Mind you, I think they say that about all blokes who dance. I bet he's gonner miss his sister.'

'I expect he will. Are you going out today?'

'No. Tom's coming round later and I said I'd do a bit of tea. Nothing special, just gonner try to show him what a good wife I'll make. What time will you be back?'

'Dunno. Look, I'll go to the pictures, I don't want to get in your way.'

Sally smiled. 'OK.'

The last thing Daisy wanted was to be around while Sally was doing her best to impress Tom.

Daisy was pleased that cinemas were now open on a Sunday and thought that it would be nice to sit in the place where her life had changed. When she got off the bus outside the Roxy she was surprised at how smart it looked. They were showing a Douglas Fairbanks film, *The Thief of Baghdad*. As Daisy stood and looked at the posters outside, she felt a great longing. She loved the pictures and remembered when she had first taken Mary and they'd gazed in wonder at the images on the screen. Then the joy of working for Mr Holden, and Charlie giving her a sandwich as he said she needed fattening up. A tear slid down her cheek. Such a lot had happened since those days. Her thoughts went to Mary. Where was she? Was she happy? Had she been back here? Daisy brushed away the tear and walked into the foyer. She didn't recognise the girl at the pay desk.

'What seat d'yer want?'

'Is Mr Holden here?'

'Na. He left months ago.'

'D'you know where he went?'

'Na.'

'What about Charlie?'

'What, the old boy who was doorman?'

Daisy smiled and nodded.

'He's dead.'

Daisy held on to the counter. 'When did that happen?'

'Dunno. Before Mr Holden left. Here, what d'yer wonner know all this for?'

'I used to work here and I thought I'd like to see them again.'

'You worked here? Here, you ain't that girl what went orf and went on the stage, are you?'

Again Daisy nodded.

'They told me all about you. Said you had a sister what run away.'

'Yes, I did. I was hoping that she had come back here looking for me.'

'Na. She ain't been back all the time I've been 'ere.'

'How long have you been working here?'

'Getting on fer nearly a year now. D'yer wonner go in and see the film?'

'No thank you.'

'It's ever so good.'

'I expect it is. Thank you.' Daisy turned and walked out.

'What yer thanking me for. I ain't done nuthink.'

Daisy didn't answer. There was no way she could sit in the cinema knowing her good friend Charlie was dead and Mr Holden wasn't around. That was another part of her life she had to close the door on.

As she walked sadly away, she thought she would go and visit her mother's grave, then she would go and see Mrs Wilson. As she passed the greengrocer's, she could see that the name Martin was still above the window, so nothing had changed there, but so much had happened to her since she worked there.

It took a while to find her mother's grave. It was very overgrown, and Daisy wasn't even sure if this was where she was buried, as there wasn't a headstone. She sat on the grass and tried to remember what her mother had looked like before she became ill. 'Do you ever wonder about Mum, Mary?' she said out loud.

After a while Daisy slowly left the cemetery. People were coming though the gates carrying flowers; she hadn't brought flowers for her mother. Like her, some were brushing away a tear.

Walking through Chapel Court, her thoughts went back to the night Mary had left. The large ugly buildings still looked the same, with rubbish and old furniture strewn about, and as she mounted the stairs to Mrs Wilson's rooms the smell of urine was as strong as ever.

When she arrived at Mrs Wilson's door, she hesitated. Everywhere looked in the same sorry state, but what about Mrs Wilson? Was she still around? Was she still alive? Would she remember her? She knocked.

It took a while for the door to open, and to Daisy's joy she could see that Mrs Wilson still lived here. She looked a little older, and as she peered at Daisy she said, 'Yes. What d'yer want?'

'Mrs Wilson, it's me, Daisy Cooper.'

'Daisy Cooper?' she repeated.

'I worked at the greengrocer's and the cinema. I had a sister, Mary. Don't you remember?'

Mrs Wilson's face lit up. 'Oh yes. Pretty little thing.' She looked along the passage. 'How is she? She's not come with you, then?'

Daisy shook her head. 'No. I never did find her. I was wondering if she ever came back here?'

It took a moment or two for Mrs Wilson to remember. 'Come on in, love. I must say you look very smart.'

'Thank you.' The memories flooded back when Daisy sat in the armchair.

'I remember now,' said Mrs Wilson. 'Young Mary ran away. Did you never find her?'

Daisy shook her head. 'I was hoping that she might have come back here at some time.'

'No, love. Would you like a cup of tea?'

'Yes please.'

'So, what you up to these days?'

'I'm dancing in a nightclub up West.'

'You've come a long way since working for old Ethel Martin.' She put the sugar on the table. 'And don't you look nice?'

'How are Mr and Mrs Martin?'

'Still going strong, but they've had that many working for 'em. They don't stay more than a month or two.'

The kettle whistling sent her back to make the tea. 'So you don't know what happened to your sister?' she called out.

'No. I tried everywhere. She must be with a nice family not to get in touch.'

'Just as long as she didn't finish up in the workhouse.'

'Don't say that. Could it be possible?'

'Dunno.' Mrs Wilson put the teapot on the table and covered it with a knitted tea cosy.

'She would have written and told me if she had.'

'Course she would.' Mrs Wilson handed Daisy her tea.

'Thank you. Are you still keeping busy?'

'Yer, they're still dying and having babies.'

For an hour Daisy sat and talked to Mrs Wilson. Then she said, 'I must be going.'

'You gotter work tonight?'

'No, we have Sundays off.'

'And you say you like it?'

'It was the best thing that ever happened to me, except of course that it meant Mary leaving. I wish I knew where she was.'

'Look, leave me yer address, and if she ever turns up I'll get her to get in touch.'

'I always hoped she'd come back to find me.' Daisy wrote out her address. 'I'm living with a girl from the club. We have a very nice flat.'

Mrs Wilson picked up the piece of paper. 'I'll just put this behind me clock. That way I'll remember where it is.'

Daisy held her tight. 'Thank you.'

'Keep yer pecker up, girl.'

'I'll try.' She kissed Mrs Wilson's cheek and left.

Daisy walked along to the bus stop. Where could she go? She didn't want to go to see her old home, as it held too many sad memories, and

she certainly didn't want to intrude on Sally and
Tom. The only other person she knew was Joe.
That was it; she would go and see him.

Chapter 31

'DAISY, WHAT YOU doing here?' Joe looked very surprised and embarrassed. He ran his hand over his flushed face, which Daisy gathered was from running down the stairs after his landlady had called him a couple of times. Although it was late afternoon he was bleary eyed and hadn't shaved; he certainly didn't look his usual smart self.

'Sorry, Joe, am I intruding?' She was trying to look up the stairs, waiting for someone to open the door to his flat. 'I was hoping you'd be on your own. I just needed a friend to talk to.'

He came out on to the pavement and pulled

the front door to behind him. 'I'm sorry, but it's not very convenient at the moment.'

'Not to worry.' She turned to walk away. 'I'll see you tomorrow.'

Her sad face told him everything. 'Daisy, wait.'

'Why? If you've got a friend up there, I don't want to intrude.'

'It's not that.' Look, I'll just get my jacket and we can go for a coffee or something.'

'Oh no. What about your friend?'

'What friend?'

'Whoever you have up there.' She nodded towards the stairs.

Joe laughed. 'There ain't nobody up there.'

'It's all right, Joe. I understand.'

'I don't think you do. Wait here. I'll get my jacket.'

As Daisy stood there he raced up the stairs. She wondered why, if no one was there, he didn't let her go in? In less than a minute he was back at her side.

'Come on.'

'What about your friend?' Daisy couldn't believe that he was going to be seen out and unkempt. Normally he was so fastidious.

'Don't worry about it.'

In the café, Daisy sat and told Joe all about what had happened that afternoon.

'So the only contact you have left now is this Mrs Wilson?'

Daisy nodded.

'That's a shame.'

'I should have gone to see them before this. Poor Charlie. I was very fond of him. And even Mr Holden has moved on. If Mary should ever come back looking for me, would she think to go and see Mrs Wilson?'

Joe patted her hand. 'Don't upset yourself.'

Daisy dabbed her eyes. 'I'm sorry. You don't want to hear all my troubles.'

'That's what I should be doing.'

'Why? You're me boss.'

'I know, and if Rhoda was here she'd have a right go at me, but then again she would be here for you.'

'I'm gonner miss her.'

'You're not the only one.'

Daisy suddenly realised that Joe looked tired and drawn.

'Have you had anything to eat today?' he asked.

She shook her head.

'Neither have I. Let's order something, even if it's only egg and chips.'

'No, thanks all the same, but I mustn't keep you away from your friend any longer.'

Joe laughed. 'What friend?'

'The one that's in your flat.'

'There ain't nobody in me flat.'

'So why didn't you ask me up? Has he gone?'

'He! Who the hell do you think I've got up there?'

'I don't know. Sorry, is it a female?'

'No it ain't, and if you must know, the reason I didn't ask you up there was because I got stinking drunk last night and I've only just got up and the place is a tip.'

Daisy began to laugh.

'What's so funny?'

'I thought you'd got a bloke up there.'

'Well I ain't.'

Daisy smiled. 'In that case, come on. Don't worry about having egg and chips here. We'll go back to your place, and after I've tided up I'll cook something.'

'You can't do that.'

'Why not?'

'Rhoda will go mad if she finds out what a state the place is in.'

'And whose gonner tell her? You? Besides, she's going to be away for weeks yet.'

'That's true.'

When Daisy opened the door to Joe's flat, the smell of tobacco and drink almost took her breath away. 'You certainly had a lot, by the look of all these empty bottles,' she said, going round picking some up.

'Yes, I'm sorry.'

'You don't have to be sorry. What you do is your affair.' Daisy wanted to smile. Ever since she'd known Joe she had been terrified of him; now she was talking to him like he was a naughty boy. She wanted to take him in her arms and comfort him. The tables had certainly turned.

'I'm really gonner miss Rhoda.'

'We all are, but that's no reason to be so down. The girls ain't gonner like it if you start taking it out on them.' She emptied the over-full ashtray.

Joe sat on the sofa and put his head in his hands. 'She's been beside me all me life. After Dad went she helped me to do busking, and then when I was picked up by someone who wanted to teach me to dance she stood by me. Me mum didn't want to know and threw me out.' He stood up. 'I shouldn't be telling you all this.' He took a glass and filled it with whisky.

'That's not going to make Rhoda come back to you.' Why did he seem so vulnerable? 'Does Rhoda know how you feel?'

He nodded.

'And?'

'She told me in no uncertain terms that it was about time I took control of my own life.'

Daisy couldn't believe this was the man who had put the fear of God into them and ruled them with a rod of iron. Then she thought about when she had lived here; it had been Rhoda who made all the decisions.

Joe must have read her thoughts. 'I'm sorry. I knew I shouldn't have let you come up here. I don't want this to get round to the others.'

'It won't. Now, I'll just wash this lot up, then I'll find us something to eat.'

'You don't have to, you know.'

'I know, but don't forget I'm unhappy and hungry as well, so we can eat and both feel very sorry for ourselves.'

He smiled. 'I always said you were like a tonic.'

Daisy smiled too. She was going to show him that she could be there for him, but not just like a sister. What she had in mind was to be like a wife.

Daisy was so happy doing things for Joe that she started singing.

'I'm glad you've cheered up.'

'So am I.' She looked away. She knew that this could be the time to try to tell him her feelings again. 'Joe . . .' She twisted the bottom of Rhoda's pinny she was wearing. 'If you want me to, I'd be more than happy to move in here with you.'

'Honestly, Daisy, I don't need a nurse-maid.'

'No, I didn't mean . . .' She stopped, then whispered, 'No, not just as a nursemaid.'

He looked surprised. 'I'm sorry, I thought . . . Daisy, I'm sorry.'

She felt deflated. 'I don't like to see you unhappy.'

'I'll be all right. I'll get over it.'

Why couldn't she make him understand that she was in love with him? She had told him once before and he'd laughed at her.

'Joe, if you don't have feelings for me, why

were you so nasty when I went to Southend with Tom?'

'What? Why bring that up after all this time? If you must know, I didn't want him taking you out. As you know, I lost Amy through him.'

'I don't think so.'

'Well that's what I think, despite what he tells you.'

Daisy didn't want to argue with him, but she knew Tom was decent and would never take advantage of anyone.

Joe felt guilty as he sat and watched Daisy cleaning up his mess. He offered to help but was told to sit down and read his paper.

Despite the horrible day, Daisy, in a strange way, was glad to be looking after Joe. She gave him a beaming smile. She knew she could make him happy, and in time he would see that.

Joe knew he had to tell Daisy that he couldn't have feelings for her, not to love her the way she wanted and deserved. She was a lovable girl and a great dancer, but that was as far as it went. But he wouldn't tell her today; she was upset, as the last threads of her past had almost been severed. The only hope of her ever finding her sister had almost disappeared. If only he could help her, but he knew he had to be sure that she wouldn't get the wrong end of the stick if he showed her any kind of affection. It was times like this that he knew he was going to miss Rhoda so much. Why did she have to get married? They had always been there for each other.

Mary was very excited as she ran down the stairs. It was the day that Penny had said was to be her birthday, and Auntie Martha and Uncle William said they were taking her out for a special treat.

'Where are we going?' she asked, as she tore open one of the presents that were in her place on the breakfast table.

'You must wait and see,' said William

'It's such a beautiful day,' said Martha as she watched Mary with pride.

Mary looked up with tears in her eyes, then ran round and kissed Martha and then William. 'Thank you. Thank you so much.' She held up a beautiful bright red patterned Chinese kimono. 'This is lovely. How did you know?'

'Well, after all you have been telling us about China every time you came home from school, and Harry's been telling us how much you love geography and have been fascinated by the country, so we thought you would like this.'

'I do. I do. I do.' She danced round the room hugging her gift. 'D'you know, they tie the little girls' feet up so they don't grow?'

'Yes, we did know,' said William.

Martha was proud of Mary's progress at school. 'Now I think you had better open Penny's present,' she said.

Mary smiled and returned to her place. 'Oh look. It's a book about China. I would love to go there.'

'Maybe one day,' said William.

'Now come along,' said Martha. 'Let's get breakfast over so that Mrs Aimes can get on with her chores.'

'When are we going to get my treat?'

'Later,' said Martha. 'Just be patient.'

Mary didn't want this day to end. She was so happy.

Chapter 32

MARY COULDN'T WALK; she just had to skip along to the car. 'Where're we going?' she asked for the fourth time. 'Is it somewhere nice?'

'Of course it is, so just be patient, young lady,' said William, taking hold of her hand.

'Rose, stop it,' said Harry.

Mary looked at him sheepishly. 'I'm sorry,' she said as she scrambled into the back seat of the car next to Martha. She smiled up at her and, reaching for her hand, held it tight. Martha swallowed the lump that was in her throat.

Johnson drove into London and they all got out of the car and began walking. They passed the shops and stopped outside a cinema that announced that *The Ten Commandments* was now showing.

'Have you been to the cinema before?' Martha asked Mary.

She shook her head. 'I don't think so.'

'It's very exciting,' said Harry.

'Come along, the programme is about to start.'

Once William had paid at the box office, he guided the children inside. The lights went down and a man came on stage and sang; some dancing girls who kicked their legs high in the air followed him.

Suddenly Mary's stomach heaved and she felt sick. What was wrong with her? She looked at the girls dancing on the stage; she had seen something like this before, but where? She slid down in her seat.

'Are you all right, dear?' asked Martha.

'Yes thank you,' said Mary timidly.

The girls left the stage and Mary was still trying to remember. When the lights went down and the film was projected on to the silver screen, she took a sharp intake of breath.

Martha patted her hand. 'There's nothing to worry about.'

Mary's head was reeling. What was happening to her? She wanted to cry out and hold her head; it hurt like something was crushing it. The noise of the lady pounding on the piano was thumping in her head and making her feel faint. She knew she had been through this before. She had been to the pictures with her sister Daisy. She had a sister called Daisy. Suddenly it all came flooding back to her and she began to silently cry. Daisy. Daisy. Where was she? She remembered that she had run away from home; that must have been when she was hit by the car and Roger and Penny found her. The piano was being played a lot softer now and she tried hard to think. Where was home? It was that horrible, horrible building; that was the place she and Daisy had called home. How could she go back there? She looked at Martha, who was intent on watching the film. How could she leave her? She loved her and William and Harry. This was her life now. But what about her sister? Had she been looking for her all this time? Did she go on the stage? Was she still alive?

The piano was getting louder again and Mary wanted to run away. The noise was filling her ears and making her dizzy. She wanted it to stop.

She wanted to cry out for it to stop. The moving images on the screen all blurred into one. She sat very still and upright; she didn't want to faint and make a fuss. What would happen to her now? Should she tell Martha what she knew? She slumped down in her seat. How could she? She knew it was selfish, but she didn't want to go back to . . . It took a moment or two for her to remember the address. Chapel Court. But what about Daisy? Had she been looking for her all this time? Was she married? Was she still living in Chapel Court? How could Mary find out?

For hours she sat there not taking any notice of the film. Her mind was going back through her life. Her mother dying, and Daisy going to those silly dancing lessons. These past two years had been full of ups and downs, but she was so happy now and she didn't want it to end.

At the end of the programme they all filed out into the sunshine.

'Rose, are you feeling all right?' asked Martha.

She nodded, and very nearly blurted out, me name's not Rose, it's Mary.

'You look very pale,' said Martha as she took hold of her hand.

'So do you think you have been to the cinema before?' asked William.

Mary quickly shook her head.

'Perhaps it was the excitement. After all, it must be a bit overwhelming seeing that for the first time,' said William.

How could she tell them? She didn't want to tell them. All these thoughts were going round and round in her head. How could she get in touch with her sister and tell her that she didn't want to go back to Chapel Court, that she loved living here with her new family? Did Daisy even still live there?

'Rose, didn't you like the film?' asked Harry, interrupting her thoughts. 'I thought it was great. Why are you so quiet? It's not like you not to be talking.'

'Perhaps you will feel better after we're eaten,' said Martha.

William smiled at her. 'Come on, young lady. I'm sure you must be hungry.'

'Well I am,' said Harry.

Martha laughed. 'That doesn't surprise me.'

They walked along talking about the film, but

Mary couldn't join in the conversation as she was filled with her own thoughts and what could be ahead for her if she told them the truth. Should she tell them who she really was?

At the club, things were normal, with Joe shouting at them and the new dancer being reduced to tears.

'Joe, why are you so horrible to Peggy?' asked Daisy after a rehearsal when the other girls had gone back to the dressing room to prepare for tonight's performance.

'She's supposed to be a dancer, but you can see how she's always behind and half asleep.'

'It's very daunting being in a new troupe, and you shouting at her don't help.'

He walked away.

Daisy followed the girls and sat at the dressing table. Why did she love Joe when all he was interested in was being a perfectionist with his dancing girls? She thought about the day she went back to his flat and the mess he'd been in. He had never mentioned it or thanked her – not that she wanted thanks, though it would have been nice – but he hadn't changed.

'You all right?' June asked Daisy as she sat next to her.

'I'm fine.'

'You look a bit down in the dumps.'

Daisy smiled.

'It's old misery-guts, ain't it? Since Rhoda left he's been like a bear with a sore head. He ought to find himself a good woman who'd give him a proper seeing-to; that might cheer him up.'

'He might prefer a good man,' said Rene.

'Is he really . . . you know?' asked Peggy.

'They all reckon he is,' said June. 'I did know a bloke who knew him when he was just starting, and his dance teacher was a right one of those.' She laughed and bent her wrist. 'My friend did say that was the only way Joe could pay for his dancing lessons.'

'You've never said anything before,' said Thelma.

'Couldn't, could I, not with Rhoda here. Anyway, my friend said he was almost suicidal when he was dumped.'

'Who, Joe or the other bloke?'

Daisy wanted to walk away. She couldn't bear to hear all this tittle-tattle about Joe.

'Joe, and it was Rhoda who kept him on

the straight and narrow. She was the brains, while he was the dancer. So there. Now you know.' June turned round and began applying her make-up.

Daisy sat quietly looking in the mirror. Was she being silly falling for a man who wasn't interested in women?

'Well let's hope this bloke comes back into his life now that Rhoda's gone.'

Daisy turned round. She wanted to say something but thought better of it. Would Joe get in touch with his friend again?

That night as they walked home, Sally and Tom were laughing and playing about as usual.

'You're very quiet tonight, Dais,' said Sally. 'Everything all right?'

She gave them a false smile. 'Course.'

'I found that new girl you've got crying round the back. I don't reckon she's gonner stay much longer if his nibs keeps on at her,' said Sally.

'And what may I ask was you doing round the back?' asked Tom.

'What if I told you nothing, would you believe me?'

'No.'

'Thought as much.'

'I hope she don't leave, she's good,' said Daisy.

'But not up to his standards,' said Tom.

'It takes time,' said Daisy.

'It didn't take you long,' said Sally.

'Daisy here is the exception. I heard Joe telling Kenny that she's a natural.'

Daisy laughed. 'What a lot of codswallop. He shouts at me just as much as all the others.'

When they got to their flat, Daisy offered her cheek to Tom for their usual goodnight kiss, then left him and Sally alone. Normally Sally would be a while saying good night to Tom, but tonight she was in almost at once.

'What's up? You two had a row?'

'No. It's just that he gets on me nerves.'

'I thought you liked him.'

'I did, but he's carrying a torch for some dame, and even though I've tried to give him everything, he's still not interested. He's turned me down more than once, so I've decided to move on. I've been seeing that new barman.'

'Oh yes, who's he?'

'His name's Steve and he's ever so

handsome.' Sally hugged herself. 'You must 'ave seen him.'

'I don't get a lot of chance to see beyond the lights.'

'Well I'll introduce you tomorrow, but don't you go pinching him. Remember, he's mine.'

As she went to her room, Daisy thought about all the different people in her life, and the complications. She loved Joe, but he loved someone else. Tom loved her, and up to now Sally had loved Tom, but now she loved Steve, so Tom was free again. Daisy was so confused. The one person she knew she loved but would never come into her life again was her sister. She was certain now that Mary had gone for ever.

Chapter 33

'ROSE, ROSE, WHATEVER'S wrong?'

Mary sat up. Her eyes were wide and staring and her face was wet with tears.

Martha held her close. 'You were shouting out again.' Mary cuddled up to her and sobbed. 'What is it, my dear? What's bothering you? Ever since you went to see that film, you've had these nightmares.'

'I'm sorry.'

'You don't have to be sorry, just tell me what it is.'

For weeks now Mary had had bad dreams. She'd been dreaming that Daisy was pulling her away from Martha and she was screaming as rats were running round her feet. Daisy was dragging her up to the flat they lived in and her mother was lying in her coffin. Mary just screamed and screamed and not for the first time woke herself up

Martha held her tight. What was it that distressed this poor child so much? She and William had been very concerned at the change in Rose. She was now very quiet, off her food and sallow looking; she had definitely lost her sparkle.

'Are you happy living here with us?' asked Martha.

'Yes,' sobbed Mary.

'Was it that film that upset you?'

Mary shook her head. She wanted to tell them but was worried they would send her back to Chapel Court. 'I never want to leave you.'

'And you don't have to.' What was it about that film that had caused this upset? Martha knew she would have to follow William's advice and take Rose to see their doctor to see if he could find out the cause of her distress. 'I'll get you a glass of warm milk and then you must go back to sleep.' Martha slipped off the bed and made her way downstairs. She was very worried about Rose.

*

For weeks now Sally had been over the moon with Steve. She never stopped talking about him, and Daisy was pleased to see that Steve appeared to be just as crazy about her.

It was Saturday night and the girls were getting ready to go home.

'Daisy, can I talk to you?' Sally called out, banging on the dressing room door.

'Course.'

'What does she want?' asked June.

'How should I know?' said Daisy, opening the door.

Sally looked very flushed. 'Daisy, you're never gonner guess,' she whispered breathlessly. 'I'm not coming home right away, I'm gonner go round to Steve's place, so I might not be home tonight.'

Daisy pulled the door to behind her. 'But I thought Steve shared with a married couple.'

'He does, but they're going away for the week-end and he wants me to go and stay with him.' She blushed. 'You know, be the little housewife.'

Daisy wanted to laugh. 'You, a housewife?'

'Well, sort of.'

'Are you sure you're doing the right thing?'

'What I do is me own affair. I don't need you to mother me.'

'I know, and don't get on your high horse. I'm sorry, but I don't want to see you hurt.'

'I won't be. Right, see you sometime.' Sally walked away.

Daisy was concerned about her friend; Sally was very vulnerable since she and Tom had split. But she had to admit that Steve did seem a nice bloke, just as long as he didn't break Sally's heart; after all, Daisy was very fond of her.

That night Tom was driving Kenny back home, so Daisy walked home alone. She missed Sally and especially Tom's company. When she went into the flat, even though it was only September, somehow it felt cold and empty. She made herself a cup of tea and sat thinking about her life. She hadn't seen a lot of Rhoda since she returned from her honeymoon, and was thrilled when she came to the club. Rhoda looked so happy, and best of all she had invited Daisy and the girls to her house next Sunday for lunch. They were all very excited about it.

*

'I've had a long talk to Rose,' said Dr Benson. 'And as far as I can see there is nothing physically wrong with her.'

Martha sat with the doctor while William took Mary outside.

'Can I get you some sweets?' asked William.

Mary just shook her head.

'Come on, let's sit over here.'

Mary took William's hand and sat next to him.

'You know that Martha is very, very worried about you.'

Mary nodded. She was frightened to speak, as she was afraid she might give her secret away.

'I wish you could tell us what's wrong.'

Tears slowly ran down her face. She couldn't keep up this pretence any longer.

'What is it? You know that we love you so very much.' William held her close and Mary began to sob.

'Rose, Rose, whatever is the matter?' Martha came hurrying over to them and quickly sat next to her.

'I can't keep this a secret any more,' Mary said between heart-rending sobs.

'What secret?' asked Martha.

'I know who I am. Me name ain't Rose, it's Mary. Mary Cooper.'

Martha took a quick intake of breath and held her hand to her mouth. 'Oh my God.'

'How long have you known?' asked William softly.

'When I was watching that film.'

'That was weeks ago. You've kept it to yourself all this time?'

She nodded. 'I'm frightened that you'll make me go back to me sister, and I don't want to go, I love you all so much.' She threw her arms round Martha, and Martha held her close.

'And I don't want to lose you,' she whispered. 'But your parents and your sister must be very worried about you.'

'I ain't got any parents, it was just me and Daisy.'

'Look, I think we had better get home and sit and talk about this,' said William.

Mary looked at William; her eyes were full of pleading. 'Please don't send me away.'

'We have got to sort it out.'

*

Mary was relieved it was during the week as Harry was at school. Mrs Aimes brought in the tea and then they sat in the drawing room.

'I think you had better tell us everything,' said William.

Mary looked from one to the other. 'You won't send me back, will you?'

Martha looked away. She knew she had to be prepared for the child to go away, as William would have to do the right thing.

'We have to find your sister and let her know you are still alive.'

Mary only nodded.

'Now, tell us where you lived and we'll try to sort something out.'

Mary surprised herself as she remembered in great detail her life before the accident. She told them about her second-hand clothes, the shoes that let in water and the smelly lav they had to share with other families. When she finished she wiped her eyes with the delicate hanky that Martha gave her and looked pleadingly at Martha and William. 'So please don't send me back.'

'Do you remember your address at this Chapel Court?' asked William.

Mary shook her head.

'You are telling me the truth?'

She nodded.

'Well the only thing we can do is go and look to find out if your sister still lives there.'

'You can't go there, it's horrible.'

'We have to find your sister.'

'What if she's moved or gone on the stage?'

'The only way we can find out all that is for us to go there and ask the neighbours.'

Mary looked at Martha. 'Please. I don't want to go back there, it's horrible. I want to stay here with you.'

'But we must tell your sister that you are still alive. She must be very worried about you.'

'Not if she's on the stage and dancing.'

'Rose, that's not a nice thing to say.'

'Well it was 'cos of her that I got run over.'

'No,' said William. 'It was because you decided to run away from her.'

Mary began to cry again, and Martha went to go to her but William put up his hand to stop her.

'I'm sorry, my dear, but we must get to the bottom of this.'

'So you're going to send me back?'

'Not at the moment. Let's see what Daisy has

to say about it. I think we should go on Sunday. If your sister's working, she should be home then.'

That night Mary tossed and turned. She wanted to see Daisy but she didn't want to go back to Chapel Court. Why did she have to get her memory back? She was happy before then.

Martha lay in bed looking at the ceiling. 'I can't believe that after all this time Rose . . . I mean Mary has got her memory back.'

'The poor child. No wonder she didn't want to tell us.'

'She must have been going through all sorts of trauma trying to keep it to herself. William, if her sister is working, could we keep Rose . . . Mary. I can't get used to calling her Mary.'

He held his wife's hand. 'Let us wait and see what the outcome of all this will be.'

'I don't want to lose her. I love her.'

'I know you do, my dear.' He put his arm round his wife and held her close. He knew he would have to go very carefully over the legal aspect of this situation.

*

It was almost midday when Tom came for Daisy; he was taking her to Rhoda's.

'I'm really excited about this. Is it a big house?'

'A fair size. I must say you look very nice.'

'Thank you, and you don't look so bad yourself.'

'Is Sally still in bed?'

'No, she's at Steve's again.'

'I only hope that bloke don't let her down.'

'She's very fond of him.'

'I know, that's what bothers me.'

'Well, you had your chance.'

'I know, but you know I couldn't feel for her what I feel for you.'

Daisy smiled. Walking along to catch a bus didn't seem like the best time to declare your love for someone, although to be fair to Tom, he never missed an opportunity to tell her whenever they were on their own. And how did she feel about Tom? Daisy wasn't sure about anything at the moment.

When they were knocking on Kenny's door, Daisy was amazed at the lovely house.

'Dais.' Rhoda rushed up to her and held her tight. 'Welcome to me humble abode.'

'There's nothing humble about this,' said Daisy as she looked round the hall at the number of doors.

'Give me your coat and I'll give you a tour later on when the others get here. Go into the front room – we can't get used to calling it the drawing room – and Kenny will give you both a drink. Joe's in there already.'

When the others arrived, the house was soon filled with laughter and music. After the tour, the girls oohing and aahing at Rhoda and Kenny's lovely house, it was time for lunch. Joe had kept himself to himself most of the time, only joining in when it was time to eat the lovely buffet that Rhoda had prepared.

'Rhoda, this is lovely,' said Daisy as she helped herself to some ham and cheese.

'Glad you like it.' Rhoda's eyes were shining.

'You look very happy.'

'I am. I'll tell you something; this sure as hell beats dancing night after night. You should try it.'

'Got to find someone to look after me first.'

'I heard that,' said Tom, coming up behind her and putting his arm round her waist. 'I keep asking her but she keeps turning me down.'

Daisy quickly looked round to see if Joe was watching, but he was busy talking to Kenny and had his back towards her.

Rhoda laughed and patted Tom's shoulder. 'You've just got to keep trying, me boy.'

Daisy moved away. 'Why did you say that to Rhoda?'

'Because it's true. You know how I feel about you, Dais, and I ain't ever gonner give up.' He swiftly kissed her cheek.

All too soon it was time for them to go. Daisy was alone with Rhoda in the bedroom, collecting her coat.

'Dais, it's lovely to see you again.'

'You too.' She held her friend close.

'You still ain't heard nothing about your sister, then?'

'I did go back to the cinema, but Mr Holden has left and Charlie died.'

'Oh Dais, I'm so sorry. You was very fond of Charlie.'

Daisy nodded. 'Anyway, I left me address with Mrs Wilson, just in case.'

Rhoda patted Daisy's hand. 'D'you know, if I

were you I'd take up Tom's offer. We all need a shoulder to cry on now and again. He's a good lad and has got a job for life driving Kenny about.'

'And he's also his manager,' said Daisy proudly.

'I know.'

Daisy closed the door. 'Rhoda. There's something I must tell you.'

She laughed. 'Is it true confessions time?'

'In a way. You see, I've always been in love with Joe, and when you got married I went to your flat to throw myself at him.'

Rhoda sat on the bed. 'Oh dear. And what did he say?'

'That he didn't want to know.'

'I'm glad you've told me, but if I'd known how you felt, I would have saved you that embarrassment. You see, Joe never had a father figure, and when his dance teacher Barry took him on as a pupil all those years ago, Joe thought he was in love with him. He never got over Barry turning him down. I believe that one day they will end up together, but only when Barry is ready to take him in as a son, not a lover. I don't think Joe will ever get married.'

'I see.'

'So what about Tom?'

'I like Tom very much, but . . .'

'Give it time.'

Kenny was banging on the door. 'Rhoda, Daisy, Tom's getting a bit fed up out here.'

Rhoda opened the door. 'D'you mind, we was just having a little bit of girl talk.'

Kenny put his arm round her waist and kissed her cheek. 'You, my dear, can do whatever you like.'

'Sorry, Tom,' said Daisy. 'All the others gone?'

Tom nodded. 'That's OK. See you tomorrow, boss. Bye, Rhoda, and thanks.' He kissed her cheek.

When they were outside, Daisy put her arm through Tom's. 'That was lovely. I'm so glad we came. Rhoda is so happy.'

Tom patted her hand. 'So am I.'

Chapter 34

'WHY CAN'T I come with you?' Harry asked Mary when they were alone in the garden.

' 'Cos I don't want you to.'

'But Rose . . .'

'I keep telling you, me name ain't Rose, it's Mary.'

'Mary, why are you being so horrible to me and talking all silly again? I thought I was your friend.'

'You are.' Mary walked away. She didn't want him to see how much she was hurting.

Harry ran to catch her up. 'Mary, Mama has said that if your sister agrees, you can still live here with us.'

Mary turned. 'But what if she won't let me come back?'

'Please don't be upset. I'll come with you and make her see that's fine. Please let me come with you this afternoon.'

'No, I can't. It's a really horrible place.' Mary was dreading the thought of going back to Chapel Court.

After lunch, a very sad Mary sat next to Martha as Johnson drove the three of them to Rotherhithe.

When the cinema came into sight, Mary called out, 'Me sister used to work there. That's where she took me to see the pictures . . .' Her voice trailed off as she remembered when she gave the flowers to the lady mayor.

'Pull over, Johnson, and I'll go and make some enquiries.' William got out of the car.

In a very short while he returned.

'Well?' said Martha.

'The young girl in the kiosk told me that the manager before this one was a Mr Holden and he has moved on, and that the man you remember called Charlie has died, but she does remember your sister coming here looking for you. She said she'd moved away.'

Mary sat very still. So Daisy had been looking for her, and she had moved.

'Did she say where?' asked Martha.

'No. She didn't know.'

'Does this mean we can go home now?' asked Mary.

'It looks like it,' said Martha, hugging her.

As they drove along the high street, Mary was pleased they were going home.

'Johnson, can you go to Chapel Court?' said William.

Mary froze. 'Why?'

'Your sister may have left her address where you used to live.'

When they approached the buildings, Mary shuddered. This was the place she had had all those bad dreams about. Now she was back here. 'Do I have to get out?' she asked softly.

'You'll have to show me where you once lived,' said William.

'Don't worry, I'll come with you,' said Martha, looking up at the drab buildings.

Mary clutched her hand as they walked along.

'Is it this block?' asked William, stopping.

Mary shook her head. 'I don't remember.'

'Are you sure?'

Mary looked about her; it did seem vaguely familiar. 'I'm not sure which block we lived in.'

'People must have talked about your disappearance, so we will have to ask someone if they remember you.'

There was still the rubbish, and scruffy kids running about, but they stopped when this party of well-dressed people came close.

'What d'yer want?' asked one boy who wasn't wearing any shoes.

Mary thought about when she had no soles to her shoes, and how Daisy worked at the greengrocer's and any evening she could just to get her second-hand ones from the market. She had never really thought about the long hours Daisy worked, trying to make things all right for her. How must she have been feeling after all these years?

William drew himself up. 'Do you happen to know this young lady?'

The children all fell about laughing.

'This young lady,' mimicked the boy. 'Just 'cos

she's got nice clothes, my mum says that don't make a lady.'

'And your mother's right, young man. So can you help me?'

He walked round Mary. 'Might do. What's it worth?'

'Would sixpence be all right?'

'Make it a shilling and I'll tell yer.'

William gave the lad a shilling. 'Well?'

'I ain't never seen her before.'

The other kids were laughing and shouting, 'Ever bin 'ad?'

'Come along, William,' said Martha. 'These children are making me nervous.'

'There must be someone round here who remembers you.'

Mary was getting worried and asked. 'Uncle William, do you want to get rid of me?'

They began to walk away and William took her hand. 'Course not, my dear. It's just that I do have to explore every angle. You see, if there is no one, we may be able to adopt you.'

Mary threw her arms round his waist.

Martha smiled. 'There must be someone round here who remembers you and is able to help us.'

A woman came running up to them. ' 'Ere, you lot. What d'yer think yer doing giving me boy money. What yer after?'

'I'm sorry,' said William.

'Don't come all that la-di-dah stuff with me. I know your sort, trying to take kids away.'

'I beg your pardon, madam.'

She folded her thick arms across her chest. 'I ain't no madam. Now move on or I'll call the police. You and yer posh ways. Yer thinks you can get away with all sorts.'

'Come along, William.'

'Just a moment. Excuse me, Mrs . . .'

'Ross.'

'You don't happen to know this young lady? She used to live round here.'

Mrs Ross looked at Mary.

'I'm Mary Cooper. Me sister Daisy used to work in the greengrocer's and then in the cinema.'

'I remember Daisy. A nice, well-mannered girl. That Mrs Martin in the greengrocer's was a right cow and no mistake. 'Ere, didn't you run away?'

Mary nodded and looked down.

'Well it certainly looks like yer done all right fer yerself.'

'Mrs Ross,' said William, 'you don't happen to know where Daisy went?'

'Na. Some said she went on the stage.'

'Thank you. Come on, Mary.'

They began to walk away.

'Just a mo. Old Mrs Wilson might know about yer sister.'

'Mrs Wilson,' repeated Mary. 'I stayed with her after me mum died.'

'You never told us that,' said Martha.

'I forgot. It was only a couple of nights till me mum got buried.'

William turned to Mrs Ross. 'Do you happen to know where she lives?'

'Next block. Over there.' She pointed towards the dirty redbrick building further along. 'Number forty-six. Everybody knows Mrs Wilson; she brings 'em inter the world, then lays 'em out when they leave it.'

'Thank you. Thank you very much. And here's ten shillings for your trouble.'

Mrs Ross smiled, showing a large gap between her stained teeth. 'No trouble.' She almost curtsied. 'And thank you, sir.' She turned and left them.

As they mounted the smelly stairs, Martha

held her handkerchief to her nose.

'No wonder you blocked all this out of your mind,' said William.

Mary was trembling when they knocked on the door.

It took a while before it was opened. 'Yes.' Mrs Wilson peered at them. 'What d'yer want?'

'Mrs Wilson?' asked William.

'Yes. Who wants ter know?'

'Mrs Wilson, do you happen to know a Daisy Cooper?'

She thought for a moment or two. 'I remember Daisy. Nice kid. She all right?'

'We don't know. Do you remember her younger sister, Mary?'

She smiled. 'She was a nice little thing. She ran away. Broke poor Daisy's heart, that did. She walked the street for weeks looking for her, but she never found her. Do you know something about her?'

'This is Mary.'

Mary had been hiding behind Martha. Tears were rolling down her cheeks. Her sister had been trying to find her. 'Hello, Mrs Wilson.'

'Mary. Mary, me little love. Where've you bin,

you naughty little girl?' She held Mary tight. 'Look, you'd better come in.'

They followed Mrs Wilson into her tidy home. 'D'yer fancy a cuppa?'

'No thank you, we wouldn't like to put you to any trouble.'

'Ain't no trouble. I likes a bit of company now and again.'

'Please, do sit down and let me tell you why we're here.'

Mrs Wilson did as she was told. Mary sat on the floor.

When William finished he said, 'So have you got Daisy's address?'

Mrs Wilson sat silently for a moment or two. 'Come here, me little love,' she sniffed as she held Mary tight. 'I can't believe that you went through all that, you poor little thing.'

Even Mary realised what a sad time she'd been through this past year or two.

Mrs Wilson took a piece of rag she used for a hanky from her overall pocket and blew her nose and wiped her eyes. 'I've got yer sister's address here somewhere. She's been looking for you all this time, you know?'

Mary sat on Martha's lap, while Mrs Wilson

scrabbled through all the papers behind her clock.

'This looks like it. Can't read it without me glasses.' She handed the piece of paper to William.

Chapter 35

MARY WAS SURPRISED when they stopped outside a very different building to Chapel Court.

'Is this right?' asked Martha, not knowing quite what to expect after the other place they had been to.

'It's the address that's on this paper. I'll just go and check.' William left the car.

'It does look rather nice. Your sister must be a lot happier living here,' said Martha.

Mary only nodded. She wanted to see Daisy again and tell her she was sorry, but what if she wanted her to come back? Although this looked a lot better than where they used to live, she still didn't want to be left alone every night while her sister was on the stage. Besides, she loved living with the Tunbridges.

William returned to the car. 'I can't see her name on the wall, and I've been up to the flat but there's no reply.'

'She might have changed her name,' said Martha. 'She might even be married.'

They sat in the car and looked around them.

'This does seem to be a much better area than where you used to live,' Martha said, patting Mary's hand.

Mary didn't reply, but sat silently wondering what her future would be now.

'I can't see anyone around, so I'll slip a note under the door.' Once again William left the car.

All the way home Mary was deep in thought. She wondered if Daisy would ever get in touch with her. In many ways she was very upset that she hadn't seen her sister. What if she'd moved? Would she ever find her? As much as she wanted to see Daisy again, she knew that her life could change once more. She had to somehow let her sister know that she was happy where she was. Now Uncle William had an address, perhaps she could write to her, and even if she had moved, the new people might send it on to her. That way she could tell her she was happy where she was.

Tom was trying to be a little more than affectionate when they got to Daisy's doorstep. He was kissing her neck and whispering, 'Please, Daisy. Just give me a chance. I can be as loving as you want. And I will give you anything you want. Please say you'll love me just a tiny bit.'

In some ways Daisy wanted to laugh at his eagerness, but that would be mean. She did like Tom, but she knew it would take her time to get over her feelings for Joe.

'Tom, you know I like you, so let's leave it at that for a little while.'

'Anything you say. But can we still go out sometimes?'

She smiled. 'If you want, not that we get a lot of time for socialising.'

Tom felt his heart melt. He loved her so much and was determined that one day she would feel the same way about him, but she needed time, and that was something he had plenty of.

He kissed her lips. 'I'll see you tomorrow at work.'

'OK.'

He watched her walk up the steps to her front door, then turned and went home to his lonely bachelor rooms. When they got married, where would they live? And would Daisy be willing to give up dancing to have babies? He grinned to himself. This was all in the distant future. At least he had a good settled position with Kenny all the while he worked at the club.

Daisy pulled the key out of the door and closed it quietly behind her. She would just make sure Sally was home before she put the bolt on. Peering into Sally's room, she could see that she was still out. Perhaps she was staying with Steve again. Daisy went into the kitchenette and filled the kettle. What if Sally and Steve wanted to get married, would he want to live here? If so, where could Daisy go? They wouldn't want her hanging around them. She went and sat on the sofa to wait for the kettle to boil. It was then that her eyes travelled to the front door and she saw a piece of paper on the floor. That was probably Sally leaving a note telling Daisy she wouldn't be home after she'd been to collect some clothes.

It must have been an afterthought letting her know. Still, that was Sally. Daisy went and picked the note up as the kettle started to whistle. She put it on the table and made herself a cup of tea.

Settling herself down once again, she read the note. She couldn't believe it. She read it over again. Mary was alive and she had been here. The family she was living with had finally tracked Daisy down. Tears fell from her eyes and she was laughing and crying all at the same time. She had to tell someone. Her thoughts were all over the place. Who could she run to? The first name that flew into her mind was Tom's. She grabbed her coat and made her way to his rooms.

'Tom, Tom! Are you still up?'

He opened the door. 'Daisy, what is it? Whatever's wrong? You look like you've just seen a ghost.'

'Can I come in?'

'Course.'

Daisy and Sally had been to Tom's rooms before.

'Have a seat,' Tom quickly threw the newspapers off the only armchair on to the floor. 'Now, what's the trouble?'

She handed him the note, as she couldn't speak for fear of crying.

After reading it, he went to her and held her close. 'This is wonderful news! After all this time of waiting and wondering, she has finally found you.'

'They don't say why after all these years, though. Do you think she's in some kind of trouble and they want to get rid of her?'

'I wouldn't think that for one moment.'

'It looks like it could be a posh address, as there's no house number, just a name. Tulip Cottage, School Lane. Sounds nice.'

'I'll ask Kenny if I can borrow the car and we can go and see her.'

'D'you think he'll let you?'

'Course he will, and if he won't, I'm sure Rhoda will have something to say about it. No, everybody will be thrilled for you.'

Daisy just let her tears fall. 'It can't be true. She must have grown. Where has she been all this time, and why wait till now to find me? I wonder what she looks like. Tom, what if she wants to live with me, what shall I do? Where can we go? Will she want me to give up working?'

'Just calm down.' Tom pulled a chair closer to Daisy. 'Let's wait till you've seen her before you start worrying about what might happen.'

'My life will have to change now. She must have been to see Mrs Wilson. She was the only one who knew where I lived. But why now?'

Tom held her hand. 'I can't answer any of your questions. Tomorrow first thing we'll go and see Kenny, then you'll be able to get to the bottom of this.'

'I won't be able to sleep.'

'Would you like me to stay at your place tonight?'

Daisy looked at him.

'No, Dais. I can kip down on the sofa and then if you can't sleep and want to talk in the night, I'll be there for you.' He held up his hands. 'And I promise there'll be no hanky-panky.'

Daisy let a smile lift her face. 'You're a good friend, Tom.'

He wanted to say, I'd like to be more than a friend but he knew this wasn't the time.

*

Harry couldn't believe it when Mary told him that they thought they had found her sister. 'Do I have to go back to school tonight?' he asked his father.

'Yes, son,' said William. 'I'm sure Mary will tell you all about it on Friday if we hear from her sister.'

'I wanted to see her.'

'She might not come here. She may have moved.'

Reluctantly Harry got in the car to be taken back to school.

That night, like Daisy, there were some in the leafy glades of Surrey who were having trouble sleeping.

Mary was tossing and turning, worrying about seeing Daisy again. Would her sister be angry with her for running away and make her go back?

Martha and William sat in the drawing room talking, trying to work out the possibilities of the situation.

'What if her sister wants to take her back?' asked Martha.

'We mustn't think about that. If she is on the stage, would she want a young girl around her?

Don't forget, she would be leaving her most nights, and then if whatever show she's in moves away, could she take Mary with her?'

'What about her schooling? She's getting on so well. William, I don't want to lose her.' Martha dabbed at her eyes.

'Now come on, dear. Don't upset yourself. I think we had better try to get some sleep.'

'I don't think I can.'

'You must. Who knows, we may get a letter in the week and maybe we could be entertaining Miss Daisy Cooper later on.'

'Do you think she would come here?'

'I don't know. We have done our best.'

'Do you think Mary will want to go with her sister when she sees her?'

'I don't know. Now come on, no more questions.'

The following morning, Tom and Daisy were up early.

'You should have something to eat,' said Tom, enjoying a piece of toast Daisy had made him.

'I can't. I just want to go.'

'I'll have to have a shave first.' He had come prepared.

'Go on then, but hurry.'

'Kenny and Rhoda won't thank you for waking them too early. Who knows what time they got to bed.'

'If I'd been here last night I would have seen her,' Daisy fretted.

'Well you wasn't, so stop worrying about it. I'm gonner shave.'

It didn't take Tom long to do what he had to, and soon they were on their way.

Kenny was half asleep when he opened the door. 'Tom, Daisy, what's wrong? The club burnt down?'

'No. Can we come in?' asked Tom.

'Course. Sorry.'

'Is Rhoda up yet?'

'Oh my God. What's happened to Joe?'

'Nothing. This is about Daisy.'

'Daisy?'

'What's going on?' asked Rhoda, bleary eyed as she came down the stairs. 'Oh my God, Daisy, you look awful. What's happened?'

'I didn't get a lot of sleep.'

Rhoda raised one eyebrow. 'I can see that.'

'You'd better come into the front room,' said Kenny.

They followed Rhoda and Kenny. When they had all sat down, Daisy told them what had happened. When she finished, they were both silent for a few moments.

'What are you going to do, Dais?' asked Rhoda.

'I've got to go and see her.'

'Will you bring her back?'

'I don't know.'

'Kenny, could we take your car and . . .' Tom didn't finish, as Kenny was on his feet right away.

'I'll just get the keys.'

Daisy began to cry, and Rhoda put her arms round her friend's neck and gave her a handkerchief.

'Thank you. I can't believe that after all this time she has found me.'

'Did the note say why it has taken so long?'

Daisy shook her head. 'I'm hoping we will be able to find that out when we see her.'

Kenny came back into the room and handed Tom the car keys.

'Thanks, boss.'

'I shall be in all day, so let us know the outcome.'

'We will. Come on, Dais, let's be off.' Tom took her arm and led her to the car.

Kenny and Rhoda stood at the door and waved them off.

'This could be a whole new life for Daisy,' said Kenny.

'I know. In her job, to have to look after a child could be a problem.'

'I suppose it could. D'you think she'll give it all up?'

'I don't know.' Rhoda closed the door. It was Daisy's dancing that had been the cause of the problem with her sister before, she thought. What would happen now?

Chapter 36

'THERE'S SOME VERY nice houses round here,' said Tom as they drove slowly along School Lane. 'Call out if you see the name of the house. It's a bit daft not having numbers.'

'So why does Mary suddenly want to leave living round here and come back to London?'

'Search me. Perhaps somebody's died and they can't look after her any more.'

'That could be it. Poor Mary. But why didn't she write to me? She didn't have to tell me where she lived.'

'I don't know, Dais. I don't have any answers for you.'

'I'm sorry, Tom.'

'You don't have to be.' He turned and gave her a beaming smile.

Daisy's heart skipped a beat. Was love creeping up on her? He was so kind.

'I think this is the place,' he said, interrupting her thoughts and stopping the car. 'We better get out here. It looks like too much cheek going down there and parking near the house.'

Daisy peered through the windscreen. 'This house is massive. Are you sure it's the right one?'

'That's what it says on the paper. Tulip Cottage.'

'It's not really a cottage.'

'I know. Come on, out you get.'

'Tom, I'm frightened.'

He walked round and opened the door. 'Why?'

'I don't know.'

'Come on, you daft 'ap'orth,' he said gently, taking her arm.

They mounted the steps leading to the front door and rang the bell. They could hear someone calling out.

'I'll go, Mrs Aimes.' Martha Tunbridge opened the door and stared at them. It took a moment or two before she said, 'You're Daisy, aren't you?'

Daisy nodded.

'Please come in.'

They stepped into the hall, and its size and beautiful furnishings almost took Daisy's breath away. Why would Mary want to leave all this?

'Thank you, Mrs . . .'

'Tunbridge. We'll go into the drawing room. I'm afraid Mary is at school and my husband is at the office. Please sit down.'

Daisy perched on the very edge of the green damask sofa and Tom sat next to her.

Immediately Daisy asked, 'Could you tell me why Mary has suddenly wanted to get in touch with me after all this time?' Her voice was very soft and trembling.

Martha smiled. 'I'll get some coffee sent in, or would you prefer tea?'

'No, coffee's fine,' said Daisy.

Martha pulled the cord at the side of the fireplace. 'This is a very long story. Are you in any hurry?'

Daisy shook her head.

When Mrs Aimes walked in, Martha asked for three coffees. 'I'll wait for the coffee to be served, then we won't be disturbed.'

Daisy clutched Tom's hand. She was very nervous. 'Is Mary well?'

'Very. She's such a lovely girl. We are all very fond of her.'

Daisy wanted to scream at her, so why wait till now to find me? But she held her tongue.

Mrs Aimes brought in the tray of coffee and put it on the glass table.

Martha smiled at her. 'Thank you. I'll bring this out later.' She turned to Daisy and Tom. 'Milk and sugar?'

'Please,' they said together.

Daisy's nerves were at breaking point and she wanted to shout out, just get on with it, but knew that wouldn't do any good.

Martha passed the coffee round, then sat back. 'Mary had an accident.'

'What? When?'

'Dais, calm down. Let Mrs Tunbridge tell you.'

'I'm sorry.'

'When she ran away from home, Mary was hit by a car and she lost her memory . . .'

An hour later Daisy and Tom were sitting almost in a trance. The loud ticking of the grandfather clock was the only sound that disturbed the air for a moment or two.

'The poor little devil,' said Tom at last. 'All those different homes and not knowing who she was.'

'It was a very sad time for her, but she's happy now.'

Tears were running down Daisy's face. 'And you say she's only just remembered who she is?'

Martha nodded. 'We took her to the cinema.'

'I used to work in a cinema.'

'I know, and it seems that triggered her memory. We took her there for her birthday.'

'That was last year. Her birthday's in November. Why wait till now?'

'We didn't know that. We chose July the twenty-third as her birthday; that was the date when Penny and Roger found her in the road.'

'But that was a few weeks ago.'

'I know. She kept it to herself. She was frightened that you still lived in Chapel Court, and she didn't want to return there.'

'So now she knows different, does she want to come back with Daisy?' asked Tom.

Martha looked uneasy. 'We are all very fond of Mary.'

'But she is Daisy's sister.'

'We know. I think it should be up to Mary to decide where she would like to live.'

Daisy was bewildered. 'What time does she finish school?'

'She should be home at three.'

'Can we wait that long, Tom?'

'Course. Mr Kenny said to take as long as you like.'

'Is Mr Kenny your boss?'

'Yes.'

'And what show are you in?'

Daisy looked at Tom. 'I'm not in a show.'

'Oh, I'm sorry. I thought Mrs Wilson said you were a dancer on the stage.'

'I am a dancer, but I work in a nightclub.'

'I see.'

Daisy could almost read this woman's mind. She could see by the way she spoke about Mary that she was very fond of her and had decided that Daisy's lifestyle was not suitable for Mary to be exposed to. 'Do you have any children of your own?' she asked.

'Yes, I have a son who is about the same age as Mary.'

'Will he be home at three as well?'

'No, he's a boarder and is only home at weekends. We didn't send Mary to a boarding school as she had had enough traumas in her life without being sent away again.'

'Why are you doing all this for my sister?'

'When I saw her in the last home, she looked so pathetically sad that I told my husband that I wanted to bring her home.'

'And he didn't mind?' asked Tom.

'No. As I said, we are very fond of her and he loves her as much as I do.'

'So you would be very upset if she wanted to come and live with me?'

Tom looked quickly at Daisy.

'Yes, I would.'

Daisy sat back and looked at the elegant grandfather clock ticking away in the corner of the room. They had another two hours to wait.

'Look, why don't we have some lunch while you're waiting?'

'No. We couldn't put you to any trouble.'

'It's no trouble.'

'No. Thanks all the same, but we can get something in the village.' Daisy stood up.

'Will you be back later?'

'Yes, if that's all right with you.'

'That will be fine.'

Daisy and Tom made their way to the front door. When they were outside, Tom took her arm. 'Why didn't you want to stay for a bite to eat? I'm starving.'

'I'm sorry, but I want to get to Mary before she does.'

'Why?'

Daisy grinned.

'Oh my God. You ain't gonner kidnap her, are you?'

'You been reading my mind?'

Martha went into the kitchen and sat at the table.

'You all right, Mrs T?' asked Mrs Aimes.

'I don't know.'

'I gather that was Mary's sister.'

'Yes.'

'So, she gonner take her away?'

'I don't know.'

'It'll break yours and Mr T's heart if she does.'

'I know. She's a dancer in a nightclub; how can she look after her?' Tears welled up in her eyes and she quickly left the room. What could she do? Martha desperately wanted William here, but she knew he was at the meeting and couldn't be contacted.

'Daisy, be sensible.'

All the while they had sat in the corner of the café nursing a sandwich, Tom had been nagging her. Now they were back sitting in the car at the end of the drive.

'How could you look after her? Besides, would you give up living in a place like that if you were her?'

'But she's me sister.'

'I know that. But how could you look after her?'

'I'd manage somehow.'

'And what about when Sally brings Steve back for a bit of how's yer father? You gonner want Mary listening to all their groans?'

Daisy sat staring through the windscreen. 'What shall I do?'

'Wait till you talk to her. Remember, you would have to leave her every night till four in the morning. How would she feel about that?'

Tears trickled down Daisy's cheeks. 'That's

what made her run away in the first place. Tom, what am I gonner do?'

'Now you've found her, there's no reason why we can't come and see her now and again.'

Daisy sobbed. 'Me life's in a mess. I don't know what to do. I promised me mum I'd look after her, and now . . .'

Tom held her close and Daisy let him kiss her tears away. 'I'll look after you. We can come and see her and take her out some Sundays; that way you'll both be getting the best of both worlds.'

'But what if she don't wonner see me ever again?'

'I think she will. Now come on, dry your tears and let's go back in the house and talk to Mrs Tunbridge. She seems a reasonable woman.'

'All right, and . . . thanks, Tom.'

'What for?'

'Being here with me.'

'I've told you before, I'll always be here for you.'

'I know.'

*

Martha was pleased to see them when they returned; she had had reservations, and had thought they might take Mary away.

'Mrs Tunbridge. I've got something to say before Mary gets back.' Daisy didn't like to say 'home', as this wasn't Mary's home.

'Please come and sit down.'

Again Daisy sat on the edge of the seat and nervously twisted her hanky round and round. 'If Mary wants to stay here, then I shall be quite happy about it. Perhaps we could come down some Sundays and take her out?'

Martha jumped to her feet and hauled Daisy up, hugging her. 'You have made me so happy. And I know William will be pleased. But I want you to be sure you are doing the right thing.'

'I don't really know.'

'Of course you can come and see her, you would be more than welcome.'

The clock struck three and the drawing-room door opened. Daisy turned slowly.

'Daisy. Mrs Aimes said you were here,' the little girl said solemnly.

Daisy walked towards her and let her tears fall. 'Mary, my love.' She held her close, but Mary was stiff and unyielding.

Chapter 37

DAISY LET GO of Mary and stood back. 'You look very well, and so grown up.'

'Are you still dancing?'

'Yes.'

'Are you going to take me away from here?'

'Not if you don't want to come with me.'

'I don't.'

'Mary, please,' said Martha. 'Your sister has been looking for you all this time, so at least be polite.'

'I'm sorry, Aunt Martha, but I don't want to leave you.' She rushed to Martha and held her tight.

'Mary,' said Daisy softly, 'I'm not here to take

you away. I have been so worried about you all this time. I didn't know if you were alive or dead.' She brushed the tears from her cheeks.

'Your sister has spent days walking the streets looking for you. I do think you should at least be nice to her.' Tom was angry with this spoilt child.

'Who are you?'

'My name's Tom and I work with Daisy.'

'Are you a dancer as well?'

'No. I'm our boss's driver and manager.'

'Is that your car in the lane?'

'No, it belongs to me boss. Everyone has been very concerned about you, and as soon as we knew where you lived, Mr Kenny said we could borrow his car to come and see you.'

'When did you move away from Chapel Court?' Mary asked.

'A long while ago. I didn't want to go at first, as I was always hoping that you would come back, but now I know why you didn't. Please, Mary. Please forgive me for whatever I've done.'

Mary stared at Daisy, then her tears began to fall. 'I'm sorry.' She went to her sister and held her close. 'I'm so sorry. It's just that I don't want to leave here. I don't want to be left on my own every night while you're dancing.'

'You don't have to leave here. Just let me know how you are. Sometimes we can come and see you, Mrs Tunbridge said we could.'

'Please, call me Martha.' She was smiling broadly. 'I'm so happy for you. You must have been at your wits' end all this time.'

'I was. I went to every hospital and police station, but Mary had just disappeared, and all the while she didn't know who she was. I shall never forgive myself for leaving her.'

Mary took hold of Daisy's hand. 'I'm sorry I was nasty to you when I came in, but I was really frightened you would take me away.'

Daisy smiled. 'I promise I shall never do that.' They held each other tight.

Martha dabbed at her eyes. 'Can you both stay long enough to meet my husband?'

'I'm afraid not,' said Tom. 'We have to work tonight.'

'Then you must come here on Sunday. You do have Sundays off, I presume?'

'Yes, and I'd like that,' said Daisy. 'Tom, do you think Mr Kenny would let you have the car?'

'I can only ask.'

'You look very nice,' said Mary to Daisy.

'Thank you, and so do you. You have grown, you're nearly as tall as me now. That's a very nice uniform. Do you like school?'

'Yes I do, and my teacher said I'm very bright.'

'Well you could always pick things up quickly. Do you remember when we used to sit round the table doing sums and reading?'

Mary nodded. 'Do you know, Aunt Martha, when she came home from work Daisy used to sit teaching me.'

'Well, it's certainly paid off. Her reports are always glowing.'

'It was funny, really. Although I didn't know who I was, I could still read and write.'

Daisy held her close. 'I'm so glad it has all worked out lovely for you.'

'Dais, I'm sorry, love, but we do have to get back.'

'Of course.'

'Everyone will be dying to know how you got on.'

'They certainly will. By the way, do you remember Joe and Rhoda?'

'They did the dancing, didn't they?'

'Yes. Well I still work for Joe, and Rhoda has married our boss.'

'What a pity you can't stay any longer. You both have got such a lot of catching up to do,' said Martha.

'We can do that on Sunday. Harry will be here then. You'll like him, he's good fun. And I can show you my room and everything. Daisy, I do love you!' Mary ran into her sister's arms, and once again Martha was dabbing at her eyes.

Daisy was very quiet as they drove home.

'When she first walked in, I thought what a spoilt brat she was, but when she knew you wasn't gonner take her away she turned out all right and was genuinely pleased to see you.'

Daisy didn't reply.

'Dais, what is it?'

'I don't know. I feel as if a great void in my life has been filled.'

'Well it has in a way.'

'I've had this day to look forward to for years. Now what have I got?'

'What do you want?'

'I don't know. But thank you for helping me.'

Tom stopped the car. 'Daisy, I promise I will

always be there for you. You know I love you, and this might not be the right time, but we could have a good life together. Please give it some thought.'

She turned and kissed him. 'I have, and now I know Mary is safe and sound and happy, I am going to give it a great deal of thought.'

Tom started the car. 'And?'

'I think the answer could be yes.'

Everybody at the club was so pleased for Daisy, and even Joe hugged her and said how thrilled he was. Daisy realised that when he held her she felt nothing. Had her feelings for him just been a schoolgirl crush?

That night while she was in the wings waiting for her cue, she looked around her. For the first time in years she was more than happy. She had found Mary after all this time, and she had realised that she did love Tom. She would tell him tonight that she was ready to spend the rest of her life with him.

The band began to play the fast jazzy number, and right on cue the girls all joined arms and high-kicked their way out in front of the crowd.

All That Jazz

The customers clapped wildly. This was the jazz age, and everybody was going to enjoy it.

Daisy smiled. She was so happy, and danced like she had never danced before.

Just
for You

DeeWilliams

Just for You

Kicking up their heels . . .
The dancing girls of the 1920s

Latin lovers and damsels in distress . . .
Stars of the silver screen

Chin-chin . . .
Classic cocktails of the Twenties

My kind of day . . .
A typical day for Dee Williams

Just
for You

© jandaphotography.com

Dee Williams was born and brought up in Rotherhithe in south-east London where her father worked as a stevedore in Surrey Docks. Dee left school at fourteen, met her husband at sixteen and was married at twenty. After living abroad for some years, Dee moved to Hampshire to be close to her family. She has written seventeen previous sagas. In this exclusive interview, Dee answers our questions about the life of a dancing girl in the Twenties . . .

1. *What was the life of a dancing girl like in the 1920s?*

These girls had to start quite young, as they needed to have the stamina and be very supple. They had to dance for hours on end, night after night, which couldn't have left them with much free time. Dancing girls were disciplined, highly trained and very professional. I would imagine they had to come from dance schools as some of the routines were very complicated. They worked long hours so dancing really had to be their life. I think all the dancing girls probably dreamed of being head girl or 'line captain' in their group; this lucky girl would have the trust of the choreographer and help him carry out his instructions to the rest of the troupe.

2. *Were the girls chosen on appearance as well as dancing ability?*

Height and weight were pivotal factors. These girls had to be tall and slim as the boyish look was all the rage, and dancers sported bobbed hair and taped bosoms. Madame Bluebell, for example, who established and trained the famous Bluebell Girls dance troupe in the 1930s, only looked for girls with extensive ballet training; a Bluebell also had to be beautiful and long legged, and 5′ 8 or taller.

All the girls wore a lot of make-up on stage and for that reason they were looked upon by some as 'good time' girls. Parents didn't necessarily approve of their daughters working on the stage, or in sleazy nightclubs. I think I read somewhere that some of them did go on to marry rich playboys though, so perhaps it wasn't all bad!

3. *What were their outfits like?*

Women's fashion at the time was for cloche hats and short, tight frocks. Long necklaces, particularly pearls, were very popular. Bone bracelets were pushed up to the top of their arms with a chiffon scarf pulled through, and white stockings and pointed shoes finished off the outfit. The clubbers loved the dancing girls in their short skirts and shimmering fringed costumes. Sometimes they wore tight-fitting cloche hats made of sequins, and headbands with feathers. The Tiller Girls and the Bluebell

Girls all wore very short skirts so that they could do their 'tap and kick' routine, which involved high kicks, in time to the music.

Jo Baker, an immensely popular American dancer in the Twenties, was noted for her banana skirt when she performed in the Folies Bergère, a Parisian music hall, at the height of its popularity.

4. *Why did dancing become so popular in the 1920s?*

Ragtime music developed into Jazz and young people in Britain rushed to dance halls and Jazz clubs to join in with these exciting new dances that had come over from America. Dance palaces and nightclubs became all the rage and young people couldn't wait to learn the new steps.

The Charleston and Black Bottom were very popular dances and it wasn't long before young women were doing them in dance halls across the country. This was just after the war, and women hadn't long had the vote, so they were feeling very liberated and free.

5. *Which were the most popular dance clubs?*

The 1920s was the golden age of nightclubs. In London, the Trocadero was the place to be seen. When the licensing laws were changed in 1921, the clubs were able to serve alcohol until 12.30 a.m. As a result of these extended drinking hours, nightclubs flourished. The drinks were often expensive, and many became frequented by the young, rich and famous. London's most popular clubs prided themselves on their exclusivity; the Kit-Kat Club and The Embassy were perhaps the most exclusive hangouts.

One of the most popular troupes, The Tiller Girls, performed as resident dancers at the London Palladium, the Palace Theatre in Manchester, the Blackpool Winter Gardens, the Folies Bergère in Paris, and many other theatres across Britain, Europe and America.

Just
for You

Latin lovers and
damsels in distress ...

The silent films of the Twenties were very popular. Italian actor Rudolph Valentino was the heartthrob of the day and women everywhere swooned over him. His role as Julio in *The Four Horsemen of the Apocalypse* was highly acclaimed and the film was one of the top grossing of all time. Ramón Novarro was sensational in Fred Niblo's silent film adaptation of *Ben Hur*, as he raced around the Coliseum on his chariot. When Valentino died in 1926, Novarro became the screen's leading Latin actor. Also in the very popular weekly motion picture serial *The Perils of Pauline*, actress Pearl White terrified cinemagoers as she was tied to a railway line or some other precarious place, seemingly unable to escape. Of course, she always managed to untangle herself or be rescued at the end of every episode, but audiences were engrossed.

There was great excitement when the talkies arrived in the late Twenties. Many filmgoers thought that comedian and film star Al Jolson was the greatest performer of all time and my mother told me that when he said 'You ain't heard nothing yet' some women fainted. She said it was the most wonderful thing she had ever seen, even better than *Ben Hur*.

When 'America's sweetheart', Canadian motion picture star Mary Pickford, married 'the king of Hollywood' Douglas Fairbanks, both male and female fans went wild over the match. The couple were greeted by huge crowds during their European honeymoon. They were the first real celebrity couple and were widely regarded as Hollywood royalty.

The plot of the 1952 film *Singing in the Rain* highlighted some of the problems encountered in the talkies by a few of the big film stars of the Twenties. For example, silent-film star John Gilbert was mocked for his funny, squeaky voice when he first appeared in a talkie. This must have been devastating for him, a huge star and among one of the highest earners at the time.

I love films and stage shows. *Chicago* is my favourite; I have seen the show three times and the film twice, and I own the DVD and CD of the soundtrack! I love the music and the costumes from that era so much, and it inspired me to write ALL THAT JAZZ. I also think that *Love Me or Leave Me*, the film about the life of singer Ruth Etting starring Doris Day and James Cagney, was a wonderful picture. That also really brings the music of the Twenties and Thirties to life for me.

As well as music and film, I'm a huge fan of dancing. When I was little I went to dancing school; some of the other pupils went on to perform on the stage as the Baby Beams, but my dad wouldn't let me and I remember feeling broken hearted. I can't remember our teacher's name, although it certainly wasn't Madam Truelove! I don't even remember where we practised. I do remember, however, desperately wanting to be a Baby Beam. I would love to hear from any past members of the Baby Beams, especially Yvonne and Barbara Fox.

I also used to do acrobatics as well as tap. When my Auntie Rose bought me a pair of red tap shoes, which had red ribbon laces that I had to tie in a big bow to stop them falling off, I was so excited. I used to tap all around the house driving everybody mad. I was very upset when I grew out of those shoes.

Just for You

Classic Cocktails
of the Twenties

Cocktail drinks became very popular with the bright young things who flocked to the dancehalls and nightclubs of 1920s London. Here are a few recipes from the era:

BUCK'S FIZZ

Named after the Buck's Club in London, where it was created. It was first served there by one of the club's barmen, Mr McGarry, in 1921. The ratio is normally two thirds champagne to one third juice.

Fresh orange juice
Brut champagne

Fill a quarter of a champagne flute with orange juice and top up with champagne. Then stir gently.

JACK ROSE

A popular cocktail of the 1920s and 1930s, its name is probably derived from the 'jack' of the Applejack and the light rose colouring from the grenadine.

½ oz Applejack
¾ oz fresh lemon juice
Grenadine to taste

Pour the ingredients into a cocktail shaker with ice. Shake well and strain into a chilled cocktail glass. Garnish with the lemon twist.

BRANDY COCKTAIL

Another classic cocktail of the 1920s. The original recipe, however, did not use Angostura bitters.

5cl brandy
2 dashes orange Curaçao
2 dashes Angostura bitters

Pour all ingredients into a mixing glass with ice and stir. Strain into a balloon glass.

Just for You

My kind of day . . .

It's quite tricky to describe a typical day for me, as every one is so different! If I've been out the night before, I check any phone messages on my answering machine after I've had breakfast. I always phone Carol, my daughter, in the morning, as she likes to know that I am all right. After I've spoken to her, I usually read my e-mails. Then I'll sit down at my computer to write. I like to write as often as possible and become completely engrossed in the story I'm telling. When I get to a sad or exciting bit I carry on through until the early evening. As a rule I try not to write too late in the day as by then my eyes (and bottom) have had enough!

If the sun is shining, however, I have to have a walk around my lovely garden. It's a good size and I love to spend time in it. I'm a really keen gardener and I can never reach the bottom of the lawn without dead-heading my flowers or pulling up a weed that has dared to show its head in my flowerbed! I am very lucky to have a gardener who cuts the grass and trims the bushes and hedges. I always help him bag up the garden waste as that way he can get much more done in the short time I've got him for. In the summer I pick up the windfalls from my three apple trees to stop the wasps buzzing around. Then I fill in the holes that the squirrels make when they're looking for nuts.

Every so often I give talks about my books, usually in the afternoon or evening. I mainly speak to library groups, the W.I., that kind of thing. The *W.I.* magazine was very kind and featured an article about me in the March issue. I was so pleased about it and I even received a phone call from an old friend in Spain who'd seen the piece. It's not always just women at my talks though, and I love it when men in the audience come up to me afterwards and tell me that I'm responsible for keeping them awake half the night because their wives won't put my book down! It is very satisfying to know that people are enjoying my writing. Apart from meeting so many lovely people, the money raised by these events goes to Breakthrough Breast Cancer. I have just received a letter from them and to date I have donated over £5,000, which makes me very happy indeed.

I have been known to do a bit of housework too although, because I live alone, my bungalow doesn't seem to get too untidy very often. I even get the vacuum cleaner out of the cupboard sometimes, and I'm sure it blinks because it's not used to daylight!

Then, of course, there's always plenty of shopping to be done!

Just for You

A snapshot of the world . . .
the 1920s

1920

- First commercial broadcast aired on radio

- Columbia Pictures is founded in America

- This year saw the births of actors Mickey Rooney, Montgomery Clift and Walter Matthau

1921

- Lie detector invented

- D. H. Lawrence's *Women in Love* is published in London

- Coco Chanel releases Chanel No.5, which goes on to become one of the world's best-selling perfumes. It is estimated that one is sold every 30 seconds

- The first edition of *Good Housekeeping* appears

- Laurel and Hardy appear for the first time together in the film *Lucky Dog*

1922

- Lloyd George replaced as Prime Minister by Conservative Bonar Law

- The BBC starts broadcasting regular daily news bulletins

- Matinee idol Rudolph Valentino stars in the film *Blood and Sand*

1923

- Stanley Baldwin replaces ailing Bonar Law as Prime Minister

- The Duke of York and Lady Elizabeth Bowes-Lyon marry. The couple would have two children, one of whom, Elizabeth, would later become Queen

- Walt Disney opens his first studio in Los Angeles

- W. B. Yeats is awarded the Nobel Prize for Literature

1924

- First Olympic Winter Games are held in Paris. This was the Olympics that later became fictionalised in the film *Chariots of Fire* in 1981

- The first Labour government comes into power in Britain

1925

- John Logie Baird invents the first working mechanical television

- Virginia Woolf's *Mrs Dalloway* is published

- F. Scott Fitzgerald publishes *The Great Gatsby*

1926

- Greta Garbo stars in her first American film, *The Torrent*

- The style guru Coco Chanel introduces her 'little black dress'

- The General Strike is called in support of British miners and affects more than two million workers around the country

1927

- Warner Brothers produces the first part-talkie, *The Jazz Singer*

- Janet Gaynor and Charles Farrell star in the film *Seventh Heaven*, for which Gaynor is awarded the first ever Best Actress Academy Award and director Frank Borzage receives the first Best Director Academy Award

1928

- The now famous Piccadilly Theatre opens in London. Its opening production stars one of the most acclaimed actresses of the period, Evelyn Laye

- The first all-talking movie, *Lights of New York*, comes out

- The Equal Franchise Act is passed, giving women equal voting rights with men; all women over the age of 21 can now vote in elections

- Emmeline Pankhurst, Britain's leading women's rights activist dies, aged 70, very shortly after women were awarded equal voting rights

1929
- Many young women vote for the first time on 30 May. This has since been referred to as the Flapper Election

- The Great Depression begins in Britain

- Penicillin is used for the first time

- This year saw the births of Anne Frank, Jackie Kennedy and Audrey Hepburn